SCOVILLE

SCOVILLE

Marlene Lee

Holland House

www.hhousebooks.com

Copyright © 2014 by Marlene Lee

Marlene Lee asserts her moral right to be identified as the authors of this book

All rights reserved. This book or any portion thereof may not be reproduced or used in any manner whatsoever without the express written permission of the publisher except for the use of brief quotations in a book review.

All characters appearing in this work are fictitious. Any resemblance to real persons, living or dead, is purely coincidental.

Paperback ISBN 978-1-909374-26-3
ePub ISBN 978-1-909374-27-0

Cover design by Ken Dawson.
http://www.ccovers.co.uk/

Typesetting by handebooks.co.uk

Published in the USA and UK

Grey Cells Press
Holland House Books
Holland House
47 Greenham Road
Newbury
Berkshire
RG14 7HY

United Kingdom

www.hhousebooks.com
www.greycellspress.co.uk

For my sister, Lavetta

THREE BLIND MICE

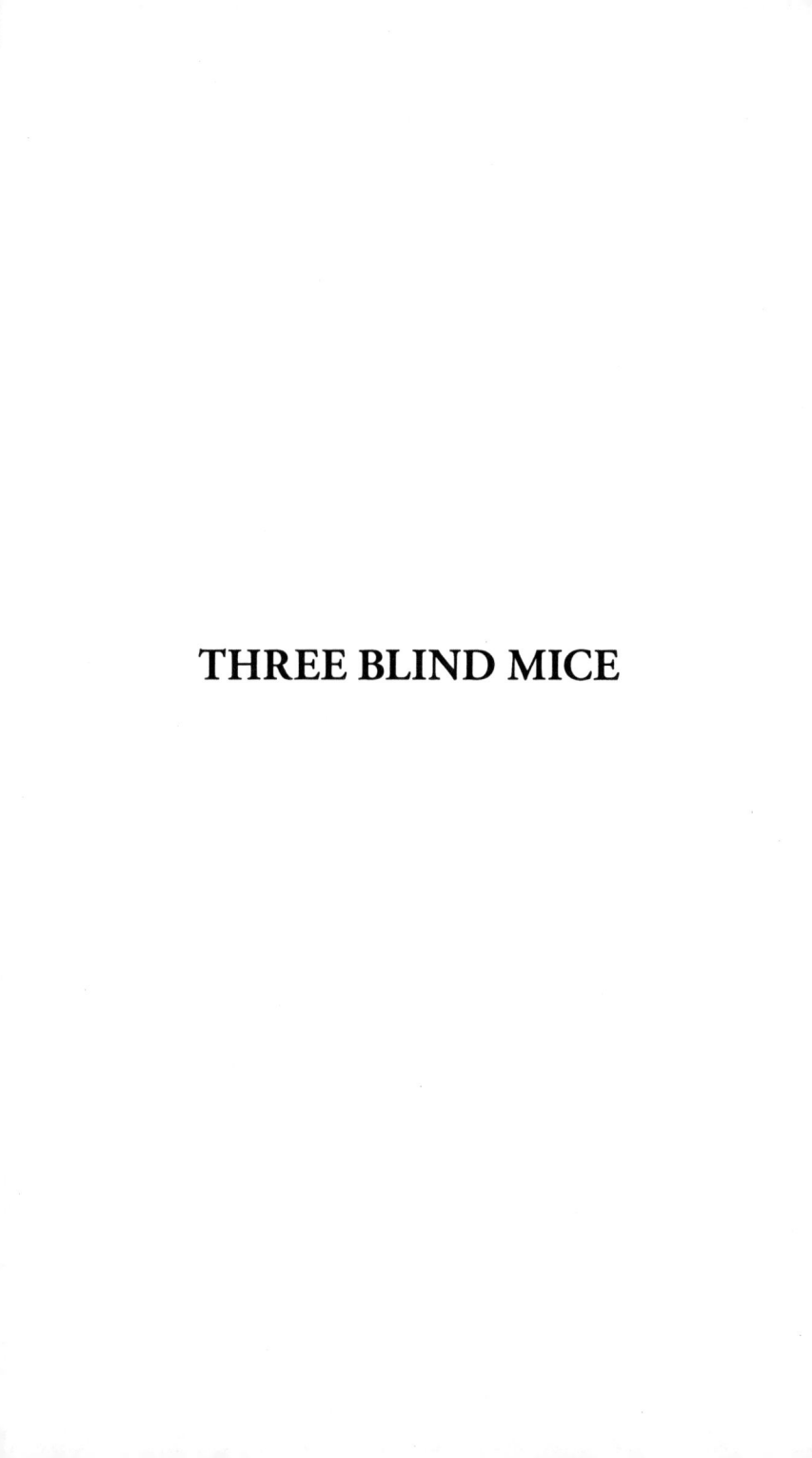

1

Humboldt Denton, a small, elderly man wearing blue jeans and a "Bowling for Dollars" sweatshirt, drove along the road at the edge of the Oregon cliff. He shifted his aging Plymouth into second and began the steep descent to Coast Highway. At twilight, the ocean below was colorless. A line of suds frothed at the edge of the gray beach.

"Do good tonight," he said, leaning toward his wife and patting her on the knee. "Hilda dealin'?"

"As far as I know."

Humboldt sighed.

"What's the matter? She too quick for you?"

"Damn right. I can't add that fast."

He turned onto a gravel road and entered Pacific Trailer Court, a small community of mobile homes tucked beneath magnificent Douglas firs. Humboldt parked in front of the fourth coach to the left, the Glynnises' mobile home. Maggie moved closer and Humboldt put his arm around her. They sat for a while and listened to the wind in the firs. The foghorn out on the jetty blew its single note every twenty seconds.

"Happy?" he asked.

Maggie nodded. "You?"

"Never better." He breathed deeply and smelled the sea and the docks and the sweet, gluey smell of the plywood mill working the night shift. "If I was young again I'd have me an outrigger and—"

"And you'd be a lumberjack and drive logging rigs and build a cannery and—"

They smiled at each other. Coming toward them along the gravel path from the far end of the court was Hilda, the dealer, a large woman of fifty. The blowing rhododendron bushes cast moving shadows on her broad head and shoulders as she walked toward the trailer, looking neither right nor left, a slow-moving freighter with the right of way. They waved, but she did not respond.

By the time Hilda reached the Glynnises' porch, Humboldt and Maggie were out of their car and on the steps behind her.

"Howdy! Howdy!" Duane Glynnis bawled out to Humboldt from the doorway, holding the screen open against the wind. Swept up in Duane's bear hug, Humboldt sent two punches, swift and gentle, to the big man's mid-section. Laughing and sparring, he tried to disengage himself. Released at last, he adjusted his "Bowling for Dollars" sweatshirt and beamed at the younger man.

Duane Glynnis was a strong, swarthy giant a few years past fifty. His thick, black hair was long at the front and sides, and he combed it and sprayed it over a thinning patch on top. His handsome face was just slightly tainted by an expression of self-indulgence.

He clapped Humboldt on the shoulder and looked around the room, roaring, "Make yourselves at home! Have some beer!" From time to time he took a large white handkerchief out of his pocket and wiped his forehead. The dark chest hairs curling under his open collar were moist.

Duane's wife, Angela, ran back and forth between the kitchen and living room with plates of cheese and cold cuts. She was considerably younger than her husband, whom she watched with nervous attention. Her smile was strained. The bright pink of her pantsuit brought out nothing in her pale eyes. Her bleached hair, teased into a fluffy nest, overpowered her thin face and body. Duane stayed near her and frequently touched her.

When everyone had their beer, Duane bellowed across the room, "Dealer! Ready?"

"More 'n likely," Hilda said. She threw back her large head and funneled peanuts into her mouth. Then, accepting an olive from Angela who had come hurrying toward her with food, she popped it in her mouth, released the damp pit into the palm of her hand, and advanced on the Black Jack table, a used piece of gaming furniture purchased from the Lucky Deuce Club during remodeling. Everyone laid down their twenty dollars.

Hilda's shuffle was fast and professional. In her thick fingers the cards appeared small. Her polished fingernails gleamed under the low-hanging light fixture. She dealt around the table and turned her top card over. It was a smiling queen. One after another she laid a strong, ringed forefinger beside each player's bet. Angela was first and stayed. Maggie took another card and stayed. Humboldt busted. Only Duane took his time, studying his cards with ponderous, low-lidded concentration.

"Hit me," he finally said. Hilda dealt him a card. He stayed on it. She turned her card over: Another queen. Duane swore as Hilda scooped up his bet. Then she collected from Humboldt and Angela. Only Maggie retained her four purple chips.

"Lousy start," said Humboldt amiably.

"I kind of liked it," said Maggie.

There was a long, serious silence.

"A hard-working group here," Humboldt declared. "Very little talking."

"Some of us gotta think about what we're doin'," said Duane. "Some of us got to work for what we get." He sneaked a look at his wife who avoided his eyes.

Humboldt checked his watch. It was only 9:25. He looked at his cards without seeing them. He wondered what was eating at Duane.

Angela lit a cigarette. Hilda reached around behind her, picked up the ashtray from the shelf, and set it in front of the younger woman.

Duane looked at Hilda through narrowed eyes. He clinked his wedding ring three times against his glass. Angela dragged quickly on her cigarette and went to fetch him more beer. Maggie arched her eyebrows in disbelief, but Hilda was more vocal.

"Who was your servant this time last year?"

"Play cards," ordered Humboldt. He snuck another look at his watch. Duane glared at the two women and at Angela as she returned with his beer.

Hilda dealt the next hand. Humboldt looked over at Duane's cards, an ace and a six.

"Give him a low card," he said helpfully. "Hit him with a four."

Hilda gave him an eight.

"Hit me again," Duane said darkly.

She hit him again. The nine of Clubs. Duane took a count and threw down his cards. He tapped his large knuckles on the felt as Hilda slid his chips next to hers.

Humboldt busted. Maggie's stack of chips increased and so did Hilda's. Angela's stayed the same. Only Duane had to buy more.

Humboldt set his chips on top of his overturned cards and wandered into the kitchen. He was helping himself to salted peanuts when he heard Angela laugh—giggle—for the first time all evening. Then Hilda laughed a rare, dry laugh.

"Hummer, can you find a towel out there?" Maggie called to him. "Duane is washing with his beer instead of drinking it."

Humboldt located a towel and took it out to Duane who was standing, unbuttoning his dripping shirt. He took the towel and mopped his hairy chest and belly with irritable swipes while Angela and Hilda snickered.

"The dealer's aimin' wild," Duane said in a tight voice.

Humboldt went back to the kitchen for more peanuts. For several minutes he heard nothing but the click of plastic chips being stacked. Hilda's stack, he thought.

Suddenly Duane shouted, "Goddammit, Hilda, whyn't you take the gold outta my teeth, too?" There was a tense silence, then a thud as something hit the carpet.

Humboldt walked to the doorway and nearly got knocked

over by Duane who was striding angrily into the kitchen, his wet shirt flapping open. Humboldt saw Angela hurry over and set her husband's barstool upright at the Black Jack table. Maggie looked disgusted. In the kitchen Duane threw open the refrigerator door.

"What's goin' on?" Humboldt asked. Duane dug in the refrigerator for a bottle of beer. He was breathing hard and sweating.

"Get a hold of yourself!" Humboldt clamped the large man around the upper arm.

"She's gotta go!" Duane shouted, straightening up with the bottle in his hand. "She's takin' everything I got!" He ran his other hand through his damp hair, then swiftly arranged strands over the bald area.

"What in the hell's the matter?" asked Humboldt.

Duane torqued off the bottlecap. "D'you see what she's doin'?" he demanded. "She's turnin' Angie against me." He jammed the bottle in his mouth and drained half the beer. "She made me spill the beer," he said. "They're laughin' at me. They're up to somethin'."

He paused and whispered fiercely, "Angela don't even look at me anymore." He moved in close to Humboldt and, tapping the smaller man's shoulder with the bottle of beer, said softly, "There's somethin' unnatural about Hilda." He pulled his damp shirt together and walked out of the room and back to the table where Hilda, unperturbed, was still dealing cards.

Humboldt stood in the middle of the kitchen floor, lost in thought. Then he walked quickly into the dining room. He was more than ready to go home.

"Let's wind this thing down," he said to Maggie. He put his hands in the side pockets of his sweatshirt and said, "My bedtime, folks. Too much excitement for an old man."

Maggie slid gracefully off her barstool and nodded good-bye to Hilda. She patted Angela lightly on the cheek. "The food was real good."

Humboldt punched Duane in the biceps. "Take it easy." They exchanged another set of punches, but it lacked spirit. Duane followed Humboldt outside. While Maggie walked to the car and got in, the two men stood at the edge of the gravel road, talking.

"Shuffleboard at the Lucky Deuce tomorrow night?" Humboldt asked.

"Yeah. Tomorrow night."

Humboldt watched him make a little clearing in the road by scraping away gravel with the side of his boot. Facing away from the trailer, Duane couldn't see Hilda close the screen, turn back into the house, and shut the front door behind her. Humboldt had an odd sense of the two women moving through strange rooms.

"What's goin' on at your house?" he asked bluntly.

Duane was silent for a moment. "Angie and I've got trouble," he finally said. Humboldt looked from Duane to the mobile home and back again.

"It's none of my business. But what kind of trouble?"

"She don't love me anymore," Duane said softly.

Humboldt took out his pocket knife and began turning it end over end in his hand. "That happens sometimes," he said. "It'll pass."

"Not this. Hilda's in there stirring the pot."

"What's that old woman doin' over here?"

"She and Angie are thick as thieves," Duane said. "I don't get it. Hilda's over here every day, every spare minute. And Angie wants it that way. Neither one of 'em wants me around."

"Hell, it's your house." Humboldt looked squarely up at the large man. "Be firm. Women like it."

"I've always been firm. Now Angie don't like it."

"Be flexible. Women like it." He grinned wryly. Duane smiled a little in spite of himself.

Humboldt had a low misery threshold. Over the years he'd

kept his health by taking immediate action before thinking. If it was him, he'd kick Hilda the hell out of his house, take Angela out to dinner, and kiss her a few times when she wasn't expecting it. That's how he'd handle it.

Duane was standing quietly now, staring at the cleared spot he'd created and nudging last little bits of gravel off of the smoothed dirt.

"Well," said Humboldt, turning toward the car, "see you tomorrow night."

"Tomorrow night," Duane replied over his shoulder.

Humboldt got in the car beside Maggie and started home up the steep, forested hill now engulfed in heavy fog. He used his low beams to find the white center line of the road. Neither he nor Maggie spoke until they got above the fog.

"Something's rotten in Denmark, as they say," Humboldt said, turning on his brights and pressing down on the accelerator. "Hilda's a trouble-maker."

Maggie said nothing.

"What's he s'posed to do?" Humboldt argued. "They're both against him."

He knew Maggie didn't like Duane. And he didn't like Hilda. That's the way it was. He and Maggie had worked around it before. They'd work around it again.

He wondered if Hilda was still at the Glynnises. Why didn't she just move in? Or Angela move out?

He wanted to turn around and go fix things, make things right for Duane. Nothing was harder for Humboldt than doing nothing. His stomach churned.

"You're upset," said Maggie.

"Damn right I am."

"I'll fix you bicarbonate of soda before bed."

Just thinking about the soda water made him feel better. He began to look forward to television.

"Maybe later I'll have a little Jim Beam. With some of that chocolate cake from yesterday."

"Jim Beam and *what?*" Maggie asked in a pained voice as they drove into the garage.

"Chocolate cake. Later." He shrugged. "It's not like mixing sleeping pills and booze."

Maggie went into the kitchen muttering, "Jim Beam and chocolate cake," while Humboldt settled into his recliner to watch John Wayne.

Tomorrow night at the Lucky Deuce he'd casually broach the subject of Hilda to Duane. Get him to open up a little, talk about his problem, like in Ann Landers. The guy just needed a little advice. Humboldt was older, with forty-five years of marriage under his belt. These big problems had a way of disappearing if you attacked them hard at the beginning, then ignored them until they went away.

He sipped his straight whiskey from the little shot glass Maggie placed at his elbow. He hadn't needed the bicarbonate of soda after all.

2

"Duane? Anybody home?" The trailer was dark. The dog next door growled. Down on Highway 101 a semi shifted into low gear at the grade. Uneasiness attacked Humboldt at the base of the spine and worked inward.

"Duane!" Humboldt banged on the door. Missing Saturday night shuffleboard was like missing Christmas. If Duane couldn't make it, he would have said something. Humboldt walked over to the pickup truck parked in the carport, but it was too dark to see anything.

He got the flashlight from his car. Opening the passenger door of the pickup, he moved the light over the steering wheel, dashboard, and objects on the seat: coffee cup, tin pouring spout for motor oil, work gloves. A can of Copenhagen. He walked around to the bed of the truck. On the floor and in the four corners he found nothing but fishing gear and a couple of oily rags.

As he ran the light around the truck bed one last time, he heard a car labor toward him from Hilda's end of the trailer park. He switched off the flashlight and waited. Technically maybe he was trespassing.

Hilda's old Chrysler ground past. She was looking straight ahead. He thought he saw someone in the seat beside her and guessed it was Angela. If they had seen his light, they didn't act like it.

"So what if they did?" he asked out loud. It was Saturday night. He was here to pick up Duane, like always. Saturday night was their beer and shuffleboard night.

Humboldt got in his car and headed back to the Lucky Deuce Club where he had dropped Maggie off earlier. As he turned onto the highway from the county road, he saw Hilda's car traveling south along 101 maybe three hundred yards ahead of him. He dropped back. It wasn't that he was following her. He just didn't want to pass her.

After a mile or so, Hilda's interior light went on. It was Angela in the passenger seat, all right. Humboldt watched the two women, their heads turning as they talked, Angela's hand gesturing now and then. The light went out.

What kind of a life did the old broad have, Humboldt wondered. Ever been married? Have any kids? Brothers? Sisters? Pets? Anything besides Angela?

He wanted to know why she'd moved here.

He wanted to know where Duane was.

Humboldt turned west when he reached the edge of town. He circled around and approached the Lucky Deuce from the ocean side. As he turned off his lights and engine, Hilda's Chrysler limped into the parking lot from the highway and straddled two parking spaces. Humboldt got out of his car and walked over.

"Followin' me?" asked Hilda, laying one fleshy arm across the top of the steering wheel and the other along the back of the seat.

"Nah. Maggie's here waitin' for me." Humboldt bent down and squinted into the car. "Who's that with you? Friend or foe?"

Hilda didn't answer, but heaved herself out of the car. Humboldt closed her door. "Where's that husband of yours?" he asked Angela who was getting out on the passenger's side. Angela shrugged. Her pale gaze strayed about the parking lot, touching everything but Humboldt. The women walked past him and entered the club.

"Goddam rude bitch," he said aloud as the entrance door closed upon Hilda's large pantsuit. He forgave Angela for snubbing him; it was the company she was keeping.

Humboldt entered the Lucky Deuce. There was a bar at one end, dance floor at the other, electronic poker game, Black Jack table, shuffleboard, and pool table. Something for everyone. Humboldt ordered a beer and looked around the large, dimly lit club for Duane. Fishermen in sweaters and knit caps slid pucks along the shuffleboard that ran down the center of the room. Loggers and haulers wearing striped work shirts and red suspenders stood in their own groups, big men with upper arms like thighs. But nowhere was there a dark giant who would have given Humboldt a bear hug, bought him a beer, and shouted confidentially, "About time you showed up!"

So he sat at the bar and drank his beer. Humboldt's brilliant blue eyes and perky expression made him look both kind and alert. Perched on the barstool, his pointed little face turned toward the room, his sweatshirt hood hanging down his back, he looked like a gray-haired elf having a night out.

As his eyes adjusted to the light he spotted Angela and Hilda sitting at a table talking. Cigarette in hand, Hilda breathed long streams of smoke into the room.

"She'll give us all cancer," he said under his breath.

"Hummer!" Maggie was coming toward him. She wore white slacks with a red silk blouse. Her fair skin, still glowing, wrinkled becomingly as she smiled. Her hair was lightly curled.

"Hello, good-lookin'."

"Why, Father." She smiled, and hugged him. "See anyone you know?"

"Nah. Not Duane. Not anyone. Are you winnin'?"

"Just hangin' in there," she replied. Humboldt ordered her a beer.

"I see Hilda and Angela," said Maggie. "Where's Duane?"

"Not here. And not at home," said Humboldt. "His truck was in the carport, though."

"That's odd," said Maggie. "Where would he go without his truck?"

Humboldt said nothing.

"Well, let's go sit with Angela and Hilda," she suggested.

"I'd as soon sit on a waffle iron."

Maggie stared at him, then at the two women. "What happened?"

"Nothin' aside from Hilda's fat-ass rudeness."

Maggie shrugged and went back to the game table. Humboldt brooded a while, then followed her.

"I don't see anyone here I want to talk to," he said, changing his mind. "I'll be home. Call me when you're ready to leave and I'll come get you," and he turned on his heel and walked out of the building.

On his way home he swung by Pacific Trailer Court again. This time lights were on at the Glynnises' and an old T-Bird was parked behind Duane's pickup. Humboldt knocked on the door. After a long wait it was opened by a tall, thin young man who looked familiar. With shorter hair and a less vacant expression he would have been almost good-looking.

"Evenin'. Would Duane be home?"

"Huh-uh," said the young man.

Humboldt remembered him. "Aren't you Duane and

Angela's boy?"

"Yeah."

"We met you on a picnic last summer."

No response.

"Up at the campgrounds," Humboldt amplified.

"Yeah."

"Your dad out of town or somethin'?"

"Yeah."

"Be back in a day or two?"

"Maybe."

"Still goin' to school in Eureka?"

"Yeah."

Finally Humboldt ran out of resources. "Okay, then."

"Yeah."

Humboldt backed his car up and retraced his path with nothing to show for his efforts. Ten minutes later, tired and disgruntled, he arrived home. He switched off the engine in the driveway and sat considering where Duane might be and why Richard had come home from Eureka at this particular time. It wasn't a school holiday, as far as he knew.

He wondered how Richard could be in college if he was as stupid as he sounded.

It was cold sitting there in the driveway. He went in the house and turned on the heat and the TV. By the light of the Saturday night movie he found the afghan on the sofa and took it over to his recliner where he half-sat, half-lay, drowsing restlessly before the television.

In a state of semi-sleep he projected a dark, charismatic figure onto the flickering screen. It laughed, bear-hugged, sweated, swore, and suddenly disappeared. Humboldt woke himself with a moan, pulled the afghan higher, and turned uneasily in his black Naugahyde chair.

Eventually he fell into a deep sleep that was not disturbed until Maggie closed the front door and switched on the table lamp beside him. He heard her walk across to the TV and turn off the test pattern.

"What time is it?" Humboldt asked, squinting up at her.

"Late. Almost two." She sat down on the footstool of his recliner.

"I must 'a slept through your call," he said thickly.

She untied his shoes. "I didn't call."

She removed one shoe and rubbed the bottom of his foot. Then she got up and hung her coat in the hall closet.

"How'd you get home?"

"Hilda brought me."

Humboldt tripped the lever on the recliner and sat upright. "Her Chrysler made it up the hill?" he asked in disbelief.

"Just barely."

Humboldt rose from his chair and began slowly wadding up the afghan.

"How'd she tear herself away from Angela?"

"She didn't. Angela came with us."

Humboldt walked across the living room and dropped the blanket in a fuzzy heap on the sofa. "Hilda keeps her on a short leash," he remarked.

"Not for long."

"What do you mean?"

"Angela's moving to Eureka. Duane left her and she's getting a divorce."

3

Humboldt was at the Glynnises' trailer the next morning at ten o'clock. Richard, pale and untidy, answered the door.

"Mornin'. Your dad back yet?"

"Nope."

"Mind if I wait inside for Maggie? She had to swing by

town. She'll be back to pick me up any minute." As he talked he opened the screen door and walked into the house. "Home for long?"

"I dunno."

"Let's see," Humboldt said, creating small talk. "You're workin' in Eureka and goin' to school, your dad said."

"Yeah." Richard played with the hairs on his upper lip.

Humboldt glanced into the living room. Things looked the same, a little cluttered, maybe. He straightened a picture on the entryway wall.

"Don't mind me," Humboldt said.

"Well… " Richard stood weakly between the entryway and the hall leading to the kitchen. He fiddled with the *TV Guide* he was holding.

"Watching TV?" Humboldt asked cheerfully.

"Yeah." Richard turned and walked back to the kitchen.

"What's on?"

"Nothin' much. Cartoons."

Humboldt perched on a stool at the breakfast bar and adjusted the angle of the mini-TV. "See okay?"

Richard didn't answer.

Humboldt was just getting involved in an old Roadrunner when Richard said, "How long is she gonna be?"

"Who? Angela?"

"No. Your wife."

"Maggie? Any minute now."

"I'm leaving," said Richard. "Gotta lock up."

"Oh, very well," said Humboldt. "You can count on me. I'll see that everything is shipshape and locked up tight before I leave."

Richard hesitated. "Whyn't you wait outside?" he asked.

"And miss the Roadrunner?"

"My mom—"

"Your folks know me. I've been here a lot," said Humboldt.

"Anyway, Maggie'll pick me up in five minutes."

Richard turned indecisively before walking back down the hall to the entryway. As soon as Humboldt heard the front door close and the old T-Bird drive away he got off the barstool and went straight into Duane and Angela's bedroom.

4

Dirty linen and underwear flew over Humboldt's head and landed on the carpeted floor to the right and left of him. He reached deep into the wicker hamper again and again, energetically producing and discarding limp gray laundry by the handful. He straightened and walked over to the closet. Half-hearing the low sound of the TV still on in the kitchen, he went through Duane's clothes for the second time like a worried mother. Still he could not find the plaid shirt smelling of beer that Duane had worn Friday night.

Humboldt jogged to the laundry room, keeping his ears open for the sound of tires on gravel. He peered into the washer and dryer. Empty. Nothing hung from the rack above the dryer. The shirt was not in the house. Wherever Duane was, he was wearing it.

Maybe he'd packed some clothes in a suitcase and left town. Humboldt pictured Duane relaxing with friends somewhere far away from Hilda and Angela, wearing clean clothes and with money in his pocket. Duane would probably call him tonight and tell him not to worry. Humboldt took a deep breath and felt better. Duane could take care of himself. The whole thing would blow over, like any other spat between a man and wife.

He closed the dryer door. It occurred to him that if Duane had packed a suitcase, his shaving kit would not be here. He walked quickly into the bathroom and went rapidly through cupboards and drawers. Now he could hear the Roadrunner's beep-beep as the little bird buzz-sawed its way along cliffs and crags and through obstacles that should have been fatal. Then, to the accompaniment of frustrated Wiley Coyote music, Humboldt's hand touched Duane's shaving kit. He rummaged through the case. Razor. Shaving cream. Toothbrush.

Discouraged, he tried to reason it out. Shirt gone. Razor still here. Maybe Duane had left in a hurry, or in some kind of mental fog. Maybe he had amnesia or something. Humboldt pictured him wandering around Portland or San Francisco unshaven, hollow-eyed, wearing his plaid shirt that smelled like beer. He saw him sitting on a curb, dirty and forgetful.

Had Duane taken any money? The Glynnises banked at U.S. Western. He was pretty sure they were on a joint account. He hurried back into their bedroom and began looking through the desk and chest of drawers. Nothing.

He hoped Duane had the checkbook, and not Angela.

Half-listening for a car in the driveway, Humboldt began scooping up dirty clothes off the floor. Blood rushed to his face and his eyes burned. Marriages broke up every day, but people didn't cut loose of everything near and dear all at once. Or have it all taken away from them. Picking the linen up from the floor, he thought of Hilda and punched the sheets and towels deep into the hamper.

For about five seconds he questioned whether or not to pull back before he got more involved. His peaceful routine was upset. For the last day and a half he and Maggie had been arguing about Duane. She didn't want him taking sides in a divorce. She didn't want him opening a can of worms because, she said, he might not be able to close the lid.

"What are friends for?" he muttered. He dropped the last sock into the hamper and firmly closed the wicker lid. "So much for lids."

He heard brakes squeal and a car door slam.

Humboldt made a lightning-quick survey of the bedroom.

THREE BLIND MICE

It looked undisturbed. As he turned to go back into the kitchen where the Roadrunner had succumbed to a game show, he saw that the clothes in Duane's closet still looked disarranged from the search. Listening for the front door, Humboldt quickly slid hangers along the pole, trying to remember how the clothes had looked before he moved them.

As he adjusted a shirt on its hanger, his eye was attracted to a small circle of light in the back wall of the closet about five feet up from the floor. He separated the hangers again and put one eye against the neatly cut opening.

Humboldt felt puzzled and flustered. He tried to think of a reason for the hole, a conduit, perhaps, for plumbing lines or electrical wiring. He could think of none.

The front door had not yet opened. Whoever had driven up was still outside. He hurriedly separated clothes hangers all the way down to the dark end of the closet until he could see another circle of light. Already he thought he knew what he would find. Bending his knees and peering for the second time, he found himself looking into the master bathroom.

He straightened quickly. The front door still had not opened. He ran his hands along the top of the clothes pole and spaced the hangers evenly. There might be time to check out the peephole from the bathroom side. He could say that he'd been watching TV in the kitchen and had just stepped into the bathroom for a minute. He could say he was waiting for Maggie, like he'd told Richard earlier.

Humboldt smelled cigarette smoke. He backed away from the closet and turned toward the bedroom door. Hilda was standing squarely in the doorframe watching him.

17

5

"What in the hell are you doin'?" Hilda asked in her deep voice. She slouched in the doorway, smoking. Humboldt felt trapped, and tried to act nonchalant.

"I'm missin' a shirt," he said, reaching into the closet and pulling out a shirt sleeve to illustrate. He was a little out of breath.

Hilda snorted. He met her contempt with a bright blue stare. She shifted her weight and blocked the doorway with one large arm braced against the jamb. Angling her right leg across her left, propping her foot up on one toe, she looked at him with a superior expression.

"Where's Duane?" he said softly.

Her eyes narrowed and she answered too quickly, "How should I know?" She shrugged her bulky shoulders.

"He was fine when I left him Thursday night," Humboldt said.

Just then Angela appeared in the hallway behind Hilda, a thin, pale figure in a beige knit outfit and an elaborate hairdo. Humboldt had not heard her footsteps. Maybe she got around by floating in the air above Hilda's pathway. Now that he thought about it, he never had heard the front door of the mobile home open and close. Maybe Angela floated through doors, too. But Hilda didn't float. He knew she'd turned the doorknob silently, lifted her heavy body on tiptoe, and crept into the house, probably looking carefully in each room as she proceeded down the hall.

"Somebody's in Duane's closet," she said to Angela, jerking her thumb toward Humboldt. Angela saw him and reddened. For a moment her colorless eyes showed emotion. Was it alarm? Anger? Humboldt couldn't tell. Immediately she brought her face under control.

"You told Richard that Maggie was picking you up," she said

in a neutral tone.

"I thought she was. She's forgetful. I'll have to call her."

Angela followed him part way into the kitchen. He smiled at her as he dialed home, and she smiled back mechanically. Not so long ago Humboldt had liked Angela's smile. He'd liked Duane's young wife, too thin for his taste, but pretty. Now he didn't know what to think about her.

Hilda was still in the bedroom, probably checking to see if he'd plugged up her peepholes. He pictured her bent at the waist, hands on knees, staring into the two bathrooms. He had a sudden urge to go into the john and look back at her, eyeball to eyeball.

Maggie didn't answer. He couldn't remember if she was going to pick him up or go home and wait for his call.

"Excuse me," he said to Angela, replacing the telephone receiver. "Indigestion." He patted his stomach and strode across the kitchen and hallway, closing the door of the guest bathroom behind him. Quickly he scanned the busy wallpaper and found the little hole he was looking for just above a white wicker doodad on a painted shelf. The shelf held two plants and a roll of toilet paper disguised by a discreet crocheted cover.

Bracing his hands on his knees, he bent down and put his eye as close to the hole as he could. It was dark. He could see nothing, not the bedroom closet, not clothing, not Hilda's eye. Just in case she was there, though, he winked.

It might be fun to pee in the hole and get her in the eye. He stepped back and studied the little opening so well hidden by the shelf and patterned wallpaper. He mused on the naughty child trapped within his old body, wishing for less self-control. He opened the bathroom door and walked out of the room with dignity.

Humboldt entered the living room, where he found Richard sitting on the edge of the sofa, studying the floor. Humboldt had not known he was in the house. Perhaps he floated, too.

"Can I use the phone in here?"

Richard stood up too quickly and hit the edge of the coffee table in front of him. The artificial flowers trembled in their vase.

"Yeah," he mumbled. He rubbed his knee and avoided Humboldt's gaze.

The older man walked across the room to the table beside Duane's chair and dialed home again. Richard turned to leave, hesitated, then turned back.

"Maggie was supposed to be here a long time ago," Humboldt lied, putting down the receiver. Richard seemed on the verge of saying something. Then, aware of his mother and Hilda coming down the hall, he put his hands in his pockets and studied the floor again.

As the women entered the room, Humboldt noticed two things simultaneously: Maggie drove up, and Richard walked over to his father's chair and sank deeply into the red upholstery. It was the most emphatic thing Humboldt had ever seen him do. Angela watched her son intently.

"Maggie's here," Hilda announced bluntly. No one moved.

Richard's features softened as he allowed his head to fall back for a moment on the head rest, his long, unwashed hair fanning out on the red velour. Against the chair his face was colorless.

Angela started to cross the room toward her son, but was prevented by Hilda's hand on her forearm. Humboldt watched the heavy-set woman with interest. She might be surprised by the bond between mother and son. It might be stronger than she realized. His interest turned to snide satisfaction. Angela might have a mind of her own. And Richard just might know more than he was telling.

Maggie sprayed gravel as she came to a stop in front of the trailer. Humboldt turned on his heel and walked out the front door, leaving Hilda to get the lid back on her own can of worms.

6

"Maybe you're wondering why I called," Angela said into the telephone, sliding the green potholder on and off its hook.

"I'm just glad you did," replied Maggie. "We've missed seeing you."

"That's what I'm calling about. Since Humboldt always keeps track of things, I wanted to tell you and him that I'm going to Eureka for a couple of days with Richard."

"Well, how nice. You already told me, though, remember? When you and Hilda drove me home the other night."

"Oh, yeah," said Angela. After a brief silence she added, "Richard's college starts."

"I guess it's that time of year again," said Maggie.

"I'm going with him. I deserve a vacation."

"Of course you do. It'll do you worlds of good."

"Well, we'll have to get together when I come back."

"We'll do that," said Maggie. "Take care of yourself and have a good time."

Angela hung up the phone. She was pleased with the way she'd sounded. "We'll have to get together." That's being sociable. She would start phoning people, not just Hilda. She would start being sociable.

She imagined herself sitting in a nice bar in town with people in their twenties and thirties, not fishermen and loggers, but office workers in nice-fitting suits. She'd be drinking a Daiquiri and smiling. It would be late afternoon. She and her friends would decide to stay and have dinner in town. Maybe Richard would drop by and join them. It would be a weekend and he would be home from college. Maybe it was Christmas or Easter vacation. Duane said they had long vacations in college.

Angela's eyes narrowed as Duane entered her fantasy. There he stood, heavy and tall and dark, watching her, waiting for her, demanding dinner, drinks, bed. Fury whipped through her daydream. She would have to leave her smiling friends and go home. He would never let her spend an evening alone. Even though she would never see him again, never needed to fear him again, still she could not spend an evening away from him, even in her imagination.

The telephone rang. She jumped. New friends calling already!

But it was the phone ringing in the TV program. Richard sat at the breakfast bar watching a smiling teenager pick up the receiver and mouth into it the pleasant words of the script.

Angela hauled out the electric frying pan from the bottom shelf of a cabinet.

"Grilled cheese?" she asked Richard tonelessly. He didn't hear her. It didn't matter. Neither of them ate much these days. Meals were a chore; cooking was a chore; living was a chore. Angela twiddled the plug into the recessed socket of the pan and looked over at Richard. His eyes were blank, his face impassive.

She was very tired. The thought of melted cheese nauseated her. She pulled the plug out by the cord and said, "You want a glass of milk or something?"

Richard shrugged. He avoided her eyes.

"When do you have to be back at school?" she asked.

"Soon."

"I know that. What day?"

"I dunno."

Angela flared. "You'd better find out!"

"I don't even wanna go," Richard said sullenly.

"Your dad wants—" She stopped herself. Richard's eyes flew to her face. The plug swung at the end of its cord like a pendulum. Duane's power over them made Angela feel faint.

She dropped the cord, walked frantically to the chair by the telephone, and put her head on her knees.

"I'll go," Richard said from a great distance.

She was having trouble staying on the chair. When she could

stand again, she would call Hilda.

"Mom?" He sounded nearer.

"Okay," she breathed.

"You want some fresh air or somethin'?"

"Yeah." She opened her eyes and saw daylight again. Slowly she sat up and the kitchen righted itself. She felt a little better. She didn't need to call Hilda after all. She and Richard didn't need anybody. Not Duane, not Hilda.

"Let's get out of here," she said. Richard was silent. "Let's go to Eureka." She stood, swaying a little.

"Now?" Richard asked.

"Right now. We've got to get away. You've got to find a job." She pushed her hair away from her damp forehead.

"Yeah, but—"

"This time it's different," she said. "I've left your dad."

Richard looked at her squarely, then stiffened and pivoted away.

"Dad's left us," he said in a tight voice. He stumbled on his way back to the barstool. Angela covered her mouth with her hand. Desperately she worked at keeping the kitchen floor from tilting again.

By 7:30 she was euphoric. They were on the road. Without Hilda, she had made the decision to leave town. It was the beginning of her new life. She and Richard could manage just fine by themselves. Angela touched her hair carefully. She encouraged it to fluff upward and outward; she would have liked to be taller than she was.

Richard drove his old Thunderbird fast along the dark highway, around curves, in and out of giant redwoods. About halfway between home and Eureka, Angela's mood changed. She looked at the black forest coldly. When she was younger the woods had calmed her, made her feel spiritual. In the past she had been able, like the trees, to reach for something more. More light and air. Sky. She'd felt religious in her striving for— what? To love and be loved. To laugh and enjoy her family. To be telephoned by friends. To dial the phone and say into it, "Just thought I'd call to say hi."

Now, however, the trees meant nothing to her. She felt numb.

Richard drove fast, with narrow concentration. They sped around the curve at Driftwood Beach. Trees whipped by in the headlights. Just beyond them, she knew, was the Pacific Ocean.

She thought of all the trips she'd made to Eureka. Pleasant trips by herself. One summer she'd driven down to the Farmers Market and filled the back seat of her car with bags of fresh vegetables. She even remembered the salad she'd made later that evening, a layered salad in the glass bowl. Lettuce on the bottom, white cauliflower next, orange carrots, then green and white cucumber slices, red tomatoes. Richard had liked it. She couldn't remember if Duane liked it or not. She really couldn't remember much about Duane from back then. Just how handsome he'd seemed when she was fifteen. And her own pain and fear and shame after they were married.

She stiffened her back and tried not to lean into the curves. She'd driven back home that summer afternoon. The ocean on her left, looking like blue glass, offered freedom, and the redwoods on her right sheltered her. But when she got home she was horrified to discover Duane's car in the garage. Just at the point that she'd started to punch the accelerator and drive on down the street, he'd opened the front door. He was thirty feet away, but she felt that he was standing directly over her, ordering her in. She parked the car and carried in one bag of groceries. The other bags stayed in the back seat.

"You didn't tell me you were going to Eureka," he'd said angrily on the way to the bedroom. She didn't reply. It was safer to give in to Duane than to argue. Over the years she'd learned to do what he wanted.

As she followed him down the hall she thought of the bags of fresh vegetables still in the car. All through the next hour, off and on, she thought of the salad she would make. If only the things didn't wilt in the back seat. She thought hard about the salad. It helped her to endure Duane.

"Richard will be home soon," she said in a flat voice at the end of it. Richard was a schoolboy then. She'd gotten dressed and carried the bags from the car to the kitchen. She made the salad and put some bacon bits in it for Richard. Supper, as usual, had been eaten in silence.

Now Richard turned on the windshield wipers. She could just make out the white line in the center of the narrow, snaking highway. She knew the trees were swaying, but she couldn't see them through the rain. It didn't matter. She didn't need to see the trees. They no longer protected her, anyway. And the heaving ocean to her right was now a dark place to drown. Nothing mattered: she was in a car; there was a storm; the road went south. That was all.

Her nerves were bad. She would call Hilda tonight. Hilda knew a nerve specialist in Eureka. Hilda would be surprised she'd left town. She'd gotten in the habit of calling Hilda a lot ever since the night…

She would not think about it. She just would not think about it.

"Where was I?" Angela said aloud. Richard turned to look at her. His face betrayed uncertainty before he extinguished all expression. Angela did not notice him.

Oh, yes. Hilda. She'd been thinking about Hilda. It was a bad habit, calling Hilda all the time. She might forget that she had secrets from Hilda.

She wanted to talk to someone, but there was no one she could tell. The windshield wipers beat a rhythm to her thoughts. Hilda. Swish. Duane. Swish.

Hilda…

She couldn't remember the roadway for the last five miles. With a start, drenched in clammy sweat, she began to pay attention. This was her new life, and it was worse than her old.

All she had was a bossy friend, a son who never talked to her anymore, bad memories from the past, and a deep, recurring fear of the future.

7

The wind came in over the ocean from the northwest, pushing heavy swells before it. It thrashed trees up and down the coast, and shook Hilda's mobile home. She sat at her kitchen table in the gray afternoon light, unperturbed: a rock in a storm.

The telephone rang. She shoved the little brush back into the fingernail polish bottle, blew on her vermillion nails, and reached for the wall phone with her dry hand.

"Hullo. Yeah, Angie. Where are you?"

Hilda cradled the phone in the folds of her neck and reached for her cigarettes and lighter. "Did you find a place?"

Angela's voice buzzed over the wire like a fly trapped in a small space. Hilda lit her cigarette and pulled the ashtray toward her, inhaling deeply as she listened.

Angela had found an apartment in Eureka. But it was too small. She hated it. Was anyone talking about her? Had Humboldt come nosing around again? It didn't matter. She was never coming home again. But she was lonesome. Would Hilda drive down tomorrow and see her?

"Give me some directions," Hilda said. She leaned toward a kitchen drawer and pulled out a pencil and note pad. She began drawing a map, squinting through her smoke. "North or south?"

But Angela's directions were wrong. Hilda tore the page off the pad and threw the crumpled paper on the floor. She started to draw a new map, but Angela was off on another tangent, talking about Duane.

Hilda threw down the pencil. It rolled off the table and landed near the paper wad.

"Goddammit, Angie!" she shouted. "Forget him. Nobody's talking. Nobody's asking questions, not Humboldt, not anybody." She lowered her voice. "He's gone. Left. Forget him, Babe." She was almost pleading now. "You're better off without him."

There was a silence on the other end of the line, then a brief torrent of words. Angela ended the telephone call abruptly. Hilda frowned and slowly replaced the receiver. She looked out at the bending alders near her kitchen window, then leaned over her hands again, slowly building up the lacquer on her hard, red nails. Outside, two strong gusts of wind aimed for the skirting around the trailer, tried to break the tie-downs. The wind hurled a heavy stick against the metal. The loud sound triggered Hilda's rage.

"Bastard!" she shouted. She placed both hands on the table and pushed herself to her feet. The trailer rocked beneath her. Now Hilda herself was a storm. Anger widened her eyes. Her lip curled. "Bastard! You're fixed!" A slight tremor of the head marked her fury and her age. She stomped into the living room and lowered herself into the cushioned trough of her armchair. Breathing heavily, she stared at the dead television screen. She saw Duane's handsome, spoiled face and his strong body.

She'd loved him the moment she first saw him in the Lucky Deuce Club. She'd just moved to town. He began to play cards regularly, always the nights when she was dealing. The first time they slept together he came to her house. The second time they went to "the ranch," his two and a half acres east of town where he kept an old trailer. There had been no third time.

Had she been too old for him? Too fat? He'd fascinated her, excited her, then dropped her. But it didn't matter now. Hilda leaned her head back on the chair. Tomorrow she would see Angela. She would take her a gift, something special, something to show her that their new life was beginning. Angela would forget Duane. Hilda would make her forget him.

She struggled out of her chair. She got her shoulder bag and jacket and walked outside. The wind had let up. It was almost dark.

Driving into town, she daydreamed about moving to Eureka herself, getting an apartment with Angela.

She slowed for the stop sign at 101. As she sat at the intersection, she reconsidered. Both of us can't leave town at the same time, she thought. Too many questions.

Now she sounded like Angela, worrying about what people would think. But it wasn't gossip she worried about. It was the police. Police and courts and lawyers and the whole shitty system coming down on your head. She didn't mind for herself so much. She could take anything that came down the pike. It was Angela who must be protected. Angela must not be touched by any of it.

Richard. That's another reason for waiting, Hilda thought, grinding the gears into first and lurching onto Highway 101. Angela flutters around him all the time, asking him this, asking him that. Well, the kid's a jerk. Gets in my way. Sooner or later he's gotta move out. Then Angela and I can make a home for ourselves, just the two of us. We can pick a spot on the map and say, "Here. We're gonna live here. Just the two of us." She was perspiring a little from hope and determination.

Hilda slowed as she entered the city limits. She drove around town looking at the shops for a while. Finally she parked in front of the jewelry store. She turned off the ignition and sat without moving for a few moments.

What should she get Angela? A ring? No. Too much too soon. Scare her away. Bracelet? Bracelets are boring. Angie don't wear them, anyway. A necklace. It's gonna be a necklace. Our necklace. She pictured a beautiful pendant on a slender chain. The chain slipped beneath Angie's blouse. Angie was letting her touch it. She was touching the chain, handling the gold pendant…

The store didn't close for another hour. She would sit for a while and think about Angie. She lit one of her long, brown cigarettes, turned on the radio, and settled back in her seat, in no hurry to end this fantasy that filled her with excitement and a sense of well-being.

8

"I don't believe Duane's in Portland!" Humboldt shouted above the music of the jukebox. He took an emphatic bite of pastrami. "I would 'a heard from him by now."

"Who said he was in Portland?" shouted Maggie.

"Jim Hampton at the lumber yard."

"How does he know?"

"His son is friends with Richard. Richard told his boy." Humboldt washed down his sandwich with a long swallow of buttermilk. He set the empty, flecked glass firmly back on the table.

"How would Richard know?"

"Dunno. I doubt if Duane called him. Him and Richard don't have much to say to each other." His face darkened. "Maybe Hilda knows and told him. She seems to be running the show over there."

"Or maybe Angela knows" said Maggie. Humboldt shrugged his shoulders and brooded.

"Want to team up?" Maggie asked brightly, inclining her head toward the shuffleboard.

"What?" Humboldt cupped his ear. The jukebox, the puck glancing sharply against mahogany, the laughter at the Black Jack table, all contributed to the din.

"Want to team up?" Maggie yelled. Mercifully, the jukebox ran out of quarters.

"Nah," said Humboldt. "My heart ain't in it."

A logger with a thick, black beard and beefy arms walked

up and down the length of the waist-high shuffleboard, tilting a large can in mid-air. As if flicking a salt shaker over a buffet of food, he delicately sifted sawdust onto the varnished table below.

"'At's good!" somebody shouted. "'At'll slow 'em down!" A black puck flew along the board, stopping inches from the end of the table. Another followed.

"'At's a pair!" somebody else shouted as the logger followed through on his shot, his heavy arm held in frozen motion over the board. "Pair 'a britches! Pair 'a britches! Go right down the middle!"

Humboldt watched the game with a melancholy expression, turning his empty buttermilk glass around and around on the formica table.

"Hey, Denton! Where's your partner?" one of the men called out.

"Hell if I know," Humboldt replied.

"You don't need him! Come on over! Show 'em how it's done!"

Humboldt smiled and waved at the players. But to Maggie he said glumly, "You ready to go?"

"Let's have a cup of coffee," she said. "One cup. Then we'll go." Humboldt reluctantly settled back in his seat. He knew Maggie wanted him to relax. She reached across the table, but he only patted her hand absent-mindedly. He couldn't concentrate on anything but Duane's whereabouts. When he wasn't trying to read Duane's mind, he was trying to read Hilda's. What was she up to?

"I wonder why Richard said his dad is in Portland." Since Humboldt wasn't going to stop thinking about Duane, she might as well think about him, too.

"Maybe someone asked him and that was the first thing that popped into his head," Humboldt answered.

"Or maybe Richard's trying to throw people off the track," Maggie said. "Richard or someone."

Humboldt hadn't thought of that. Maggie surprised him. Maggie often surprised him.

The coffee came and Humboldt emptied two packets of sugar into his cup. He added cream up to the brim and slowly stirred the mixture. Suddenly he removed the spoon and slammed it down on the table. "I'm going to Portland," he announced. Maggie jumped a little in the booth. Forty-five years of living with Humboldt had not quite accustomed her to his sudden impulses.

"What in the world for?" she asked, astonished.

"To be sure Duane isn't there."

Maggie stared at him. "How can you be sure that Duane *isn't* in Portland?"

"I've got to do something, even if it's wrong," Humboldt said. His eyes sparkled, and color returned to his cheeks. He had a job to do. For a man who had built bridges and operated two-hundred-ton cranes, retirement was very tame.

Maggie took a swallow of coffee before saying tartly, "I don't understand how you can be sure a person is *not* in Portland."

Humboldt ignored her comment. He looked through her and past her. They both knew he had decided. He might argue about it, explain, justify, cajole; but he was going to Portland. "He's got a fisherman friend up there. His friend's boat is called the Minnie T. Or the Molly C. Something like Minnie. Or Molly. Or Maggie," he added smoothly. "The Maggie D. Prettiest boat in the harbor."

Maggie didn't smile.

"Anyway, I'd know it if I heard it." Humboldt wisely retired into silence. Watching her as she ran her forefinger around and around the lip of her coffee cup, he waited for the persuasive speech she was preparing.

Finally she said, "Why don't you wait a bit? Things will blow over. He'll be back with a good reason for being gone, and you'll wonder why you stayed awake at night worrying. Furthermore," she said, "you're not a young man anymore. You have your own health to think of. All this stress—"

"Bullshit!" Humboldt said. Maggie had gone too far. She'd called him old. For a man of sixty-eight he was in perfect health, and he felt twenty years younger than he was. She should know that better than anyone.

"Well, what are you going to do when you don't find him?" she asked without a trace of sarcasm.

"A friend's in trouble," he said heatedly. "I feel it. I know it. And I'm not too old to do something about it."

"You didn't answer the question!"

"I don't have to answer the question," he snapped. While Maggie was a very intelligent and practical person, she sometimes missed the point. "Do you know what friends are for?" he fumed.

"Yes, I know what friends are for! They're for staying out of your business until you ask for help!" The Dentons sat stiffly, glaring at each other across the formica tabletop. Finally Maggie thrust her purse under her arm and stood up. "I'll be at the Black Jack table."

"Yeah. Take your purse. I don't need you to lose any more of my money," Humboldt said ungallantly.

"I'll win with my own! And don't wait for me. I'll catch a ride with somebody later."

"You'll do no such thing," said Humboldt, digging in his pocket for the car keys. He threw them down on the table in front of her.

"How will you get home?"

"Don't worry about me," he answered. "I'll find a way." She wavered, then picked up the keys and walked briskly over to the card game. Humboldt upset his coffee cup as he left the table. He strode across the room to the door and out into the parking lot.

Piss on Maggie's logic, he thought to himself. I'm gonna find Duane and I'm gonna find him my way. I hope I haven't waited too long to start looking.

The dealer took Maggie's last chip at 10:20. Maggie decided to call it a night. She had not enjoyed herself. Fighting with

Humboldt made her unhappy. And she'd lost $25. She stepped out of the Lucky Deuce Club and braced herself against the cold wind that had suddenly whipped up over the ocean. She made her way to the Plymouth and headed onto 101, struggling to keep the car on the dark highway.

Maybe Duane *is* in trouble, she thought between gusts of wind. Then again, maybe he has business out of town. Or even in town. Maybe he's got a girl friend. It wouldn't surprise me. Maggie was furious with Humboldt for getting involved. She gunned the motor, then yanked the steering wheel to the left as the wind nearly blew her off the highway.

Hummer wants to take a trip, she continued to herself as she reached a stretch of county highway that was protected from the west wind. Well, let the stubborn old fool go. Tomorrow's not soon enough.

The lights were still on in the house when she turned into the driveway. The rhododendron bushes in the front yard were blowing wildly, and she could hear the wind in the giant spruce. Humboldt had opened the garage door for her. She drove in, got out of the car, and ran to the front of the house where she pulled her potted begonias onto the protected porch. Then she dashed back into the garage and closed the automatic door. He'd left the door from the garage to the house unlocked for her. She put away her keys and passed through the kitchen into the living room.

"Hello," she said.

"Hullo." He was in the middle of dialing. Maggie patted her windblown hair and hung up her coat. Humboldt had a fire going in the woodburner. The wind howled about the corners of the house.

"Coffee or Jim Beam?" she called from the kitchen. If he was going to Portland she'd give him a good send-off.

"Both," he called back.

There. He'd reached his party. A motel in Portland? He didn't state any name but she knew he was talking to someone out of town. In spite of modern communications, Humboldt persisted in yelling over the wire whenever he talked long distance. She noisily filled the coffeemaker with water and coffee, set out mugs, poured whiskey into two shot glasses. Really, she wasn't the slightest bit interested in his phone call. Let the silly old bastard go off on a wild goose chase. Without her. She set cream and sugar down hard on the serving tray and wondered how many fishing boats there were in Portland, and how many bars with shuffleboard. She wondered how long it would take Humboldt *not* to find Duane.

There. He'd hung up the phone. Maggie carried the tray of drinks into the living room and set it on the table beside his chair.

"Looks like we're in for some weather," he remarked conversationally.

"Looks like it."

"How was Black Jack?"

"I lost $25."

Humboldt winced but merely said, "Bad luck." He leaned back in his recliner. "Anybody there I know?"

"Not a soul. Coffee?"

"Thanks." Maggie filled his cup. They handed the spoon back and forth, creamed and sugared each other's coffee, talked a little. As they exchanged civilities their argument began to fade. They were good at civilities. They were also good at arguments. They'd been practicing both for years.

"I'm awful grouchy these days," Humboldt said tolerantly.

"You can say that again."

"I'm sorry," he said.

"Well, I'm sorry, too." She moved over to the arm of Humboldt's chair. He pulled her carefully onto his lap.

"Hurt your back?"

"No. Your knee?"

"Never better." They settled close together, feeling the

warmth from the woodburner and from each other.

A few moments later Maggie broke the contented silence with a whisper: "Who were you talking to on the phone?"

"Wouldn't you like to know," he whispered back.

"I was just curious."

"It was Angela."

She leaned back to look him in the face. "In Eureka?"

"Uh-huh."

"How did you find her number?"

"I have ways."

"Well?"

"Well, what?"

"What did you learn?"

"Not a whole hell of a lot." Humboldt curled a lock of Maggie's gray hair around one finger.

"Did you tell her you're going to Portland?" she asked.

Humboldt picked up his shot glass abruptly and drank. "I'm not going to Portland," he said, wiping his mouth with the back of his hand.

"Oh?" said Maggie.

"It would be a wild goose chase," he said.

"Oh?"

"I think the answer is right here in town."

"I see," said Maggie.

Humboldt studied his wife. "Where do *you* think Duane is?" It was the first time he'd asked her opinion on the subject.

"I think Duane is staying with someone in town," Maggie answered. "Maybe a girl friend."

"He doesn't have a girl friend," Humboldt said simply. "He's happy with Angela. Or was till Hilda screwed things up." Holding his shot glass up to the light and squinting through it, he said, "Do you know what Angela said over the phone tonight?"

"No."

"She said, 'Ask Hilda where Duane is.'" Maggie looked

skeptical. "Hilda knows," Humboldt said darkly.

"Or Angela wants you to think so," said Maggie.

He looked at her sideways. "You've got a suspicious mind."

"I'm suspicious of people who point the finger at their friends," Maggie said.

"I'm suspicious of people who move in where they're not wanted," retorted Humboldt

"Angela hasn't stopped her."

"Maybe not, but she's gone to Eureka. Probably to get away from Hilda."

Maggie thought for a minute. "What makes you think Hilda's moved in to the Glynnises'?"

"For one thing, she drilled peep holes in the closet so she could watch people in the bathroom." His face twisted with distaste.

"You're kidding!"

"No, I'm not. I saw them myself."

"When?"

Humboldt tried to sound offhand. "Oh, one day when I happened to be looking through Duane's closet." Maggie moved off of Humboldt's lap and sat on the footstool in front of him. She zeroed in.

"Humboldt Denton! Have you searched the Glynnis house?"

"Yes," he said. "I searched every room and I don't know any more now than what I did before I looked." He ignored her disapproval and added, "In fact, I know less." Then in a low, worried voice: "I can't find the shirt Duane wore last Thursday night."

"You can't find the shirt…" Maggie repeated.

"The one he spilled beer on."

"Oh, that one. Angela probably washed it."

"I looked. It wasn't in the laundry room or anywhere in the house that I could see."

"Angela probably knows where it is," said Maggie.

"I think Hilda's the one who knows," said Humboldt.

They gazed at each other. In silence they picked up their cold coffee cups and carried them into the dark kitchen. Outside, the wind was rising. They could hear large drops of rain splatting on the metal vent above the stove. Through the kitchen window they watched back-and-silver clouds roll and boil in front of the moon. All else was swallowed up in wet blackness.

"Duane is somewhere out there," Humboldt said quietly, gesturing toward the stormy night. "He needs help."

Though Maggie did not disagree, she felt with dreadful certainty that somebody would try to prevent Humboldt from finding him. Unlike her husband, she wasn't sure who.

9

At midnight the storm slammed in from the sea full-force. It tore fishing boats loose from their moorings and shattered plate glass windows in town. Up on the county heights where Humboldt and Maggie lived, the wind broke off tree limbs and scattered them about the landscape like toothpicks. Humboldt was sleeping soundly through the storm, but Maggie lay awake listening to each gust hurl rain against the glass as if it were a giant hand throwing gravel at the windows.

It was one o'clock when the telephone rang. Alarmed, Maggie struggled with the bedclothes and tried to reach across Humboldt for the phone, but he was already awake, fumbling with the receiver and making it jingle annoyingly each time he dropped it.

"Hello?" He listened intently. There was a long silence. "I can't hear you." Another long silence. "I can't hear you!" he shouted. "Will you speak louder? We've got a hell of a storm goin' on. I can't make out what you're sayin'."

"Who is it?" asked Maggie, turning on the lamp at her side

of the bed. Humboldt motioned for her to be quiet. Evidently his caller finally made himself understood, because Humboldt sat bolt upright in bed, his hair standing in all directions above his pink, creased face. Maggie propped two pillows behind his back, then bent toward her bedside table, peering at the clock near-sightedly.

"How do you know that?" Humboldt yelled above the snarl of weather outside.

"Duane?" Maggie mouthed. He shook his head. She slid back down under the covers and lay straight and rigid.

Two telephone calls in one night, she thought to herself. She felt that Humboldt was leaving their calm, contented life far behind and embarking upon a senseless adventure without her. Oh, to have him puttering about at routine tasks rather than searching for an unpleasant man who, she thought, didn't want to be found. She wished with all her heart that the telephone had not rung.

"Where?" Humboldt shouted. He nodded several times energetically. "Okay. I'll be there." He hung up the receiver and sat very still for a moment against the pillows and headboard before he jumped out of bed and jogged over to the closet. He threw off his pajamas and was half-dressed before Maggie could cry, half rising from her prone position,

"Humboldt, you can't go out in this weather!"

"Got a call. Don't understand it. Have to go out."

"Tonight? In this storm?"

"Yes. In this storm."

"Then I'm going with you," she said, already out of bed and running to the chest of drawers.

"No, you're not. You're staying right here." Humboldt's voice was loud and firm. Maggie ignored him and yanked slacks and sweater from the bottom drawer.

"You're not going!" Humboldt exploded.

Thrusting her arms through the sleeves and her head through

the neck of her sweater, Maggie asked breathlessly, "Who was that on the phone?"

"I'll tell you later." Humboldt sat on the edge of the bed tying his shoelaces. "I can't tell you now. I can't talk about it at all."

Maggie hesitated in front of the chest, shivering. "This is the worst storm of the year and you're going out on a secret mission? What if you don't come back?"

"You've been watching too much television," Humboldt said. He gave her a quick kiss and ran down the hall.

Maggie zipped on some boots, grabbed her raincoat and purse, and ran after him. She tore open the back kitchen door and rushed into the garage. Through sheets of rain she saw that he'd backed out and was already heading down the mountain.

She jumped into her Plymouth and followed him toward town.

10

Humboldt drove faster than Maggie even in good weather; and now in the heavy rain she lost him again and again on the curves of the county road. Once she reached 101 she barely glimpsed his taillights as they dipped down the far side of the hill by the radio tower. She turned right onto the highway and followed him, her fingers white on the steering wheel and her body tensed forward as she strained to see through the rain slanting sharply in the headlights.

"Slow down, Hum-boldt. Slow down, Hum-boldt," she whispered in time to the windshield wipers. The small red lights of his truck appeared and disappeared ahead of her. It was cold in the Plymouth, but she was driving too fast to fiddle with the heater and vent.

Suddenly, to her astonishment, she was almost upon him.

He must have slowed considerably and she nearly stopped in order to stay well behind him.

Then she saw the City Limit sign, familiar and reassuring. She could not believe they were already in town; she'd never come down off the mountain so fast. In another few hours, she reminded herself, it would be daylight.

He's just meeting someone for coffee. For years he's been meeting people for coffee, people he likes, people who like him. No one in the world wants to hurt Humboldt. She almost smiled with relief.

But a moment later her inner voice turned doubtful: Maybe no one wants to hurt him, but what kind of information can't wait until morning?

She tried to calm herself by concentrating on Humboldt's slow-moving taillights. He was turning right. She switched off her headlights and followed him down a dark, narrow street. Here and there she could just make out a small frame house or mobile home that came right up to the asphalt. Two travel trailers on a vacant lot were lighted and appeared to be lived in.

Maggie saw Humboldt park his truck almost at the end of the block. The door opened and closed. She assumed he'd gotten out, but she could not see where he went. Slowly, with her headlights still off, she eased up the street until she was about three lots back from his truck. She turned off the motor and sat perfectly still, her hand on the cold keys. Rain drummed on the vinyl top of the car.

Lifting the hood of her raincoat over her head, she stepped out of the car and into a muddy puddle that had collected in the cracked blacktop. Swearing under her breath, she softly closed the door and waded out of the pothole, dirty water seeping in and around the soles of her high-heeled boots. She stayed in the shadows of the trees and began walking fast. She had no idea where she was going. Just drawing close to Humboldt's truck made her feel better.

She stopped beside his pickup directly across the street from the trailer she believed he'd entered. One end of the coach faced her, and the length of it extended back into the narrow, deep lot. The room closest to her was lit by a light bulb in a lamp that had no shade. Dirty, ill-fitting curtains obstructed her view of the trailer's interior. She stood quietly, hoping to see Humboldt in the window. She saw nothing. A car drove by. She stepped deeper into the shadows and watched it pass. The muddy splash covered her coat.

In the center of town the fire whistle began shrieking in sets of three blasts. Sirens picked up the wail and carried it toward some disaster. She waited, terrified that the emergency might be here, might be Humboldt. The sirens seemed to stand still. The whistle finally stopped and the screaming of the trucks and police cars gradually faded into the distance.

Maggie drew a shaky breath. Time passed. Ten minutes became twenty. Surely there had been time enough for cups of coffee or messages or warnings or threats or whatever the hell disappearing people give to old friends in the middle of the night.

Should she go back to the car and wait? Or should she try and find him? She stepped into the street toward the trailer, still undecided.

"How in the hell are you?" asked a voice beside her. She jumped. Humboldt stepped out of the shadows.

She stared at him in disbelief. "Is that you, Humboldt?"

"Pretty damn likely," he replied. He gave her a big, wet hug that lasted a long time.

She drew back and looked at him. "How did you know I was here?"

"I saw you in my rear view mirror."

"How?"

"Your parking lights were on."

"You're kidding."

"No, I'm not."

"Well, how did you get out of the trailer without me seeing you?" She gestured across the street.

"I wasn't in it."

"Oh." Words could not cover her foolishness. "Well, where have you been?"

With a thumb he pointed vaguely down the street. Then he said, "Let's go home." He put a heavy arm around her.

"You're shaking," she said, turning toward him.

Humboldt nodded. "I don't feel so good." Maggie circled her arm tightly around his waist. They walked slowly to the car.

"Let's come back for the truck tomorrow," she said as he opened the driver's door for her.

He shook his head. "Leave your lights off till we get on the highway. Follow me home." He closed her door. While he walked to his pickup, she started the Plymouth and, by the light of a distant porch light, turned around and waited for him to drive ahead.

Humboldt slowly passed her. For the second time that evening she followed him out onto the highway, squinting through the windshield wipers and wondering why Duane couldn't talk to Humboldt in broad daylight.

11

At three o'clock in the morning Humboldt Denton sank back in a tub of very hot water. His head ached; his body ached; his heart ached.

"Well, Duane," he whispered into the steam, "I'll be go to hell. Look what they've done to you." Maggie came into the bathroom with two cups of warm milk. She set Humboldt's cup on the edge of the tub beside his back brush, and placed her own beside the sink. Then she sat down at the vanity and plugged in her electric curler.

"You gonna fix your hair this time of night?" Humboldt asked hoarsely. As he spoke, he adjusted the hot water faucet with his left foot.

"I can't sleep."

"That makes two of us." Humboldt sank deeper into the bath. Maggie fiddled with her hair, took a swallow from her cup, then set it down decisively. She turned toward Humboldt.

"What happened tonight?" she demanded.

"I talked to an old geezer named Tommy Jorgensen."

"Who's he?"

"An old guy around town. He's in pitiful shape. He knew Duane." Maggie waited. For a few seconds Humboldt said nothing more. Then he slowly rolled toward her in the water. His eyes were bloodshot and his face was damp and red. "Duane's dead," he said. Slowly he rolled away from her again. He covered his face with his hands, white and puckered from the hot soak, and cried.

Maggie drew in her breath sharply and dropped to her knees beside the bathtub.

"Humboldt," she murmured, tears running down her face. She stroked his damp hair. He sat up and rested his forehead on his drawn-up knees. Maggie reached for the wash cloth and began soaping his back. Sprinkles of tears and bathwater flew through the air as Humboldt raised his head and shook it violently.

"Murdered!" he cried out.

"Hummer!" Maggie put her arms around him and laid her face against his wet shoulder. They stayed there for some time, shocked and weeping.

Finally Maggie got up stiffly and sat back down on the vanity stool. She pulled a hand towel from the rack and aimlessly dabbed at her face and arms.

"Who, Humboldt? Who did it?"

He hunched forward in the bathtub, his legs still drawn up. "Tommy wouldn't say. He's afraid to."

"How does he know about it?"

"He saw it happen." Humboldt turned on the cold water and splashed his face. He cupped his hands under the running water and drank noisily.

Maggie handed him his cup of milk. "It's probably cold by now," she said dully. "I'll heat it up."

"Can you put some chocolate in it?" he asked.

"Sure."

"And a couple of marshmallows."

"Okay."

"I'm gonna shave and get dressed," he said. "It's almost morning." He stood up carefully and dried off. He took his time shaving, then padded into the bedroom. What do you wear to report a murder? he asked himself. He answered: same damn thing you wear anywhere. Shirt and pants.

As he dressed he thought about what he would say to Scoville at the Sheriff's Office. He knew the man slightly and had played shuffleboard with him once or twice at the Lucky Deuce.

Humboldt pulled open the bedroom drapes. Outside it was still pitch dark, with no light at all to the east. He went into the kitchen where Maggie was buttering toast.

"You're going to the police," she said matter-of-factly.

"You betcha," he said. "Well, not the police. The Sheriff. I know Jim Scoville." They sat down across from each other at the breakfast bar. "Besides, I think it's a matter for the Sheriff."

"What exactly did this Tommy Jorgensen tell you?" Maggie asked, playing with her cup handle, turning the cup this way and that.

"Just what I already told you," Humboldt said irritably. "I'm feelin' better now, Maggie. I don't want to get riled up again. Let me tell you later when I've got somethin' to tell." He finished his hot chocolate and chewed his marshmallows.

Maggie cut her piece of toast in half. "I can wait," she said, her face coloring slightly.

"Good," said Humboldt. He cleared the dishes off the bar and set them in the sink. "I'm gonna have a look around the place and see what damage the storm did last night."

"Lots of damage last night," said Maggie, sounding tired and resentful. Humboldt looked at her quickly, then went outside into the dawn. It was still too dark to see much, but the air smelled fresh and sweet. He walked down to the mailbox to see if the paper had been delivered. He needed something to do. It would be four hours yet before he could talk to Scoville; it seemed more like four years.

The Sheriff's Office was on ground level at the back of the old stone courthouse. Humboldt parked on the side street and approached the polished double doors along a sidewalk flanked by chrysanthemums.

"Yes?" said the young man in uniform at the window.

"Is Detective Scoville in?"

"He should be in any minute," said the officer. "What's your name?"

"Humboldt Denton." The young man finished writing down the name. His large hand paused on the paper.

"Purpose of visit?"

Humboldt thought. Curiosity crossed the young man's face as he waited. "A matter to be investigated," Humboldt finally said. The officer scribbled a few more words on the pad and asked Humboldt to have a seat.

"He knows me socially," said Humboldt as he turned back to the waiting room. He stood at the bulletin board and read the notices: hotline for runaways. A police auction coming up before Christmas. He sat down in a straight-backed chair and leafed through a pamphlet called 'Your Stake in Law and Order.' The officer behind the window was chatting with two secretaries; no sirens, no handcuffs, just a young man and some pretty girls laughing.

"Mr. Denton?" Jim Scoville was entering the lobby through a door marked 'Detective Scoville, No Admittance.' He came over to Humboldt and shook hands. "How are you, Humboldt?" he said cordially and gestured to indicate that Humboldt was to precede him back through the same door.

Detective Jim Scoville was seven years away from retirement. He had thin brown hair; his body was thin and brown, too. A sinewy man, stronger than he looked, he seemed to have a deep year-round suntan in this rainy north country.

"Good to see you," Scoville said once they were in his office. "What's on your
mind?"

"I've got some information for you," said Humboldt. "It's a terrible thing." Scoville waited. "It's got to do with Duane Glynnis, a good friend of mine. I think you've met him." Scoville said nothing. Humboldt cleared his throat. "Well, at first it seemed like he just disappeared."

Scoville reached for a toothpick in a miniature barrel that had the words 'Durango, Colorado' printed across it

"When did you see him last?"

"About two weeks ago. We played cards with him and his wife on November 10th, and that's the last I seen him." Jim Scoville moved his toothpick expertly from one corner of his mouth to the other.

"You haven't seen him since?"

"Nope." Humboldt swallowed and leaned forward in his chair. "And I ain't ever gonna see him again." Scoville's toothpick came to a rest. He waited. Humboldt lowered his voice. "Somebody saw Duane murdered."

Scoville took the toothpick out of his mouth. He reached for a lighter and flicked it on with his thumb. He stared at the flame and sighed. Humboldt kept his attention on the detective. He couldn't guess what Scoville was thinking. The man was courteous, efficient, and private. He didn't seem very interested in Duane Glynnis, or if he was, he kept a poker face.

"Who saw it?" Scoville asked without expression, still

studying the flame.

"There was a witness. This witness told me," Humboldt said evasively.

Scoville stood up quickly. "Wait a minute." He walked out of the office and returned immediately with the Sheriff.

"Sheriff Naider, Humboldt Denton," Scoville said, looking at each in turn. The two shook hands and Scoville pulled up another chair at the corner of his desk. The Sheriff, a younger, plumper, paler man than Scoville, sat down.

"How did you get in touch with this witness?" Scoville pulled a pad of paper from his desk drawer. The hand holding the pen was brown and dry, the fingernails broad and cut short.

"I didn't. He called me."

"Tell us about it."

Humboldt slowly started talking, self-conscious because of the notes Scoville was taking. Gradually words came more easily. "The call came late last night. I could hardly hear him. He said he knew something about Duane Glynnis and that he wanted to talk to me."

Scoville interrupted him. "Do you know where the body is now?"

Humboldt shook his head.

"How well do you know this witness?"

"I've seen him with Duane a few times," said Humboldt. "He knew Duane and me were friends."

"Go ahead."

"Well, I met him at his place right after he called. And he told me what he saw."

"Does he know you're talking to us?" asked the Sheriff.

"Yeah. I told him I was going to the Sheriff." Humboldt paused uncomfortably. "He doesn't want the law involved, but I told him I was gonna follow through on it."

"Exactly what did this witness tell you?"

Humboldt paused. "Where does this put me legally?" he asked. "And the guy who told me? Where does it put him?"

"It puts you as the person reporting a possible crime, and it puts him as a witness."

"He doesn't want anyone to know who he is," said Humboldt. "He saw it. He's afraid. And he's old and sick."

"How old and sick?" Scoville and the Sheriff asked almost in unison.

"Real old and sick. But he's sharp as a tack. You don't have to worry about that." Humboldt suddenly felt defensive. Maybe these guys think Tommy's too old to witness a crime, he thought to himself. Maybe they think I'm too old to report one. Piss on 'em.

"It's too late for your witness to pull back," Scoville said quietly.

"But if he's that old and sick," said the Sheriff who had been thinking, "he might not have to testify in person. We may be able to take a statement from him and use it later in court." Warming to the subject he added, "He might even die before trial and we'd need to have the statement, anyway."

"If it's prosecuted," said Scoville cautiously.

"He doesn't want the killer to know he saw anything," Humboldt said, getting back to the main point. "He doesn't want to testify at all." These guys were talking in circles as far as he was concerned. And already putting Tommy in the ground, for Christ's sake.

"If the judge thinks there's good cause," said the Sheriff, "he might let this witness go confidential."

"What does that mean?" asked Humboldt.

"Testify confidentially to the judge. Or the judge might just read the statement. We'll get the court reporter to make an official transcript."

Humboldt slumped back in his chair. This was more complicated than he'd thought. Tommy Jorgensen was caught in the chain of events, poor old duffer. Just like himself.

Scoville read his thoughts. "Duane can't find his own

murderer," he said.

Humboldt wavered, then stood up. "I'll go talk to the guy," he said grimly. "If you can assure him of secrecy, he might talk to you."

"Like I said, it's too late for him to back out," said Scoville unhelpfully.

"Well, what d'you wanna do? Go over there and interrogate him right now?" asked Humboldt with annoyance.

"We'll give you an hour to talk to him," said the Sheriff, carefully expressing no threat. Scoville laid down his pen and walked with Humboldt to the office door. He put out his hand, exchanged a strong handshake, and thanked him for coming in.

Humboldt crossed the lobby and exited the building. He hurried down the walkway flanked by flower beds. His pickup was parked in a two-hour parking zone; the meeting had taken fifteen minutes.

He jumped in his truck and shifted into first, turned sharply into the light stream of traffic, and drove toward Tommy Jorgensen's street on the north edge of town. Scoville and the Sheriff were suspicious of Tommy, maybe even suspicious of himself. They weren't giving him much slack. Humboldt had an hour to persuade Tommy to tell the law what he knew. He looked in his rear view mirror and wouldn't have been surprised to see a Sheriff's car tailing him. For all he knew, there was a plainclothesman in an unmarked car behind him at this very moment.

They'd better treat old Jorgensen with respect, he thought angrily as he ground the gears. Now I remember why I never cared for cops.

12

Eureka has many fine old nineteenth-century homes. Angela and Richard were not living in one of them. Like the other rundown Victorian houses on the block, theirs had been carved into numerous small apartments with implausibly divided rooms, make-shift closets, and tiny kitchens added as an afterthought.

Hilda cruised past the fading mansions in her old Mercury. On her second swing around the block she located Angela's street number painted on the peeling porch. Tenants' cars lined the street. She found a parking space and propelled her car in a series of back-and-forth jerks until rubber rasping on cement announced she could come no closer to the curb. She rested behind the steering wheel for a few moments, then grasped her overnight case and emerged into the bright, chilly November air.

The aging woman approached the house and slowly climbed two flights of outside stairs. She arrived at Angela's door and knocked loudly, perspiring and out of breath. Angela opened the door; she was eating something, and her mouth was full. She'd cut her hair. Without a word, she turned back into the apartment.

"You hungry?"

"I ate on the road." Hilda followed this short-haired stranger through a narrow hallway back to the kitchen. She set her case down by the kitchen table and walked over to the coffeepot. She poured herself a cup, leaned back against the sink with exaggerated familiarity, and studied Angela.

"You don't have to stand," said Angela without expression.

"I've been sittin' all day," said Hilda. There was a long silence. Angela chewed.

"When did you get your hair cut?"

Angela shrugged. "Few days ago." More silence.

"Nice place you got here," Hilda said.

Angela shrugged again. The silence persisted. Finally Angela broke it. "I got a job," she said through her sandwich.

"Bully for you." It had not occurred to Hilda that Angela might manage on her own. She moved out of the way while Angela cleared the table and stacked her dirty dishes in the sink. "What doing?"

"Part-time in the public library."

"Oh," said Hilda, unimpressed. "You gonna stay here, then?"

"Yeah. For now."

"You cut your hair," Hilda repeated.

"Yeah. Like it?" Angela ran water into the sink. She lifted her head coquettishly, then stopped halfway through as if the gesture no longer applied to her.

"It's cute," said Hilda uncomfortably. She reached into her purse for a cigarette and felt the small gift box that contained the gold necklace. She cursed herself for bringing it.

"You have to work today?" she asked.

"From 1:00 to 9:00."

"Library!" Hilda snorted. "Library or a bar? When's your day off?"

"Sunday."

"If I'd 'a known that, I wouldn't 'a come until the weekend," she said bitterly. Angela said nothing.

"Hey, Babe," said Hilda, "aren't you glad to see me?"

"Sure," said Angela. Hilda lit the cigarette, waved the match in the air, and looked around the room for an ashtray. Tears were at work somewhere behind her eyes. Angela had already forgotten her. She'd been dumped.

Wordlessly Angela led the way through a narrow hallway toward the front of the apartment. Hilda followed. On the way she found a glass ashtray that said "The Big Win" on it and carried it with her to an easy chair in the living room. She lowered herself into the chair, leaned back, and inhaled heavily on her cigarette. Angela perched on the couch opposite her. Without the fluffy hairdo, she looked thin and colorless. She rocked back and forth on the edge of the worn sofa.

"What's the matter?" asked Hilda. She suddenly wanted to touch the high-strung woman across from her, take care of her, love her.

"My nerves," said Angela.

"Did you call the specialist I told you about?"

"I didn't need to. I was feeling good for a while. It comes over me all of a sudden."

"Do you still have your Valium?"

Angela shook her head. "I ran out."

"I've got some." Hilda took pills from her purse. "Here."

Angela accepted them. "I'm better when I'm at work," she said. There was another long silence. Angela looked down at her hands and suddenly cried, "This thing is filthy!" She jerked a soiled antimacassar off the arm of the sofa and threw it on the floor. She reached for the one on the far end and gestured furiously at the furnished room. "Filthy!"

Hilda watched her and waited before saying carefully, "You don't have to stay here, you know." Angela looked at Hilda and resisted the message for several seconds. Then her vision slid off of the older woman's eyes and she jumped up.

"I've got to get ready for work," she exclaimed, and rushed out of the room.

Hilda ground out her cigarette in the ashtray and sat without moving. Disappointment, then anger gathered in her large body. Was this what she'd driven two hours for? Dreamed and planned for? Gambled on?

When Angela returned a few minutes later, Hilda was standing at the front door, her overnight case in her hand.

"Next time don't ask me to come see you unless you mean it," she said.

Angela's eyes widened. "I didn't know I had to work."

"You're treating me rotten!" Hilda exploded. "I risked everything for you, and you don't give me the time of day!" The veins in her forehead stood out.

"Risked?" Angela breathed softly, stepping backward toward the hallway and kitchen.

"*You know*," Hilda said hoarsely. Her eyes smoldered. She smiled without pleasure and whispered, "It's a little late to pretend."

Angela bolted for the hall. She ran down it and threw herself into the bathroom, slamming and locking the door behind her.

In the living room Hilda picked up the glass ashtray, hurled it against the wall, and stormed out of the apartment.

13

Humboldt shifted down to second and turned his truck onto the narrow street where Tommy Jorgensen lived. By daylight the neighborhood looked shabbier than it had the night before. The old man's house was set far back from the road between two lots containing a travel trailer each. Tommy still had a few old cars in his back yard, their broken-out windshields covered with black Vizqueen and cardboard. By glassing in his porch, Tommy had converted the front of his little house into a dubious living room, warm as a greenhouse and transparent as a fishbowl.

When Humboldt arrived he found Tommy lying on a gray bedsheet that covered the narrow day bed. He was wearing trousers and a striped pajama top. Beer cans, pop bottles, and filled ashtrays littered the floor. Piles of newspapers overflowed the end tables.

"Had breakfast yet?" Humboldt asked loudly as he sat down on a dirty chair.

"Nah. I don't eat breakfast," said Tommy.

"Come on. Let's go down to the café and get something to eat."

"I don't want no one to see us together," said the old man.

"What's the matter? Ashamed of me?"

Tommy Jorgensen smiled and creaked himself up into a sitting position. He set his swollen feet on the linoleum and said shrewdly, "Been to the police, have you?"

Humboldt nodded.

"I been thinkin'," said Tommy. He took a packet of cigarette papers from his pajama pocket and pulled one out, holding it delicately between his calloused fingers. Leaning to one side, he came close to straightening his right leg so that he could reach deep into his trouser pocket for the tobacco pouch. Slowly he pulled out the leather bag. With one hand he opened the drawstring mouth and shook some tobacco into the little trough of paper. He pulled the drawstring tight with his teeth and placed the pouch back in his pocket. He hadn't spilled a shred of tobacco.

"Yup. Been thinkin'." Humboldt waited. "Don't want folks to know I seen a man killed and didn't stop it. Ashamed of myself." He rolled the cigarette and licked the edge of the paper. Then he laid one end of the crooked, gray cigarette on his lower lip and struck a kitchen match on his thumbnail.

"Especially by a woman," he added, exhaling smoke.

Hilda. Humboldt sucked in his breath. He'd known it all along. He was deeply, furiously satisfied.

Tommy looked down at his body. "Wish a person would get stronger and smarter instead of older." He bowed his head. The smoke curled upward from the ash crawling out the end of the cigarette. "I'll help put her behind bars," he finally said. He covered his eyes with his nicotine-stained hand and lifted his head sharply. "Couldn't help Duane!" he suddenly cried in a high, cracked voice. He sobbed once. Humboldt stood up, unable to speak, and walked quickly to the telephone. He arranged and rearranged the stack of magazines and phone books on the rickety table and finally said hoarsely,

"You can help Duane. Nobody needs to know except the

police. And the judge later."

"Attorneys?"

"I don't know. Maybe," said Humbolt.

"Oh, shit," said Tommy.

Humboldt dialed the Sheriff's Office. Tommy inhaled one last time and ground out the cigarette.

"They'll be here in half an hour," said Humboldt.

"Hope they turn off the dang-fool sireen," said Tommy

"They won't be in a Sheriff's car."

Tommy Jorgensen stroked his whiskers and studied the floor

"Got a coffeepot?"

"Yeah. On the stove. Coffee can's on the table."

"Wanna shave and put on a shirt?"

"Sounds like a good idea," said Tommy as he pushed himself off the day bed and shuffled toward the bathroom in his frayed carpet slippers.

"What's he doin' here?" Tommy asked belligerently. He was sitting on the day bed smoking. He eyed the court reporter and stenotype machine with suspicion.

"I asked him to make a transcript," Detective Scoville said, tilting his head slightly toward the court reporter. "If the judge can read what you have to say, you might not have to come to court." Tommy grunted and looked skeptical. The detective nodded to the court reporter who raised his right hand and directed the old man to do the same.

"You do solemnly swear to tell the truth, the whole truth, and nothing but the truth, so help you God?"

Tommy Jorgensen wheezed and said, "I do."

"Tell us what you know about Duane Glynnis' death, Mr. Jorgensen," Scoville said after the court reporter was seated behind his machine.

Tommy slowly rubbed his pink, shaved chin. His eyes watered. He pulled fresh cigarette papers out of his shirt pocket. "It was up on the ranch, what Duane called 'the ranch.'" He dragged the pouch out of his trouser pocket. "He had a garden up there. Nice big vegetable garden. Grew fine tomatoes, squash, all kinds of vegetables. Kept his chickens, Rhode Island Reds, up there. Well, he'd come up there and work his garden and feed the chickens and just get out in the open."

"How often did he go up there?" asked the detective.

"Quite often. He was up there three or four times a week." He fell silent, stubbed out the cigarette, and commenced rolling another. The reporter stopped writing. Humboldt leaned forward. His hatred of Hilda burned his chest. He wanted her dead. Not just dead. Murdered. Knifed. Her neck snapped.

Tommy began talking again in a slow, steady flow of words, interrupted now and then by a puff on his new cigarette or an easing of his suspenders.

"Like I say, he'd come up there to work his garden—"

"What were you doing up there?" asked the detective in a neutral tone.

"Well, I stay up there in his trailer through the warm months."

"When did you come back to town?"

"Oh, been 'bout a week." Tommy slowly crossed one leg over the other, helping it along with a hand under the knee. "It was a warm day," he continued. "Kind of uneasy weather. One minute the sun was shinin' and the next it was tryin' to rain. Duane come up there about seven in the evening. Walked around his property. Fed the chickens. Had a smoke with me. It looked like it was gonna come up a storm.

"So I says, 'She's gonna storm,' and Duane, he says, 'I better get on down into town.' I think he asked me if I was fixed okay for grub and such. He always looked out for me." The old man paused and swallowed.

"So I says, 'Thanks, I am,' and he takes off. Well, sir, I seen headlights—"

"Pardon me, sir. Where were you when he left?"

"At the trailer. He walked down to get in his car."

"Where was his car?"

"A ways down the hill. See," said Tommy Jorgensen, slowly knocking his cigarette against the edge of an ashtray, "the trailer is up in the woods, maybe an eighth of a mile up in the woods. The garden and chickens is down in the clearing."

"Is there a road up to the trailer?"

"Nope. Just a path. Steep path up the hill." The old man fell silent.

"I didn't mean to break your train of thought," said Scoville.

"All right," said Tommy. "Where was I?"

"You saw the headlights."

"I did," agreed Tommy. "So I goes down to see who's there. I knowed it wasn't Duane's lights 'cause I seen these ones comin' up from the highway.

"I got closer to the clearing and I heard some talk, a man and a woman arguing. It got real heated. I stopped where I was. Didn't go all the way down. Hard for me to climb."

"How far away were you?"

"Oh, mebbe forty yards up the hill."

"Was it dark?"

"Comin' on fast, and the sky was stormy. If it wasn't for the headlights bein' on I wouldn't a made 'em out."

"Could you tell who they were?"

Tommy shifted on the day bed. The court reporter's hands hovered above the keyboard, his eyes fastened on empty space. "Duane and Hilda," the old man said after a long silence. Jim Scoville raised his eyebrows in a question.

"Hilda Weatherall," said Tommy.

"Did they see you?"

Tommy shook his head. "I stepped behind the trees."

"What happened after you saw them arguing?"

Tommy Jorgensen fell silent again. He looked at Humboldt without expression. Reaching into the pocket of his flannel shirt, he pulled out a small pill box and put a tablet underneath his tongue.

"You feel all right, Mr. Jorgensen?" the detective asked.

"I'll never feel good again," the old man said matter-of-factly. He lay back on his pillows, slowly pulling one leg at a time up onto the day bed. He motioned for Humboldt to wedge another pillow behind him.

The detective stood and turned toward the front of the glassed-in room. He looked into the yard that was dominated by a large Douglas fir. Farther out, the street was in sunshine. Back here all was in shade. He ran his hand over his thinning hair and surveyed as much of the street as was visible from the house.

"See anyone?" asked Tommy.

"No." A moment later Scoville added, "I've got a man parked down the block."

"He ain't in a police car, is he?" asked Tommy.

"Unmarked car," said Scoville. He turned back toward the room and sat down. He glanced at the court reporter and nodded for him to resume. Tommy Jorgensen continued as if without interruption.

"Hilda just yelled and screamed. Duane yelled back, but he couldn't hardly get a word in edgewise. She was like a crazy person." Tommy closed his eyes and lay quiet for a moment. "I think she's a witch," he finally said. "Some people don't believe in 'em." He looked at Humboldt thoughtfully. "I believe in witches.

"Well, so she's carryin' on, havin' a fit, like, and then she reaches into her purse like she's gonna get out keys or a comb or somethin', like women do, and then she just…" He paused. "She just—" and he raised his hand and pulled the trigger on an imaginary handgun.

Humboldt turned to the window and saw a bird fly up from the lawn. He watched it carefully, noted the color of its breast, the length of its beak. One part of him wanted to soar beside the bird and forget everything. The other wanted to drive to

Hilda's house and kill her.

"Would you describe in words what you just did, the gesture you made, for the benefit of the court reporter?" asked the detective.

"She pulled a gun out of her purse and shot Duane," Tommy said.

"Could you see her shoot him?"

"I seen where they was standing. I seen the gun. I heared it. And I seen Duane..." Tommy couldn't go on.

"What happened then?" Scoville asked after a respectful interval.

"Duane went down right now," Tommy said. He wiped his eyes and cheeks with the back of his hand. "He didn't move after that, that I could see."

"What happened next?"

"Hilda stood there a minute, then she run back to her car and drove away."

"How did she drive?"

"Fast."

"What did she do with the gun?"

"Took it with her, I guess. I looked for it later. Couldn't find it."

Detective Scoville, impartial, barely interested, dry-skinned and sinewy, moved the story along with the question he'd asked a thousand times in his career: "What happened next?"

"Well, like I say, Hilda drove off and I got down to Duane as quick as I could. He was dead. There wasn't no reason to get help for him." Tommy rubbed the gray bed sheet with his thick fingers and turned his head to one side on the pillows. "He needed the help before that." The room was silent until he started to talk again.

"Then I got winded and sick-like, and walked back up to the trailer. That's all."

"Is there a phone in the trailer?"

"No, sir."

"Did you have a car?"

"Truck. But it was on the blink."

"How did you get around when your truck wasn't running?"

"Duane was gonna tow me into town the next day."

"Is your truck still up at the trailer?"

"No. My daughter's boyfriend come over from Coos Bay and towed it to his garage."

"Where is it now?"

"Coos Bay. They'll be bringing it over directly."

The detective paused. "Mr. Jorgensen, why didn't you drive Duane's car into town for help?"

Tommy avoided the detective's eyes and stared hard at the top button of Humboldt's shirt. "Sick," he finally said. "And scared," he added under his breath. "Of a woman." He snorted in self-contempt.

Detective Scoville cleared his throat and went on. "So the body was there all night?"

Tommy nodded.

"Mr. Jorgensen, where is the body now?"

"I don't know."

Detective Scoville showed some slight curiosity. "It's not still in that clearing, is it?"

"Nope. It was gone when my daughter's boyfriend got there the next morning."

Jim Scoville looked closely at the old man. Then he glanced at Humboldt. Humboldt looked back.

"Was there any blood on the ground?"

"Blood, all right. More'n you'd expect."

"What do you mean?"

"The ground was covered with it." The old man lowered his voice. "Looked like a slaughter yard. Like a hog was butchered." His voice cracked. "It run downhill."

Humboldt fought nausea.

"Did you see any flesh? Anything?"

Tommy shook his head.

"Can you take us out there this afternoon?" asked Jim Scoville.

"Make it later in the week," said Tommy. "I ain't feelin' good."

"We need to see the area, try to find some evidence. It's been too long already," said the detective. Tommy nodded and seemed half asleep.

"One more question, Mr. Jorgensen. Why did you call Humboldt instead of coming to us?"

Tommy was silent for a long while. "Sick. I was way down for a while." Uncharacteristically, Scoville nodded in sympathy.

"Longer I waited, more ashamed I got."

The detective paused. His brown, wide-nailed fingers tapped the arms of the chair, betraying feeling. "What were you ashamed of?" he asked reluctantly, glancing over at the court reporter.

Tommy Jorgensen closed his eyes again. He swallowed and said quietly, "Of not helping Duane."

"And why did you call Humboldt Denton?"

"He was a friend of Duane's. He was a friend of mine, you might say."

"How did you know him?"

"He come out to Duane's property with him once in a while. Seen him any number of times here and there."

"In town?"

"Yeah."

"Where?"

"Redwood Lumber. Two Guys Salvage. Different places when I was still gettin' out."

"Thank you, Mr. Jorgensen," said Jim Scoville neutrally, and stood up. The court reporter put his machine in its case and folded up the tripod. In the silence Humboldt also stood and, after shaking hands with Scoville, went back to Tommy's kitchen and jammed a can opener into a can of soup for the old man's lunch.

14

Scoville opened his office door, looked into the waiting room at Humboldt Denton, and nodded his head a quarter of an inch. From him it was a full statement. Humboldt rose and entered the detective's office.

The tall, thin man bent over his desktop and pulled a toothpick from the little ceramic barrel. Still standing, he began gently to explore his gums.

"Something's come up," he said, closing the door. "It's the damndest thing I ever saw." As if the expression of so much emotion had drained him, he sat down. He parked the toothpick in a corner of his mouth and looked up at Humboldt.

"We found Duane Glynnis' body."

Humboldt didn't sit but fell into the chair across from Scoville. The detective withdrew his toothpick.

"The body's been cut up," he said. Humboldt looked puzzled.

"Butchered," Scoville said softly.

"It's been cut?" Humboldt asked.

"Cut up."

When the words registered, fury whipped through Humboldt, followed by a sick wave of weakness. "Hilda," he uttered, trying to get his breath. He half-stood.

Scoville lifted one hand. "I need you to identify the body, Humboldt," he said quietly. "Can you drive up with me?" Humboldt swallowed a solid, sour lump that burned all the way down to his belly.

"Where to?" he asked.

"The Glynnises' trailer court."

"The trailer court," Humboldt said stupidly. He could not grasp the information.

"Come on," said Scoville. "The back way." They walked out to the Sheriff's parking lot and got into a marked car. The air in the closed automobile was hot and stale. Humboldt rolled down his window.

"Warm for November," remarked Scoville. Humboldt concentrated on breathing regularly. As soon as Scoville got onto the highway, he drove fast. Neither man talked. Scoville turned off 101 and shot up the gravel road leading to the trailer court. As they climbed, white dust rose behind the car and settled on the brush at either side of the road.

Pacific Trailer Court was deep in shade. It felt degrees cooler up here than in town, and a faint breeze was blowing off the ocean, drying Humboldt's forehead and neck. Scoville stopped in front of the fourth trailer to the left. The two men got out of the car and walked through the aluminum carport into the back yard.

Humboldt saw an officer standing at the rear of the yard where the woods began. Ten or fifteen neighbors were clustered nearby, hushed and motionless.

Without a word Humboldt followed Scoville into the woods. Dead alder leaves still wet from the storm stuck to their shoes. They walked for three or four minutes, then Scoville stopped in a small clearing. Humboldt came up beside him and saw a man in uniform standing under a Douglas fir about ten yards ahead. The man was in shadow. As they began walking toward him, Humboldt noticed the white handkerchief over the man's nose and mouth. At the same moment that the stench reached him, Humboldt saw a small bundle by the man's feet, much smaller than a body.

He was slow to understand that the bundle was what he had been brought to see. When he understood that, he gagged. Scoville motioned for him to take out his handkerchief. Humboldt controlled the retching and followed Scoville across the ten yards. Scoville stepped to one side and pointed at the foot of the tree. The police officer standing guard reached down and folded back the tarp. After a few seconds the flies resettled.

Humboldt was puzzled. He looked at Scoville. The detective's skin and eyes were very dark above the handkerchief.

The police officer, a young man, stood stiffly. The guy looks damn silly standing at attention with a hankie over his face, thought Humboldt. He was irritated. He also had an odd desire to laugh. Then he looked down. On the tarp were pieces of a body still clothed. He saw a sleeved arm, bloody at the shoulder joint where a shiny white socket showed through. The torso was still in a shirt, the collar buried in dried pulp and blood. It was a shirt like Duane's. Humboldt shot an anguished look at Scoville and turned to leave. But Scoville's hand was on his arm. He was pointing to the head at the edge of the tarp.

"Can you identify that?" he murmured through the handkerchief.

It was a head, and yet it was not a head. "What the hell?" Humboldt said, looking at it carefully.

"It's been boiled," Scoville said in a flat tone. At first Humboldt was merely astonished. Then he drew back and let out a deep, primitive sound. He looked at it again. Boiling had not removed the hair. Duane's eyes, now opaque, stared out at his murderer in a horrible, final view of the world; whiskers bristled on the soft, cooked chin; stringy muscle and moist fat laced the gray cheeks, gray as roast pork, gray as dried gravy.

It had been Duane. Humboldt was afraid of fainting and falling forward onto the tarp. He averted his eyes, nodded, and walked weakly away from the clearing. He tripped, caught his balance, and proceeded deeper into the woods. He leaned against a tree and vomited. Scoville followed him and turned him back toward the trailer court. They removed their handkerchiefs from their faces.

"Is that him?" asked Scoville. Humboldt nodded, white-faced. They walked single file. Through the trees they could see the people standing in the Glynnises' back yard.

"Not this way," said Scoville. They went around to the northeast edge of the trailer court where they cut through someone's yard and walked the eighth of a mile back to the

Sheriff's car. The stagnant air of the vehicle smelled to Humboldt like the bundle in the woods. He began sweating again. He lowered his window and leaned back against the seat. Within minutes they were once again racing along the edge of the sharp coastal cliffs. Humboldt turned toward his open window and tried to breathe deeply. He looked for boats, rocks, anything to keep his mind busy. But his mind would not stay busy. It simply remembered over and over again his friend's mutilated body. He fell into a deep depression that would not lift.

15

Maggie laid down the crust of her sandwich and stared at the door that Humboldt had just slammed shut. She heard the automatic garage door open and the car door slam. Then the engine whined, ignited, and the car screeched into reverse, its tires peeling away from the garage floor.

She hadn't seen him this angry in a long time. In the early years of their marriage his hot temper had often made her cry, and once, she recalled, it had saved her life. But usually it had simply got him in trouble.

She made herself a fresh cup of tea and carried it into the living room. Sinking into an easy chair, she surprised herself by breaking into tears. She felt shaky and as vulnerable as a bride. No one could make her as happy, or unhappy, as Humboldt. And evidently no one could enrage him more than she herself.

They'd been eating lunch and talking about Hilda's court hearing to be held soon.

"I don't think I'll go," Maggie had said.

"Suit yourself."

"Are you going?"

"Damn right." He stared at the sandwich he was having trouble finishing. "Duane was my friend."

"I know," Maggie said. "But I hate to embarrass Hilda. It's like a sideshow with people coming to gawk."

"It's a freak show and she's the freak. But suit yourself."

Maggie poured more coffee.

"Why are you so concerned about Hilda's feelings, anyway?" Humboldt's tone was controlled. "She didn't care how Duane felt."

"Two wrongs don't make a right."

Humboldt dumped sugar in his coffee. His hand shook slightly. "You never did like Duane, did you?"

"No. I think he made life hard for Angela."

"What makes you think that?"

"Just from things he said to her. The way she looked and acted."

"Women made him nervous," said Humboldt.

"Well, he made me nervous," said Maggie. "So demanding."

"Suit yourself."

"I'm sorry he was killed," she said.

Humboldt picked up the morning paper still resting on the table and put it down again. He looked strangely at his wife. "You're sorry," he said.

"I don't feel it as deeply as you do." Maggie massaged her forehead. They sat in silence. "I'm tired of this whole Glynnis affair," she added.

"Glynnis affair!" Humboldt stood up quickly. "More like Hilda's affair, I'd say!"

"Whoever's affair it is, I wish we'd never gotten involved!" Maggie snapped back. Then she said something she regretted as soon as the words were spoken: "Duane is no great loss to me."

The room turned cold, unfurnished, unfamiliar. The Dentons faced each other as strangers. That was when Humboldt spun away from her and slammed the door to the garage behind him. Maggie remained standing at the breakfast bar, a stunned expression on her face. Humboldt's anger had shocked her, but she was even more shocked to discover how little she cared that Duane Glynnis was dead.

Now, sitting in the easy chair, dried tears on her cheeks and the cup of cold tea beside her, Maggie turned the painful business over in her mind. She'd tolerated Duane because he was Humboldt's friend. Humboldt liked almost everybody. Her husband looked for the best in everyone and found it. She couldn't do that with Duane. Yet she would never have wished Duane dead, much less murdered. His death still seemed unreal to her. Unlike Humboldt, she could not grasp the fact that Hilda had killed him. And mutilated him. That was beyond comprehension. That was impossible to think about.

Maggie considered Hilda. What was her past? Did she have a family? Children? What did she think about? The woman was private as a stone wall. Somehow deprived. Depraved.

Maggie picked up her cup and carried it into the kitchen. She emptied it down the sink and began aimlessly moving cups and plates about in the thin suds of the dishwater that was now as cold as the tea.

"It's a tough thing to see," said Scoville as he poured Humboldt a beer. The two men were seated in a booth at the Lucky Deuce Club. Scoville held onto the cold, sweating pitcher. "You were the logical person to identify him."

"Him?" said Humboldt bitterly. "More like 'it.'" He took a mouthful of beer and was surprised to find it was just what he needed. He set the mug down hard, exhaled loudly, and leaned back against the vinyl-covered booth.

"Toothpick?" asked Scoville, extending one toward Humboldt. Humboldt refused it and watched Scoville pull his out of its wrapper and twirl it carefully between two lower teeth.

"We have a theory," said Scoville.

"I have a theory, too," said Humboldt instantly. "Women are a breed apart." The detective gave that statement some thought.

"I learned that a long time ago," he said.

Humboldt tried not to think about Maggie, but he kept

hearing her words, "He's no great loss to me." He was furious that she could be so cold-hearted. He was cruelly hurt that she did not comprehend the tragedy of Duane's death.

"Women stick together," Humboldt said cryptically. Scoville remained silent. Humboldt drank his beer with savage gulps. At that moment it seemed to him that Hilda and Maggie were killers, he and Duane the killed. Scoville, on the other hand, stood safely above the smoking pit where women hurt men, murder men, cut up men.

"Does this finish the case?" he asked.

"No way," said Scoville.

"What more do you need to know?" asked Humboldt testily.

"Who cut him up?"

"Hilda," said Humboldt.

"Did she?" asked Scoville with mild interest.

"Of course. She'd know how to hack someone up. She could do it."

"Proof?" inquired Scoville. Again Humboldt was speechless. The idea that Hilda might not have been the butcher upset him almost as much as the crime.

"What do you know about Angela Glynnis?" Scoville asked.

"Angela Glynnis?" Humboldt repeated stupidly. "Angela Glynnis?" He studied his beer. "A sweet woman who had marriage troubles. A weak woman," he added.

Humboldt saw Scoville's attention go slack. He felt he had somehow disappointed the detective. Well, tough shit, he thought. If he doesn't like my answers, let him get his own. Humboldt shoved his mug hard a few inches away from him. The foamy liquid sloshed up to the lip. When it had settled, Scoville poured them both more beer.

"Like I say," said Scoville, "what can you tell me about her? You knew the family."

"I'm beginning to think I didn't know them at all," said Humboldt.

"Parts of the body were cooked," Scoville said matter-of-factly, "after it was brought to the trailer."

"What trailer?" asked Humboldt, not grasping Scoville's meaning.

"The Glynnis trailer," Scoville said patiently.

"They found him in the woods," insisted Humboldt.

"After the head had been cooked in the trailer," Scoville repeated without emphasis.

"How do you know?" Humboldt asked. He was angry. He'd stuck his neck out to find Duane's killer and he was being menaced from all sides, Maggie sympathizing with Hilda and now Scoville drawing a picture that Humboldt didn't understand at all.

"We found blood on the side of the stove. And fresh signs of scrubbing."

"So what?" Humboldt's voice was plainly insolent.

"Duane's wife or son might be involved," Scoville said. Humboldt didn't speak or move. Only his eyes narrowed as he took in what Scoville was saying. He rejected the words immediately. Hilda was the killer. That was all he knew.

"Hilda is the killer," he said. "She practically lived there the last few weeks. She probably did live there after she killed Duane. Got rid of him and took his place." Humboldt shuddered. "She cooked there, probably," he added with care. "But Hilda is the killer," he repeated.

"Hilda is the killer, all right," the detective said. Humboldt relaxed slightly. At least Scoville was backing him up on something. "Have some beer." The detective filled their mugs.

"Sandwich?" asked Scoville indelicately.

"Nah. I'll go home and eat."

"Maggie will fix you something," said Scoville as a statement of fact. "Myself, I'll have a sandwich." He asked the waitress for a hot pastrami in a roll.

"You married?" asked Humboldt.

"Nope."

"The good life," said Humboldt suggestively.

"Don't know," said Scoville. "Nothing to compare it to."

"Compared to Duane," said Humboldt.

"Well, yeah," Scoville agreed. "But compared to you, I don't know." Scoville drank some more beer and set the mug back down. "She took his place?" he asked as if without interruption. "What do you mean?"

Humboldt shrugged uncomfortably. "Well, you know, she just took over. Something funny going on in that house." Scoville waited. Humboldt leaned forward and blurted out, "Hilda's a queer." Scoville said nothing. "She's a dirty old woman. She drilled peep holes into the bathrooms so she could watch. I seen 'em myself. They're in the closet."

Two lumbermen had started up a game of shuffleboard. The clack of the pucks and the players' remarks filled in the background of Scoville's silence. The hot pastrami arrived.

"Not to change the subject," said Humboldt, feeling a little better now that he had made Hilda's character clear to the detective, "how did you know where the body was?"

"A dog found it," said Scoville, taking an unperturbed bite of his food. "A neighbor's dog."

"I see," said Humboldt. He didn't want to know more.

"Did you notice the ground between the house and the shrubs in back?" asked Scoville.

"No," said Humboldt.

"It had been spaded recently. Have a theory they might have started to bury him there, then changed their mind."

"They?" said Humboldt. "She." He was beginning to grasp the mayhem and burial as facts. Wicked woman, he thought to himself. He rubbed his eyes.

"Goddam, this isn't gonna go away, is it?" he said.

"Nope," agreed Scoville. He ate tidily. In a few minutes the sandwich was gone.

"I'll drop you back at your car," Scoville said. The two men slid out of the booth. Scoville paid the cashier and they walked out of the dark club into the bright afternoon, blinking and adjusting to the painful light of day.

"Can you come to the office for a few minutes?" Scoville asked Humboldt. "I want to ask you some questions about Hilda and Angela."

Uncharacteristically, Humboldt thought before he answered. He didn't want to go home; he didn't want to see Maggie. And he was miserable not seeing her. He ached. He felt battered. It's a terrible thing, he thought to himself, when a man doesn't want to go home.

"Sure," he replied too heartily. "There's no place I'd rather be right now. And there's no hurry. I've got all the time in the world."

16

"Richard doesn't live here," Angela breathed to the Sheriff's deputy standing outside her door. Her pale green eyes were opened wide. The filmy white negligee she wore, bought several years earlier, looked odd with her boyish hair-cut.

"Do you know where he is?" asked the deputy.

"No," she answered in a small voice.

"Ma'am," he said in a nervous, tactful tone, "I'm from the Sheriff's Office, Crescent County, Oregon. Your husband's body has been found." He eyed her warily. When she didn't scream or faint he continued. "You're wanted at headquarters here in Eureka to answer some questions."

So what, Angela thought. I'll do what has to be done. She lifted her chin at the deputy but avoided his eyes.

"Wait here," she said, and started to close the door.

"Don't make any calls," he warned, stepping into the living room. He held out an official-looking paper toward her but

Angela didn't look at it.

"All right, Officer," she said. "I'll be right out."

She closed the bedroom door behind her and dropped her filmy garments on the floor. "Control" she whispered as she pulled on a sweater, corduroy pants, and a wool jacket. The officer knocked on the bedroom door.

"Hurry it up, ma'am." She hooked a leather purse over her shoulder and said,

"I need to use the bathroom."

"Make it snappy," said the deputy.

"I will, Officer." Angela went into the bathroom, took a piece of paper from her shoulder bag that had Richard's new phone number on it, and tore it up into bits before flushing it down the toilet. She washed her hands and returned to the deputy who indicated for her to precede him down the stairs and outside.

If I don't know what happened, no one else will, either, Angela thought as she walked toward the Sheriff's car. But what about Richard? She began to worry. They would find his apartment sooner or later. She must get word to him to leave Eureka.

But they don't need him, she reminded herself. Hilda's in jail. They've got their murderer. They won't need Richard and they won't need me, either.

Once inside the Sheriff's car, Angela rested her head on the back of the seat. She began to imagine the questions they might ask. Then, lifting her head, she tried on a facial expression and mouthed a possible answer. She stopped suddenly as she met the deputy's eyes in the rear view mirror. She turned her head sharply and looked out the window. It occurred to her that she should be sociable. She leaned toward the grill that separated her from the deputy. He met her eyes again in the rear view mirror.

"How do you like living here?" she meant to ask.

"I've got one son," the officer replied. Now Angela wasn't

sure what she had asked him. Had he misunderstood her? She sank back against the unpadded vinyl. He probably plays catch with his little boy, she thought to herself, in front of a nice house with a big yard. She closed her eyes carefully and laid her hand over her unquiet chest.

When the Sheriff's car stopped, Angela opened her eyes. The officer came around to her door and escorted her out of the car. She followed him down some stairs that led to below-ground level. They walked through a grubby basement entrance and into a large room with a cement floor and block walls. Fluorescent lights buzzed overhead. She followed the deputy into a room that was small and bare. A single light bulb dangled from a long black cord in the ceiling and swayed slightly above a brown rectangular table. Seated at one end of the table was Richard.

Staring at her son, Angela sat down at the end of the table opposite him, but he did not seem to notice her. The deputy took the straight chair in the corner. The door opened and a tall, thin, suntanned man entered the room. He looked vacantly at Richard and Angela, nodded to the officer in the corner, and bent his frame into a sitting position on the folding chair between the two.

Jim Scoville removed the rubber band from his small, drab green notebook and turned to a lined page that had not been written on. He entered the date. Then, stretching the thick rubber band twice around his palm, he gave Angela and Richard their Miranda warnings.

"I am Detective Scoville with the Crescent County Sheriff's Office. What you say here can and will be used against you in a court of law," he droned. He informed them they had the right to consult a lawyer; that if they couldn't afford one, the court would make a public defender available to them.

"Oh, yes, a public defender," said Angela. She tried out a smile on Detective Scoville.

"Can you call the P.D.'s Office and ask two attorneys to

come over here?" Scoville said to the officer sitting in the corner.

"We'll use the same one," Angela said quickly.

"You'll have to have separate attorneys," said Scoville in a flat tone.

Her smile vanished. "Why?"

"Your interests may be in conflict."

"What?" she asked.

"What's good for you might not be good for him," said Scoville laconically. Angela studied his face, but it was too bland to be informative.

The officer returned to the room and took his place in the corner again. Jim Scoville fiddled with the rubber band around his hand. He took a toothpick out of his shirt pocket and set it in the corner of his mouth. From time to time he flipped back in his little notebook to read an entry. Then he stared into space.

Angela shifted in her chair and looked at her son. Richard's face was colorless. He did not meet his mother's eyes. Angela pushed her chair back and crossed and recrossed her legs.

"Oh, for Heaven's sake," she said. But the other two didn't seem to hear her.

After ten more minutes of silence the sound of footsteps reached the room. The officer in the corner stood up and opened the door for a young woman and a man, each carrying a briefcase. Detective Scoville suggested by a nod of his head that the woman attorney talk to Angela.

Richard said to the natty young man approaching him, "I don't need an attorney."

Everyone paused. "I don't need one," he repeated. His voice shook.

"Fine," said Scoville. The attorney turned uncomfortably between the two.

"He needs an attorney!" Angela said loudly. "He's got his rights!"

"You are not required to say a word," said the young attorney to Richard. "In fact—"

"Yes," agreed Scoville. He studied the light bulb.

"I'm gonna get this over with," Richard spoke in the direction of his mother.

"Fine. Let's get on with it," said Scoville.

"You don't know anything!" Angela yelled. She looked at the attorney. "Do something!" she screamed at him.

The young attorney put his back to Angela and said to Richard, "I advise you to remain silent until we've had a chance to talk."

"I want to talk to you," Richard said to Scoville.

Scoville picked up his pen. "Okay," he said. He motioned for the police officer to take Angela away.

Frantically she jumped up from her chair, tears streaming down her face. She started to run toward Richard. The officer in the corner grabbed her by the upper arm and began propelling her toward the door. Angela almost shook him off, twisting and turning, all the while yelling, "He didn't do it! Hilda did it!" Her thin body writhed as the officer pushed her into the hall.

When she'd been removed from the basement of the building and her screams no longer echoed down the hallway, Richard said, "I buried my dad." He crossed his arms on the table, laid his head upon them, and began to sob.

Scoville regarded his toothpick and waited. The young attorney pulled Angela's empty chair close to Richard and sat down. When Richard's crying ended, Scoville walked to the door and asked someone in the hallway to bring a pot of coffee. Richard sat with his hand supporting his head, looking straight ahead. His eyes were now dry and red.

Scoville turned toward Richard and asked, "Where did you find the body?"

"In the back yard," Richard said. "Partly buried." He shifted his gaze and looked at Scoville steadily.

"Where in the back yard?"

"In a flower bed close to the house."

"How did you know the body was there?"

"Two dogs."

"What were the dogs doing?"

"Sniffing and digging." Richard started to break down again, but pulled his face together. "I heard the dogs out there. Went out with a flashlight. Threw some rocks at 'em." Now nothing could stop the flow of words. "With the flashlight I saw something, like a cloth or something, partly covered with dirt. I went over and saw…" Tears ran freely down his cheeks as he continued to look at Scoville. Scoville waited and did not turn away. "… him."

"How did you know it was your father?"

"By the shirt," Richard whispered. "And the ring on his finger. And his boots." He breathed loudly but was dry-eyed now.

"How did you bury him?"

"Out in the woods."

"No. How?"

"With a shovel." Richard ran the back of his hand over his eyes.

"Where did you get the shovel?"

"From our carport."

"Did you take a flashlight?"

"Yeah. Covered it with my handkerchief."

"Did you kill your father?" asked Scoville.

"No." Tears started again.

"Thank you," said Scoville. "That's all we need for now." He turned to the deputy who had returned to the room and was now turning off a tape recorder.

"Book him," Scoville said. Turning back to Richard he said, "You're under arrest. Aiding and abetting. Concealing evidence. Your attorney will be in to talk with you later. I'll come down, too."

The deputy handcuffed Richard and led him out of the

room. Scoville wrapped the rubber band twice around the drab green notebook and put it in his shirt pocket. He scraped his chair back from the table, unfolded his tall, thin body into a standing position, and walked out into the hallway, closing the door behind him.

17

Humboldt brushed his teeth savagely. I'll be damned if I ask her again, he said to himself. I'd just as soon go alone, anyway. He spat.

Why the hell doesn't she just look at things straight? It's simple. Basic. Hilda killed a man; she cut him up; she's a bitch. Nothing hard about that. But Maggie has to look at everything from ten points of view.

Piss on it. Facts are facts.

He heard Maggie walk down the hall. When he entered the bedroom a few minutes later, she was standing at the dresser with her back to him.

"I'm going, too," she said. She fastened her earrings. Humboldt grunted and looked at his watch. He transferred the car keys and change from his Levis to his dress pants.

"Glad you're comin'," he said grumpily when he'd finished. Maggie met his eyes in the mirror.

"I'll go warm up the car," he said.

Maggie nodded.

Half an hour later the Dentons entered the north wing of the courthouse, the wing built before the turn of the century. They climbed the shallow old steps of the oak staircase to the second story and pushed open dark, scarred double doors. The doors seemed small. In fact, everything about the old courtroom seemed small: the benches for spectators, the jury seats, even the judge's high-backed chair. Maybe people were smaller in those days. Better, too.

The courtroom was well-heated and smelled of warm dust in old wood. Steam radiators clanked horribly now and then beneath long, narrow windows. Reminds me of a schoolroom, Humboldt thought sourly. He hadn't liked school much. He'd liked court even less. Once when he was twenty he'd been in the defendant's chair charged with a felony, until the D.A., after two days of a jury trial, couldn't make it stick.

I don't have no love for them bastards, he said to himself, thinking of the lawyers and the judge and the law enforcement. Still, there was Scoville. Humboldt felt uncomfortable. He had no love for the prosecution; yet the D.A. and the judge were the only ones who could give Hilda what she deserved.

Humboldt hoped the black-robed judge would worry the hell out of Hilda. He wished those little jury seats from the past century were filled right now with twelve large jurors who hated killers. He wished this were the trial instead of the preliminary hearing.

A small door near the jury box opened from the other side. Spectators in the gallery shifted on the wooden benches, then grew still as they watched the first prisoner emerge: small-boned Angela in a gray wrap-around jail dress that was the color of her eyes and the circles under them. She and her attorney, a young woman with long, black hair, sat down behind the counsel table, the backs of their chairs toward Humboldt and against the low railing that separated the spectators from the defendants, their lawyers, the court reporter, and clerk. The bailiff walked back through the side door and disappeared.

Everyone waited. The silence in the courtroom tightened. Suddenly, there she was. Hilda stood in the small doorframe. She was both more and less than Humboldt expected. A larger person than he remembered. More ordinary-looking than she should have been. Less ashamed. He looked at her once with loathing, then turned away. He didn't want to be sick, not here in the courtroom. His saliva turned thick and gummy.

"Hummer?" Maggie whispered. "Are you all right?" She put her hand on his knee and moved closer to him. She pressed against his side and drew in a deep breath. Humboldt didn't answer.

She'll be sick, too, he thought fleetingly. Let her find out all about Hilda. He heard the side door close. He heard Hilda and her attorney sit down at one end of the counsel table. Maggie's breaths were short and shallow now, and Humboldt relented. Poor girl, he thought: she knows about the murder, but she hasn't faced it. He put his hand over hers.

"All rise," said the bailiff. "The Honorable James T. Berger presiding… "

Humboldt lifted his eyes in time to see a black-robed figure step through the door behind the judge's chair and take the bench. As the noise of bodies seating themselves in the courtroom subsided, Scoville slipped in and sat down beside the District Attorney at the counsel table.

"I ask that Detective Scoville be designated my investigating officer," said the D.A.

"So designated," said the judge. "Call your first witness."

"Your Honor," said the D.A., "before I begin direct examination I would like to make a brief request."

"Proceed."

While the District Attorney shuffled his papers, Humboldt looked at Hilda. She was sitting—no, lounging—between Scoville on the left and a young lawyer on the right.

"Slob. Bitch," Humboldt said under his breath as he took in Hilda's wrinkled gray wrap-around and her spread position in the chair.

"What?" whispered Maggie, leaning closer. Humboldt didn't reply.

"Your Honor," said the D.A., straightening up from an exchange with Detective Scoville, "we request that the testimony of our first witness be read into the record from a transcript of his deposition. The witness is advanced in years. As I understand it, he is in the hospital at the present time."

That was news to Humboldt, but it didn't surprise him.

The judge nodded. "For the record, I met this morning in Chambers with the District Attorney and the defense attorney, and I am aware of the situation with this first prosecution witness."

Without shifting her body or even turning her head, Hilda said something to her attorney in a rough, audible voice. Humboldt couldn't catch her words.

"I am convinced of the age and infirmity of this witness," continued the judge, "and over the objections of defense, I am going to grant the District Attorney's request."

Bunch of bullshit, Humboldt thought to himself. Secret meetings in Chambers. Legal games. Tommy seen what he seen. That's what matters.

While the judge went through more mumbo-jumbo, Humboldt shifted his attention to Hilda's lawyer. The fellow had sleek hair and sat too close to Hilda. Smug son of a bitch, thought Humboldt to himself, makin' money defending scum.

Hilda's attorney rose to his feet. "Your Honor, for the record, I object to the reading of this testimony on the grounds that defense is precluded from cross-examining the witness."

"This is not a trial," said the judge. "It's a preliminary hearing. For reasons previously stated, I am going to let it in."

"Furthermore," said the lawyer, turning somewhat toward the gallery, "we are denied the opportunity of inquiring into the witness's reputation for truth and veracity."

"Your objection is on the record," said the judge.

The court reporter climbed the steps leading to the witness stand and began to read Tommy's deposition. Maggie, sitting beside Humboldt, didn't stir. The judge leaned forward and listened intently.

To Humboldt, the straight reading of the transcript was very dry. He already knew what it said, and words were inadequate to describe the event. His Honor doesn't know how bad Tommy feels, Humboldt thought to himself. He didn't see the old man's face when he turned on his dirty pillows and cried.

Humboldt gazed on Hilda. She betrayed no interest in the proceedings. She sat with her head sunk into her shoulders, a great, gray turtle, heavy-lidded and impenetrable.

For relief Humboldt looked out the long, narrow windows along one side of the courtroom. It was a gray, wintery day, cold and threatening rain. Inside, the courtroom was warm with its clanking radiators and the body warmth of citizens seated close to each other on old wooden benches.

Humboldt looked around him. How come most people can get along together and she can't? he asked himself.

As the reporter drew close to the part where Tommy saw Duane shot, Humboldt brought his attention back to the testimony. Why in the hell did they make Angela sit through this? Concern for Duane's widow washed over him, followed by a wave of grief that pounded him, and nearly sank him. He felt old and eroded. He didn't know how to help Angela.

The court reporter stopped. The reading was over.

"Any further witnesses?" asked the judge.

"No, Your Honor. The People rest," said the District Attorney.

"We will take the noon recess," said the judge. "All parties reconvene at 1:30." Humboldt watched Hilda as she plodded just ahead of the bailiff, looking neither right nor left. When it was Angela's turn to leave she tripped on the rug and looked out at the audience with an embarrassed smile.

Humboldt and Maggie side-stepped along the bench until they stood in the center aisle. Jim Scoville, still seated at the front of the courtroom, closed his little notebook, slowly stood up from the counsel table, and walked back to meet them.

"How long's this hearing gonna go on?" Humboldt asked.

"Probably be over sometime this afternoon. Never can

tell," replied Scoville. He nodded to Maggie and smiled. Then he turned back toward Humboldt. "Talk to you a second?" he asked.

"Sure," said Humboldt. The men stepped aside.

"Those peepholes in the bathroom you talked about," said Scoville in a low voice.

"Yeah?" said Humboldt.

"Do you know who drilled 'em?"

"Had to be Hilda."

"If it was Angela's and Duane's closet?" Scoville pursued the question.

Humboldt shrugged. "She practically lived there toward the end. It's her. She's a queer, you know."

Scoville gave it a moment's thought. Then he smiled once more at Maggie and loped back across the courtroom toward the bailiff's side door. Humboldt and Maggie watched until the tweedy figure with the thinning hair and prominent shoulder blades ducked through the little door and disappeared from view.

18

At 1:30 Angela Glynnis took the witness stand. Humboldt watched her small, peaked face turn toward the clerk. His temper flared. They've got no goddam business bringing her into this, he fumed. The reason and cause of it all is sittin' right there at the end of the table.

With one pale, fine-boned hand upraised and the other behind her grasping the flap of her jail wrap-around skirt, Angela took the oath.

She hurried up the three steps to the witness box and sat down quickly in the straight-backed chair. Almost immediately she jumped up to straighten the skirt, fastidiously arranging it behind her and sitting down carefully so that the free edge lay just so. Hilda's attorney looked at the judge who nodded for him to begin.

"Mrs. Glynnis?" said the attorney tentatively.

"Yes?" Angela answered with a smile.

"You are the wife of Duane Glynnis, now deceased. Is that correct?"

Angela's smile vanished. She looked surprised, confused, and then resentful. She did not answer.

"Respond to the question, please," the judge instructed her.

"No."

"No, you are not the wife of Duane Glynnis?" asked the attorney.

Angela shook her head.

"You'll have to answer audibly for the record," the judge said.

"Yes, I'm not," said Angela, moving uneasily in her chair. The judge sighed. Hilda's attorney tried again.

"Are you married or divorced?"

"Divorced," Angela answered breathily.

"How long have you been divorced?"

"I don't know."

"Have the divorce papers been filed?"

"No. But we were going to before—"

"Your Honor," Angela's attorney said, stepping up to the counsel table, her long black hair swinging silkily, "I am concerned about my client's right against self-incrimination."

"As I am," said the judge. "I would suggest you make yourself available to the witness. Perhaps you can stand beside the witness box."

He turned to Angela. "Mrs. Glynnis, your attorney is going to stand near you so that you may confer with her, if necessary."

"I don't need a lawyer," Angela said defensively.

"Nevertheless, you do have your Fifth Amendment right," said the judge, sitting back in his chair. "You may proceed."

"Thank you, Your Honor." Hilda's attorney coughed and

jingled loose change in the pocket of his well-cut slacks. He thought for a moment, then lifted his head confidently, back on track.

"Were you separated?" he asked.

"Yes." She vacillated. "No."

"You were in the process of separating?" he suggested.

Angela nodded.

"Your Honor," interrupted the young woman attorney, "may I have a moment to confer with my client?"

"Surely," said the judge.

Humboldt crossed his arms over his chest and leaned back reflectively. He watched Angela's attorney bend over the low side wall of the witness box. As she whispered intently her black hair hung and swayed in the air, hiding Angela's face from view.

At the end of the counsel table Hilda and her attorney were also whispering. It's a double-edged sword, Humboldt mused uneasily. Either woman can be made to look real bad; like a murderer. The attorneys know it. Hilda knows it.

Finally both attorneys finished advising their clients. The judge asked the court reporter to read back the last question.

"You were in the process of separating?"

"Yes," Angela answered in an unwilling voice.

"Do you know my client Hilda Weatherall?" the attorney asked, changing tack.

"Yes," said Angela instantly. She pointed swiftly and straight-armed at Hilda sitting in the defendant's chair.

"How long have you known her?"

"Two or three years," she said clearly. She pushed herself up and out of her chair and straightened her skirt again. She looked in Hilda's direction with an odd little half-smile.

"To your knowledge, were Duane Glynnis and Hilda Weatherall acquainted?"

"Oh, yes," Angela answered immediately.

"How well acquainted were they?"

"They were acquainted pretty well."

Humboldt grew impatient. Slick, young attorney wants to make a triangle out of it.

Wish she *had* been a little jealous, he reflected sadly on second thought. At least she would of cared.

"What kind of relationship did they have, Hilda and Duane?" the lawyer asked in a bland tone.

Angela's eyes narrowed. "Hilda hated Duane," she said.

Suddenly Hilda moved. In one motion she heaved herself and her chair off the floor and turned toward the witness box. She landed facing Angela directly. Angela recoiled.

"Were they ever friends?"

"I guess," she said quietly

"More than friends?" He waited suggestively.

"No."

"When did they stop being friends?"

"I don't know."

"What makes you think their relationship became unfriendly?"

Angela licked her lips. "Different things."

"What do you mean, 'different things'?"

"Oh—" she brushed a speck off of her sleeve "—Hilda didn't like it if Duane was around when she came over."

"When you say 'came over,' do you mean to your home?"

"Yes."

"Yours and Duane's home?"

"Yes."

"You weren't separated at that time?"

"No."

"Who did she come to see?"

"Me."

"Did Duane invite her there?"

"No."

"Did you invite her there?"

"Well, she didn't need much invitation."

"Just answer the question," the judge broke into the cross-examination.

"I forget the question," Angela said nervously.

"I withdraw it, Your Honor," said the Attorney. He paused for thought. "Did she ever say anything to you that led you to believe she didn't like Duane?"

"She didn't have to. I knew."

"Just answer yes or no," the judge said irritably.

"Oh, well, yes." She looked sideways again in Hilda's direction. "She told me she'd be glad when he moved out so we could visit."

"And did he move out?"

"He never had a chance." Humboldt watched in disbelief as Angela popped up out of her chair and re-wrapped her skirt, drawing the loose edge tight behind her. She carefully sat down again.

She acts like she's more concerned about her County dress than about her dead husband, he thought to himself. He swallowed hard and wished for a recess.

The attorney paused and took a new tack. "When was the last time you saw Duane Glynnis?"

Angela hesitated. She darted a look at Hilda, then at her lawyer. "Let's see," she said, lowering her head. She was silent for several moments. "Thursday."

"Which Thursday would that be, ma'am?"

"The last time we played cards."

"Could you look at the calendar on the wall and fix the date for us?"

Angela studied the calendar. "November 10th."

"What time did you see him?"

"We played cards that night."

"And did Duane Glynnis spend all that Thursday night at home?"

Angela stopped fiddling with her skirt and seemed to retreat within herself. "He played cards," she finally said.

"Did he sleep at home that night?"

"I don't know," she said without expression.

"Is there any particular reason why you don't know?"

"No."

"Well, did you occupy separate bedrooms? Or, for example, did he sleep elsewhere?"

"Yes."

"Which?"

"Separate rooms."

"By the way, speaking of rooms," the attorney slouched a little and examined a hangnail, "did you ever see any peepholes in the bathrooms of your home?"

Humboldt watched Angela's face go through a series of changing expressions. At first, blankness. The question did not seem to register. Then she grasped the meaning. Next she passed it off as trivial. Finally, her face burning, she betrayed knowledge of what he was talking about.

"Holes?"

"Peepholes."

Angela bit her lip. Her eyes darted to the far corners of the courtroom. "I don't know about any."

It was a lie. Humboldt fought a profound uneasiness.

"Aren't there some small holes drilled in the wall between your closet and the two bathrooms?" Hilda's attorney pried patiently.

Suddenly Angela scooted forward on the witness chair and thrust her red, angry face toward Hilda. "She told you about that!" She began coughing in a frenzy. "That's none of her business!" She half-rose in the witness box, then fell back, choking and gasping for breath.

"Your Honor—" said Angela's attorney, leaning toward her client. But the judge was already speaking.

"We *will* maintain order here!" The bailiff, who had jumped to his feet at Angela's outburst, was standing midway between his desk and the witness box.

"We will take the afternoon recess!" the judge nearly shouted. "Reconvene at three o'clock!" He looked at Angela and her attorney, and said pointedly, "We will proceed in an orderly fashion until this preliminary hearing is concluded," and departed in a swirl of black.

Humboldt was shaken. He stood up quickly and half-guided, half-pushed Maggie between the benches until he stood in the center aisle.

"I need some air," he said.

"Want company?"

Humboldt shook his head.

"I'll save you a place," she promised. He squeezed her arm, then strode up the aisle, through the dark double doors, into the old north wing. He made his way to the lobby and hurried out the main entrance of the courthouse into a stiff wind blowing from the southwest. He began walking rapidly toward the ocean a block away.

Humboldt felt deeply unsettled. If the peepholes were none of Hilda's business, then Hilda didn't make them.

Who did?

He descended the cement stairway at the bottom of Third Street and crossed the wide strip of sand that lay between town and the boat basin. He turned north and walked along the shore, past the Coast Guard tower, past the jetty, until he reached the deserted beach and a view of the open sea.

The dark ocean heaved and churned. The sound of it in his ears was like the rush of his own blood. He stopped for a moment to watch the gray waves with their dirty froth slam against the shore. A seagull hung in the storm, unable to fly forward and unwilling to land.

Humboldt bent his head and walked faster. He could not rid his mind of the grim prisoners in their gray dresses. What had Duane done to deserve those two? What was the point of it all, of working, of trying to be happy, when it all ends anyway? Worse for some than others. But it ends.

He walked for several more minutes, his white hair whipping about his head. Before turning to cut back through town, he paused on the shore to look at the horizon. Nothingness. On one side of him, damp air and a few scattered little buildings. On the other, the restless, angry sea.

What's the point? his mind cried out.

He began walking back. The sound of the waves slowly receded. "I'm old," he said into the wind, and barely heard his own voice. He checked his watch. The hearing was bound to be over soon. Maggie would be wondering where he was. Soon they could go home. He straightened his shoulders against the wind and braced himself for the courtroom and the two gray women.

Angela smiled weakly at the judge as she took her place once more in the witness seat.

"These peepholes," continued the defense attorney, relentless and single-minded, "how long have they been in existence?"

Angela shrugged her shoulders. The attorney waited for his answer. The judge sat motionless and attentive.

Finally Angela turned a little to one side and closed her eyes. She ran the heel of her hand across one eyebrow and said tiredly, "A long time." The courtroom was still.

"How long?"

Angela slowly lifted her head. Her face rumpled softly and she began to cry like a small child who makes no effort to hide her tears. She looked straight at the attorney and sobbed.

"Water for the witness," the judge said gruffly to the bailiff. Both women's attorneys were whispering rapidly to them. It seemed to Humboldt that Hilda was asking her lawyer to stop the questions, or at least to do something different. The lawyer argued with her. Finally she settled back in her chair and the attorney straightened to address the witness.

"Mrs. Glynnis, who caused those holes to be placed in the

wall between the closet and bathroom?"

Angela took her hands down from her face. "Duane," she whispered.

Humboldt's temper flared briefly. "It's a set-up," he uttered without conviction. Angela was crying softly again, while Hilda sat with her head leaning into one hand.

"Mrs. Glynnis," said the defense attorney gently, "did Duane Glynnis subject you to embarrassment and abuse of a sexual nature?"

Angela looked down and nodded yes. Humboldt was stunned. He watched and listened, unable to think.

"Please answer audibly."

"Yes!" she sobbed, and stood as if to leave.

"I have more questions," said the lawyer firmly. "Can you please remain seated?" Angela sat back down obediently. She looked at her lap and waited for him to continue.

"That abuse has been going on for years, has it not?" he continued in a gentle, knowledgeable tone.

Angela nodded again.

"And no one knew what you suffered?"

"No one," Angela said softly.

"You cooked and cleaned for him all those years?"

"Yes."

"You bore his son?"

Angela nodded.

"You were at home every day keeping house and making life comfortable for Duane Glynnis?"

"Yes." Angela had stopped crying. By now she was answering questions in a subdued, almost sing-song voice.

"And sometimes it was very difficult, but you tried to be a dutiful wife?"

"Yes."

"Even though he asked you to do things you didn't want to do?"

"Yes."

"And on Friday, November 11th, did you see Duane Glynnis?"

Angela nodded. "He was dead then," she added sincerely.

Still standing near the witness box, Angela's attorney lunged forward. "Object! Object to the... "

"I want that answer on the record!" shouted Hilda's lawyer. The two attorneys nearly screamed trying to be heard over each other. Angela looked from one to the other, baffled.

The judge spread his hands and bore down on the high wooden bench. "Sustained as to the last part." He settled back in his chair. "Proceed."

"Did you see your husband on Friday, November 11th?" asked Hilda's attorney as if nothing had transpired between questions.

"Yes." Angela appeared mildly surprised at the attorney's forgetfulness. "I told you that."

"Where was he?"

"At the ranch."

"Is that some acreage outside town where he has a garden and so forth?"

"Yes."

"What time of day was it?"

"Early evening."

"Was it dark?"

"Yes."

"What was his condition when you saw him?"

Angela's attorney stiffened.

"Simply answer the question," the judge cautioned Angela. "Do not elaborate."

"Well, he was dead," said Angela matter-of-factly.

"Was he disfigured in any way?"

"Huh-uh," Angela said, her hands still, her eyes empty.

"Is that a 'no'? asked the judge.

"Yes," said Angela. "That's no."

"Why did you go looking for him?" questioned the attorney. She shrugged evasively. "He should have been home," she finally said.

Unexpectedly Hilda's attorney sat down. "No further questions," he said.

"Any more defense witnesses?" asked the judge as Angela and her attorney descended the steps from the witness box.

"Yes, Your Honor. Call Richard Glynnis to the stand," said Hilda's lawyer.

The bailiff had taken two steps toward the side door when Angela jumped in front of him and, holding her skirt tightly together in back, screamed up into his face, "No! Don't bring him in here! Leave him alone! It was me! It was me!"

Forgetting her skirt, she grabbed the bailiff's arm with both hands, then let go of it and charged into him with her right shoulder. At first he seemed dumbfounded; then, recovering, he whipped a set of handcuffs out of his back pocket. He snapped them on Angela, whirled her around, and pushed her into a chair.

Humboldt watched it all happen within the space of five seconds. He breathed hard through his nose as if he were helping the bailiff, and watched Angela throw her head onto her knees in a violent bending motion, and heard her cry out incoherent words between sobs.

Hilda sat stoically, a stone pillar. Whatever had happened the night she shot Duane, she was now a vessel large enough to hold her powerful feelings. Angela, on the other hand, was beside herself, her self escaping from her own frantic grasp as she yelled Duane's name and was half led, half carried out of the courtroom by the bailiff and a deputy sheriff.

As soon as the judge called for a recess, Humboldt jumped to his feet and pulled Maggie up with him. "Let's go home."

"But it's not over yet," she said.

"It is as far as I'm concerned," he retorted. Maggie pulled away from his grip.

"Let's see this through," she said.

"You stay if you want to. Pick me up at the Lucky Deuce when you're done."

He turned and hurried up the aisle. The dark double doors swung hard and unevenly for a long time after he passed through.

19

Humboldt stirred cream into his third cup of coffee. He'd drained the first cup fast. Angrily. The second one was slower. Now he settled back in his booth and sipped at the sweet, tan cupful, aware of the noises in the Lucky Deuce Club, yet not a part of them. Fishermen, kept indoors by a rough sea, stood around the bar drinking and staying just this side of rowdiness. The shuffleboard game was filled.

"Oh there you are!" said Maggie, sliding into the booth beside him. She was out of breath from the wind.

"All over?" he asked.

Maggie shook her head. "They'll finish tomorrow." She glanced around the room. "Jim Scoville's going to join us in a minute."

Pushing sugar, salt, pepper, and a hot sauce bottle aside, they looked up at the television mounted high over the bar. The local news was just coming on.

"There's Hilda again," said Maggie.

Humboldt grunted. "It showed the same thing last night." They watched the woman being hustled down the courthouse steps by a matron from the jail and a deputy sheriff. Brazen, Humboldt thought. She didn't bother to hide from the camera.

"Look at that," he said, shaking his head in disapproval. "Brazen. Any other prisoner would have the decency to cover his face."

Maggie cut short her laugh when she realized he wasn't being funny. Together they watched the footage, commonplace by now. There was Scoville standing in the background during a frantic interview with the D.A. in a crowded hallway. Then the camera cut to Angela just stepping into a patrol car. She sidled sadly toward the viewers and slid gracefully into the back seat. But the close-up of her face through the window showed a thin, strained neck and the knot of muscle at the corner of her jaw. She stared straight ahead as the car glided forward.

Scoville came in and sat down across from the Dentons. He nodded and reached for the menu.

"Gonna wrap it up tomorrow, huh?" said Humboldt grimly. Scoville nodded again.

Hilda's face filled the television screen, the columns of the courthouse rising gracefully behind her large head. Those near the bar quieted and watched the woman murderer whose blunt, heavy features seemed sculpted by a powerful artist.

"She ruined the Glynnises," Humboldt said softly, fiercely. "She tore that family up by the roots."

"She killed him, all right," agreed Scoville. "She's nailed." Maggie ran her finger around the lip of her cup.

"And hacked him up," Humboldt persisted.

Scoville read his menu. "The D.A.'s charging Angela with that" he said with studious disinterest.

Humboldt looked at him in disbelief. "What for?"

"She went around the bend," Scoville explained briefly.

"She hated Duane," Maggie interjected.

"Why?" Humboldt asked, angry and amazed.

"Humboldt," said Maggie in the manner of one patiently illuminating darkness, "you heard her this afternoon. He abused her." Humboldt seemed not to comprehend. "He was rotten to her," she concluded, trying to sum it up.

"That's what Hilda's attorney wants you to think," Humboldt said. He didn't give a hoot about Maggie's patience or logic. He stirred his coffee unnecessarily. "And what are those peepholes supposed to prove, anyway?"

"Part of the whole picture," said Scoville calmly. "Peeping Tom. Voyeur. All that."

Humboldt glanced sickly around the room. He brought his attention back to the table but did not speak.

"We talked to her doctor," said Scoville.

"What for?" Humboldt asked again.

"She had a history of sexual abuse."

"What does that mean?"

"Internal problems," Scoville said unwillingly. "Lacerations. Scarring."

"Jesus," said Humboldt. He went pale. Still he wrestled with his thoughts. "Who's to say it was Duane?"

"Angela told the doctor it was him."

Humboldt chuckled bitterly. "Why didn't this smart doctor do something about it while Duane was still alive?"

Scoville shrugged. "Angela was afraid. Embarrassed. Told him she would handle it herself. Consenting adults." Scoville shrugged again. "She handled it."

Humboldt's expression underwent disgust, then profound melancholy. The waitress came. He waved her toward Maggie and Scoville who each ordered. Humboldt roused himself to ask for more coffee.

"How're you gonna prove she did it?" he asked Scoville.

"We've got blood samples from her car trunk and her kitchen."

Humboldt threw his weight back against the booth and stared up at the television without seeing it. At length another thought came to him. "Somebody framed her."

"No." At this, Scoville's detachment slipped. He cleared his throat and looked away. "We have a witness," he said hoarsely.

Humboldt's question was cautious, even courteous: "Who?"

"Richard."

Humboldt looked at the detective, stunned. Maggie covered her mouth, biting down on the napkin she held in her hand.

Scoville stared hard into space. The waitress brought food. No one noticed.

"How?" Maggie whispered.

"He went looking for his folks that night," Scoville said in a controlled tone. "He found them." The detective gave his plate a quarter turn. "He didn't tell us until yesterday that he saw his mom… " He pushed back his plate. "He saw her… " He could not finish, yet he tried once again. "It's depraved," he whispered.

The lower part of Humboldt's face shook, threatened to crumble. He massaged his cheeks and jaw hard; tried to hold together the undermined structure.

"All this time," Maggie whispered, "Richard knew it." She held Humboldt's hand tightly.

"Richard will testify tomorrow," said Scoville. He took a sip of water. "Hilda went out to the property to find Duane. She found him. She killed him and left. Angela came looking for him, found him, and—dismembered him. Richard went out to find his folks, saw his mother—doing the work, helped her load the body in her car trunk, and they drove back separately to the mobile home." Scoville looked away. "He put it in the back yard."

"And the cooking?" Maggie formed the words with care.

"Angela." Scoville coughed. "She must have brought—the head—into the kitchen."

Humboldt rubbed his temples repeatedly. "With Richard?"

"Evidently not. Richard says he drove around in his car for a long time. Came back. Decided to move it to the woods."

Humboldt lifted his shoulders and looked helplessly at Scoville. "Richard might be the one who done it. Maybe even planned it in advance."

The detective acknowledged Humboldt's statement with a doubtful sideways glance. He'd finished talking.

Maggie wiped her eyes. "A person can take just so much," she said. "I wish Angela could have asked for help. Confided in someone."

"She told Hilda," Humboldt reminded her.

"Hilda can't help herself, much less anybody else," Scoville summed up. They turned their attention to the table, to the television, anything that could distract from the degradation.

Scoville picked up his knife and fork. Slowly, methodically, he began to eat. Maggie took a small bite of her hamburger. Humboldt ate one of her French fries.

"What's going to happen to them?" he asked, returning to the business at hand.

The detective looked speculative. "Up to the jury. Myself, I think Angela will get off easier than Hilda."

"Richard?" asked Humboldt. Scoville shrugged uncertainly.

"Look at you two," the detective said ruminatively. "Then look at the people you played Black Jack with."

Humboldt's face softened as he studied his wife. He waited for her to answer.

"I have Humboldt," she said, and brushed his chin with the back of one forefinger. "And luck," she added. "It's the cards you're dealt."

"How you play 'em," said Humboldt. "And—" he paused to look around the room, "you've got to stay in the game." He straightened his shoulders and called the waitress over. "I'll have a steak, medium. The dinner. With dessert."

ALWAYS ON THURSDAYS

1

From Geraldine's stout little house, the ocean could be heard pounding the Oregon coast, particularly after ten in the evening when highway traffic decreased and the night grew still.

One night in February, 1983, Geraldine sat at her lighted window proofreading a court transcript. Down at the harbor the voice of the disinterested fog horn alternated with the wash of surf, systolic and diastolic pulse of Brooks Beach.

Humboldt and Maggie Denton always looked for the light in Geraldine's window when returning home from visiting their grown children in California. If she was still awake, they would stop in town to see her before winding five miles north along Pacific Coast Highway to their redwood home on the cliff with its high, sweeping view of the ocean.

"Let's not bother her," Maggie said as Humboldt removed the key from the Plymouth's ignition. "She's working."

"Nonsense. Let's bother her. She'll be glad to see us." Humboldt came around and opened the door for his wife. It had been drizzling ever since they crossed the California border into Oregon. As they climbed the damp steps to the cottage, Geraldine turned on the porch light. She knew the sound of their car. "You're back!" she said, and opened the door wide.

"Ready for some hot chocolate?" Humboldt pulled three envelopes of instant cocoa from his jacket. "But if you're busy..."

"Never too busy for hot chocolate," said Geraldine. "I've missed you."

"Exactly what I told Maggie," said Humboldt. Geraldine had adopted the Dentons as her parents in Brooks Beach. They often visited her in the cottage whose front door faced the two-room post office across the street. Her back door nestled against the alley and the Knotty Pine Tavern. Coast Highway lay just beyond.

"Seen Guy lately?" Humboldt asked as the three of them

walked to the kitchen.

Geraldine shook her head. "Haven't seen him." She took milk from the refrigerator. "Marshmallows?"

"I never say no to a marshmallow."

Minutes later she stood waiting for bubbles to form at the edge of the pan. Lowering the flame, she said again, less certainly, "I haven't seen Guy for a while."

Maggie folded her hands on the table. "Is he still in town?"

"As far as I know."

Geraldine poured the chocolate. Maggie lifted her mug and the other two followed suit. "Here's to home. We've had a lovely trip, but it's good to be back." The clink of ceramic was satisfying.

"You found your family well?" Geraldine asked. But adult children in California were not as interesting to talk about as a good-looking man with curly hair and brilliant blue eyes who, without trying, drew women to him.

"The kids are fine," said Maggie. "So you haven't heard anything about Guy?"

Geraldine didn't answer but sat gazing intently into her cup of hot chocolate.

"We saw him just before we left for California," said Humboldt.

Maggie laid a hand on her husband's arm. "Let's talk about something else." Outside, the drizzle was turning to rain, accompanied by rising wind.

Humboldt scooped up marshmallow froth floating on his cocoa. "Tell you what," he said, "after we're finished here, let's go over to the Knotty Pine and play a couple hands of Black Jack."

Maggie brightened. In glum agreement, Geraldine drank her chocolate. A half hour later they were crossing the back yard to the alley behind her narrow garage. Several cars had overflowed the highway frontage parking onto the packed dirt behind the

Knotty Pine.

"Feelin' lucky?" Humboldt asked Maggie, buttoning his windbreaker and hunching against the weather.

"Not lucky. Skilled," Maggie said. "I feel skilled." But before she could start the next sentence, Geraldine grabbed her by the arm and pulled her back. A car idling behind the garage roared to life, and, spitting gravel, reversed out of the dead-end. Whoever was in the passenger seat held a large purse against the window to hide her face.

"Lovers' lane," said Humboldt.

"The slum behind the Knotty Pine," Geraldine murmured, dismissing her garage, her house, and, it seemed, her life. The car backed into the street at a reckless speed, shifted sloppily into forward gear, and squealed off toward Coast Highway. Maggie pulled Geraldine to her.

"I'm sorry I bought here," the younger woman said, her voice muffled in Maggie's shoulder. "A lovely residential neighborhood this is not." They crossed the alley. Under the blinking sign advertising beer, Geraldine's skin glowed pale gray-green. Chestnut hair pulled back from her forehead lacked vitality.

Her husband, the curly-haired, blue-eyed Guy Falkenburg, had enough vitality for both of them.

"Do you remember the night we were here and saw Guy drinking with the dark-haired woman?" Geraldine said as they crossed the dirt lot beginning to be spotted with hard drops of rain.

"Which dark-haired woman?" said Humboldt, and recoiled from his wife's sharp elbow.

Even though the tavern was almost on Geraldine's property line, Guy never conducted his dalliances anywhere but the Knotty Pine. He couldn't control its location any more than he could control his behavior. It was the liveliest establishment in town, the place where he could find not only Black Jack and pool, but the best-looking women in Brooks Beach.

"That might have been her in the car just now hiding behind

her purse," Geraldine said, passing through the door Humboldt held open.

"Don't think about it, honey," Maggie said.

The younger woman stayed close behind the Dentons, shielding herself from the clack of pool balls and the smells of deep-fried cod; from a curly-haired man with overflowing charm who might be dancing with another woman.

For the past six months, Guy had been squandering his abundant maleness. It would never occur to him that his wife might want to stay away from the Knotty Pine but find herself attracted, unable to resist. Might try to avoid her back bedroom facing the alley and bar because it made her think of him. Might have to struggle against wanting him every moment of every day and night. It would never cross his mind that he was ruining her happiness.

"Do you know anything about the woman?" Geraldine asked. "Do you know where she lives?"

"No, but it's probably a distance away," Maggie said, looking around the room, distracted. "She's not here every night."

Humboldt spoke sharply. "And you are?"

"I'm not here every night," Maggie said, offended, "but I'm here often enough to know she always comes on Thursdays."

"Tonight's Thursday," Geraldine said.

"Then you'll find her here," Maggie said with confidence, "along with other Thursday regulars. Dr. Brown. Guy."

On Thursdays Dr. Brown played Black Jack in the card room. Guy Falkenburg stayed up front, playing pool, talking to women, dancing. Both Maggie and Geraldine knew that he took his personal magnetism for granted. To him, sexual energy, popularity, good looks were the most natural qualities in the world. Women would always find him.

But Geraldine knew that women didn't hold Guy's attention for long. What held his attention was illegality. Fascinated by crime, he flirted with the law: cheated, dealt drugs, and stole.

It wasn't that he didn't fear the consequences. In fact, he longed for consequences, as a plain man longs for a beautiful woman. He both longed for and feared prison. Guy admired men who had personal knowledge of prison. To him, there was a maverick, fugitive romance in criminality. Risk terrified and attracted him, and he loved playing the odds. So far, he'd won.

2

Maggie had a sixth sense about people and a mind given to theorizing. "There's something going on at the Knotty Pine," she said under her breath as she and Geraldine moved toward the Black Jack table at the back of the tavern. "Guy may be playing with fire."

"Guy likes to play with fire," Geraldine murmured back.

"There's tension here on Thursday nights," Maggie said. "Something in the air."

"Something to do with Guy?"

"I don't know. I can sense it, though. A knot at the Knotty Pine."

Geraldine felt both pity and anger for her husband. Frequenting another woman's bed, he might fail to calculate forces at work in the low building here across the alley. Rolling along on his usual wave of luck and physical well-being, he might fail to consider whether the woman he was sleeping with had her own reasons for being at the tavern every week. Glancing about, Geraldine tried to guess at motives and ambitions behind the men's beards and women's makeup; behind the loud laughter and rough language in the pine-paneled room.

The first time she'd seen her husband with the dark-haired, smoky-voiced Rhonda Rhinehart, he'd pushed back his chair and left the woman sitting at the table by herself. His glass with its beer still sudsing stayed where it was, suggesting his return.

But Geraldine knew Guy well enough to know it meant no such thing. The woman might believe he'd come back to her table, but Guy went where he wanted to go.

Gratified by his languorous approach, happy to see him ignoring the other woman in favor of herself and the Dentons, Geraldine had slowly kissed him, then made bold eye contact with the loamy woman across the room while letting her fingertips graze her husband's hands, arms, hair. He hadn't returned her touch.

Flushed now with humiliation, lifting her chin high, Geraldine followed Maggie into the back room. Guy belonged to her. She shouldn't have married him, but she didn't care. She'd been giddy with lust. Wild with love. She still was. She thought she could separate sensible days from hectic nights, could always get up in time for work, and could negotiate with dawn, stirring under her husband's touch, the gray light brightening until too soon the alarm clock rings.

As long as she held a good job, enjoyed the friendship of the Dentons, and owned her tidy little cedar-shingled cottage intelligently purchased in her own name, she could maintain a precarious stability. She was not without resources. Or, she admitted, a tendency toward self-deception.

Behind them, Humboldt paused to watch a crucial shot at the pool table. Seeing that Maggie and Geraldine had already disappeared into the card room where Eppie Epperson dealt Black Jack every night, he ordered three beers before returning to the group of men focused on the pool table.

"Good to be back," he responded when the nearest logger in work shirt and red suspenders leaned on his pool cue and welcomed him home. "Good to be back in Brooks Beach." And back with men, he added to himself. Two weeks with Maggie, three daughters, and four granddaughters, was enough. Not that he didn't love family. Still, he missed his buddies. He'd been an ironworker all his life, and couldn't do without male camaraderie. His eyes wandered over the room. Rhonda Rhinehart was nowhere to be seen. Neither was Guy. The difference between himself and Guy was thirty years. Thirty years and one woman: Maggie. After marrying her, Humboldt had stopped drinking, gambling, womanizing. With a mixture of envy and contentment he watched younger men struggle with the testosterone throbbing through their systems.

Carrying three mugs of beer by the handles, he reached the door to the back room and nudged it open with his foot. Just as Maggie had said, Dr. Brown was seated at the table, smoking and studying his cards. He was a physically powerful man, with hips extending over the seat of the high stool; long, heavy legs crowding against the base of the table; wide shoes hooked around one rung. His silences were dark and dissatisfied. From her standing position behind the table, controlling the doctor's strength and mood by her attention, Eppie dealt the cards with nimble certainty. As much as anyone could, Humboldt thought, she kept him happy. Her red-lacquered fingernails gleamed against the green felt tabletop.

In between hands there was desultory conversation about the change in weather. The fisherman in thick sweater and knit cap wanted to fish cod the next morning. Dr. Brown murmured something about mud slides in the Siskiyous. Humboldt guessed the two-lane mountain road was always on his mind; the doctor needed to make it back to Medford in time for morning rounds at his private hospital.

"Is she gonna lay down?" Eppie asked, tilting her head toward the Pacific as another gust of wind rattled the single window in the room.

"Nah. No fishing tomorrow." The fisherman tapped the green felt. "Hit me." Eppie dealt him a card. He stayed. She turned her card over, swooped up the fisherman's bet, and collected from Dr. Brown. Only Maggie retained her chips.

The wind grew stronger. Twice the electricity flickered. Small-boned and versatile, Eppie Epperson didn't seem to mind working past midnight. Postmistress by day, card dealer by night, she kept a watchful eye on the table, alternately tidying a stack of chips and smoothing the sleek blade of auburn hair curling from temple to jaw. At the other ear, her hair swept up, anchored by a metallic comb that glinted under the low-hanging light fixture.

The only sounds in the room were the clink of chips and spatter of rain at the window.

Geraldine paid her losses, eased down from the high stool, and wandered out into the bar where the large, pine-paneled room contained no well-built husband playing pool or sitting at a table with another woman. No disruption to her monotonous heartbeat.

Back in the card room, Humboldt was beginning to feel sleepy. He knew Maggie could play all night and still get up at six the next morning to make breakfast. Except they were retired and had no need for six-o'clock breakfasts anymore. Musing on his ironworking days, on Maggie's thirty-year accounting job at her brother's plumbing shop, he wished they had a reason to get up at dawn.

"Let's wrap 'er up," Eppie said at one o'clock and began snapping rubber bands around bills and locking the money box that rested under the table at knee-level. The Dentons found Geraldine in the bar. She followed them outside. Humboldt turned up his collar against the rain.

"What's that?" said Maggie as they stepped into the alley. The only light came from the neon beer sign behind them. Humboldt moved closer to what could be rags or possibly a rug lying on the gravel. Geraldine thought of an animal stretched full-length.

"Gunny sack?" Maggie asked. "Several gunny sacks?" Humboldt was already standing over the bundle.

"Get out of the light," he said sharply, and squatted down. Lifting a piece of fabric, he peered closely, then let it drop. Still on his haunches, he lost balance. "I can't stand," he said. The women bent down and grasped him by the arms. Struggling, he stood.

Geraldine bent over the form. Under the thin blanket, the dark-haired woman's head rested on a satin pillow whose white tassels spread evenly over the gravel. The eyes were sunken. "My God," Geraldine breathed. With a rush of logic she thought of Guy who hadn't been at the Knotty Pine tonight. Fearing for him, for his uncontrolled emotions and unruly habits, she choked on bile that flooded her mouth.

Walking carefully around the body, staggering a little, the three crossed the alley and the strip of grass to Geraldine's back door.

Inside, Humboldt passed through the kitchen and on to the hallway between the bedrooms. He picked up the telephone and dialed the operator. "Sheriff's Office," he said.

In the kitchen, the women stood waiting for him. Geraldine plugged in the coffee maker. Soon all three were sitting at the kitchen table, silent with shock. The smoky scent of coffee filled the room. Every now and then sounds of the Pacific washing over the beach reached the little house and alley.

"Like I said," Maggie said softly, accepting a cup from Geraldine, "Rhonda Rhinehart is always here on Thursdays."

3

It was Friday morning. Scoville opened his office door in the old wing of the Courthouse and motioned Humboldt from the waiting room. They shook hands. "What have you gotten us into this time, Humboldt?" he asked, motioning to a chair on the other side of the scratched desk that swayed a little when Humboldt bumped it with his knee.

But Scoville already knew. As detective in the Sheriff's

Office, he'd accompanied the sheriff to the alley between the Knotty Pine and Geraldine's house the night before. What he meant was, *do you know anything about the murder in the alley like you knew about the last felony in Brooks Beach?*

"No idea," said Humboldt. "It's just chance that we found her. Like I told you last night, I don't know her."

Scoville leaned forward over his desk and picked a toothpick out of the little ceramic barrel labeled 'Durango, Colorado.' "Your wife does, though?"

"If Maggie doesn't know her," Humboldt said, "she knows somethin' about her. She knows somethin' about everybody."

Scoville reached beneath his sports jacket and pulled a small green notebook from his shirt pocket. Reviewing a page, he frowned. "Can't hardly read my writing."

"Bad light in the alley," said Humboldt.

Scoville squinted and massaged his gums with the toothpick.

"Name's Rhonda," Humboldt reminded him. "Rhonda Rhinehart."

Scoville wrote a methodical note. Humboldt scanned the lean face, the sharp Adam's apple, the dark eyes that surveyed surroundings without warmth or hostility. The detective changed his toothpick to the other side of his mouth and stared above Humboldt's head. "So you don't know anything about her?"

"She comes on Thursdays," Humboldt said grudgingly.

"No idea why?"

"No idea."

Scoville turned a page in the notebook. "How well do you know Eppie Epperson?"

"Seen her around town for years," said Humboldt. "Every day at the post office. Everybody knows Eppie."

Moving down a list, the detective lifted his discount-store pen and let it hover. "Geraldine Manahan."

"You saw her last night."

Scoville didn't dispute it. "What do you know about her?"

"Friend of Maggie's and mine. Moved up here from California a couple years ago."

"How long have you known her?"

"Almost from the first day she arrived."

"Any idea why she picked Brooks Beach?"

"Came up with Guy Falkenburg."

"B-U-R-G?" Scoville asked, writing the name.

"Dunno. Never was much of a speller."

"What does this Guy Falkenburg do in Brooks Beach?"

"Retired."

"How old is he?"

Humboldt pulled a thread from his raveling jacket cuff. "Maybe forty."

"Early retirement," said Scoville.

"Yeah," said Humboldt.

"This Geraldine," said Scoville, "was she in the Knotty Pine the entire time you were there last night?"

"Sure she was. No way is she a suspect."

Scoville didn't agree or disagree.

"You can count her out as a suspect," Humboldt repeated. "And you can count Guy out, too."

Scoville's questions continued without perturbation. "This Geraldine Manahan is a court reporter?"

"Yup."

"Not the regular one, though?"

"She helps out," said Humboldt. "Does depositions."

Scoville nodded. "I've passed her in the hall."

He shifted and tipped his chair back against an inner door behind him that led to a hallway connecting the holding cell, jail, and both courtrooms. Through this door Scoville passed at least once a week for Friday criminal calendar when the County's fresh batch of defendants, wearing orange jumpsuits and locked at the ankles and wrists, were led to the courtroom. There they took temporary seating in the jury box and waited to plead guilty or innocent in front of the judge.

"What's this Geraldine's connection"—Scoville cast a detached glance at his notes—"with Guy Falkenburg?"

"Technically they're married. But they don't live together anymore."

"Hers is the house behind the Knotty Pine," said Scoville.

"Yup. You can count them both out," Humboldt said.

"Where does Guy stay?"

"At the Tide Pool Motel, when he's not up working on his property."

"Interesting forms of life wash up at the Tide Pool," Scoville said. "Where's his property?"

"North of town. Point Jade Road. He's at the summit."

"Has he built on it?"

"Nope. Has a trailer. Got a helluva view of the pond."

Scoville laid the little notebook on his desk. With the toothpick shifting ruminatively, he crossed his arms and stared out the window at the rain lashing the Courthouse. Everyone in Brooks Beach knew that commercial fishing boats were tied up today, bobbing wetly in the harbor, halyards ringing, hulls squealing against tires hung low on the docks to prevent splintering.

"Is Eppie Epperson married?"

"Nope."

"Seeing anybody?"

"According to Maggie, she and this Dr. Brown have something going."

"Who's Dr. Brown?"

"No idea, really."

Scoville smiled. "Ask Maggie?"

"Ask Maggie." Humboldt stood. "Are we done?"

"Sure," said Scoville, also standing. "But you know this isn't the end of it."

"It is as far as I'm concerned," said Humboldt. "One murder

was enough for me."

"That was two years ago," said Scoville. "The Sheriff's Office gets out of practice if we don't have something serious to investigate every other year."

"No reason for me to stay in practice," said Humboldt. "I'm not the Sheriff's Office." He left the same way he came in. Standing behind his desk, Scoville watched as the rain blowing in from the ocean turned to sleet. It slapped the wood and windows of the Crescent County Courthouse in waves. Intimately familiar with coastal weather, he viewed the blustery walk to the parking lot a block away without dread.

4

"If he thinks he's going to rope me into his murder investigation," Humboldt said that same night, drinking a hot toddy in front of the late news, "he's got another think comin'."

"He didn't rope you into the investigation two years ago," Maggie said in mild reproach. "If anything, you roped *him*."

"Let's not talk about the past," Humboldt interrupted. Maggie shrugged and sipped her sherry. When she was playing cards down in town, she drank beer and whiskey with the best of them. At home, however, on the cliff overlooking the Pacific, seated with her husband in front of a fire and the television, her floor-length velour robe flowing from shoulder to slipper, she liked being elegant. In spite of a working class practicality, Maggie reached for the stars.

"Did you pick up place cards for the dinner with Geraldine and Guy?" she might ask in the days when the four of them socialized regularly.

"I forgot 'em," Humboldt would respond, "but I remembered the beer. Guy and I like beer."

"And Geraldine and I like place cards."

"For a chili dinner?"

But he would pick up place cards. One time Maggie labeled them Henrietta, Archibald, Herbert, and Regina. They'd laughed and played roles. That was in the good days before Guy moved out of his wife's little house.

"How about a trip down the hill for a night of cards and loose women?" Humboldt might suggest.

Laughing, Guy would rise from the table and pat his flat stomach. "Wonderful dinner, Mags." Geraldine would stand, too, moving beside her husband to be near his smile, height, wiry curls. With inconspicuous movements she would touch his arm, his hand, and he would look down at her and warm her with his blue eyes and ruddy face. He looked more like a sea captain than a dealer in salvage.

"Guy's dealing in more than salvage," Humboldt said one night after drinking too much at the Knotty Pine. But no matter how cleverly Maggie quizzed him, she couldn't shake his sense of loyalty. To Humboldt, men were a fraternity. Nothing could or should come between them.

"Have you talked to Geraldine since last night?" Humboldt asked as Maggie set the sherry glass on the end table and gathered the long velour skirt about her.

"I tried. She's not saying much. I can tell she's worried."

"Do you think Guy was in town last night?"

Maggie nodded. "I heard he was at the Tide Pool." The television program sputtered.

"Technical difficulties," Humboldt murmured.

"You bet," Maggie said.

"He should-a stuck with Geraldine," Humboldt said.

"Sure he should have," Maggie said. "But he didn't."

"They could get back together," Humboldt said without confidence.

"Sure. The outlaw and the court reporter." They sat staring glumly at the blank screen.

"Call her," said Humboldt.

"I won't have to," said Maggie. "She'll call *me*."

The telephone rang. Humboldt answered. Within seconds he'd hung up. "Guy called Geraldine," he said. "From Mexico."

"Was that Geraldine?" Maggie said, hurt.

"Yeah. She didn't give me time to ask questions." He gazed into the fire. "Why Mexico?"

"That's where Guy goes when he's afraid."

"He didn't waste any time getting there," said Humboldt. "Afraid of what?"

"The law, of course. He goes to Mexico whenever he's afraid of the law."

"You make it sound like a regular thing, Maggie."

Her silence resonated.

As a young man, Humboldt should have gone to Mexico more than once. Instead, in his twenties he'd found his way to Wyoming where he worked off board and room at his uncle's sheep ranch until the statute of limitations ran out. Maggie had joined him there for a weekend before returning to her job in Brooks Beach.

"Guy needs an uncle in Wyoming," Humboldt mumbled.

"If Guy went to Wyoming, his uncle would be in a nursing home," Maggie pointed out. "Our friend is getting a little old to have these scrapes with the law."

"Geraldine's getting a little old to fall for an outlaw," Humboldt retorted.

"You like the outlaw quite well," Maggie reminded him. "We both do."

They sat in worried agreement. Distrustful of sheriffs and courts, they hadn't quite adjusted to their late-in-life respectability supported by Humboldt's solid ironworker's pension and Maggie's fertile imagination.

"Do you think he's really in Mexico?" Humboldt asked.

"Would he lie?"

The answer lay between them, unspoken and agreed upon.

5

Detective Scoville learned from court records that Rhonda Rhinehart had a married name. In Medford, she was Rhonda Brown. New names, modified names, assumed names might reflect an evolving personal identity, but in Scoville's experience, it usually reflected a desire to hide.

At the Knotty Pine the next evening he approached Humboldt. "Maggie playing cards tonight?"

Torn between having company at his single table and being questioned again, Humboldt looked up at the detective without encouragement.

Scoville pulled out a chair and sat down. "Nasty night out."

Humboldt nursed his beer.

"Water's rough," Scoville added a little later.

A hissing sound came from behind the bar where fresh cod had just been dropped into the cooker. Smell of hot fat drifted through the Knotty Pine. Near the side door, the shuffleboard puck hit the wooden end of the table with a high, crisp ring.

Humboldt put his elbows on the table. "Any leads?"

The detective scanned Humboldt's face with calm scrutiny. "Yes," he said.

Humboldt took his elbows off the table and put them back again. "Like what?"

"Rhonda Rhinehart is Rhonda Brown."

Humboldt gave a small jerk of the head toward the back room. "Married to Dr. Brown?"

"Yes," Scoville said without interest.

"Maggie thought there was a reason they were both here every Thursday." Humboldt put his hands on the edge of the table as if to push off and head immediately for the card room where his wife so often sat on a high stool beside the man who was now a brand-new widower. Brand-new murderer, more than likely.

Scoville lifted an eyebrow. "Is the doctor playing cards tonight?"

Humboldt shrugged.

"Would you go look?"

Returning with a cold, pitying smile, Humboldt said, "He's here. Leaves Medford two days after his wife's murder so he can get over the mountain in time for Black Jack."

The leathery contours of Scoville's face remained impassive.

"It's not even Thursday."

Scoville slowly crossed his long legs in the aisle between the tables.

"Some hell of a husband," Humboldt added. "No respect." Bristling with morality, he forgot that he, himself, never honored death. Never went to visitations, funerals, or wakes. Told his daughters to take care of everything if Maggie preceded him in death; that he would be on a long trip, unable to attend any funeral. When his daughters asked him where his travels would take him, he said, "Nowhere. There'll be nowhere for me if your mother goes first."

Humboldt waited for Scoville to show contempt. But Scoville, life-long bachelor, felt unqualified to comment on the marriages he saw in his line of work.

Humboldt shifted gears. "Why the name change?"

"Don't know."

"Why did she come over to Brooks Beach once a week?"

"Don't know that, either."

For a man who hadn't wanted to be questioned, Humboldt lingered at the table. Eventually he was forced to volunteer an answer. "Maggie thinks both Dr. Brown and this Rhonda whatever-her-last-name-is are having affairs."

"Wouldn't surprise me," said Scoville.

Finished with his beer, Humboldt stood. He wanted to get word to Guy not to come home for a while. To stay in Mexico.

Scoville took a swallow of beer. "How well do you know Guy Falkenburg?" he asked.

Humboldt sat back down. "Somewhat well."

"Why is he separated from his wife?"

Humboldt focused for a minute on a light fixture across the room. "I

don't know, Jim." He'd never called Scoville by his first name. Talking about Guy eased him into man-to-man conversation he'd been missing; his life had narrowed since Guy stopped coming around. "She's crazy about him, but he doesn't like to be tied down."

"That little house too domestic for him?" said Scoville. "Too close to the Knotty Pine? I guess you can hear the music and voices from across the alley."

"Yeah, you can." Humboldt hadn't thought of it that way. In bed with Geraldine, Guy might have been preoccupied by the tavern, those pool and shuffleboard and Black Jack games, those women, so close to his wife's property. The Knotty Pine trespassing on their bedroom.

"She owns the house in her own name," said Humboldt.

"I saw it," said Scoville. "Crescent Title Company."

"She didn't lean on him financially," Humboldt said. "He liked that. Of course," he added thoughtfully, "she leaned on him in other ways."

"Love," Scoville said in a neutral tone. "Sex."

Humboldt stood, yawned ostentatiously, and turned toward the card room.

"Maggie'll be waiting," Scoville said. Leaning back in his chair, he watched the older man stroll toward the back of the tavern. Soon after the game of Black Jack ended, he knew, the Dentons would be in a worn Plymouth, driving the Coast Highway up five winding miles to their redwood house overlooking the ocean.

He sat idly with his beer. After a half hour or so he stood, slid his chair back under the table, and left the Knotty Pine Tavern, noting the absence of Guy Falkenburg on his way out.

6

"Mornin'," Humboldt said to Eppie Epperson as he picked up his day-old mail from Box 302. Only rarely did he and Maggie skip the daily drive to town. Sometimes, though, they lay abed, ate a late breakfast, and watched an old movie on the movie channel. They liked black-and-white films with stars like Laurel and Hardy, Fred Astaire and Ginger Rogers, Clark Gable.

"How's it goin'?" Eppie replied. She'd already put up the Monday morning mail. Now she was busy polishing a glass display case on the wall. The unlocked door swung on its hinges as she cleaned one side, then the other. No matter whether she was dealing cards or polishing glass, her movements were quick and efficient. Day or night, her fingernails were strong, bright, and unchipped.

"Can't complain." Humboldt pulled several envelopes out of his box, shut the little silver door, and spun the miniature combination lock back to zero. "Any news about our crime?"

She paused and looked over her shoulder. "*Our crime?*"

"Our Brooks Beach crime."

"Haven't heard anything." Half-obscured by the polishing cloth, her red fingernails flicked into and out of view.

Humboldt absently studied the return addresses on his envelopes. "Detective Scoville talk to you yet?" he asked.

"Nope. Has he talked to *you?*"

Humboldt retrieved a rubber band from his wallet and snapped it around the envelopes. "A little."

"About Guy?"

"Guy Falkenburg? Not to me."

"Might be a good place to start," said Eppie. She closed and locked the glass door.

"What makes you say that?"

Eppie passed through the swinging door in the counter that led to the business part of the post office where she'd been putting up mail for twenty years. She didn't look her age: fifty. Lithe, even sinewy, she handled her two jobs with ease: never late, never sick, never overwhelmed by impatient customers or a cheating card player. She knew who to call for help, though she seldom did. She never raised her voice.

"I'd love to talk," she said, turning to face Humboldt across the counter, "but I don't have time just now. I only meant that Guy's been out of town for the last day or two."

"Didn't notice," said Humboldt. "Don't see him as regular as I used to."

"Geraldine gets his mail," Eppie said. The bell hanging high on the door rang as Humboldt left. A few minutes later it jingled again. A cool breeze pushed aside the overheated air of the narrow post office. Originally a family-owned bank, during the Depression it had been deemed too small and insignificant for a Works Progress Administration mural.

"Morning, Geraldine," Eppie said.

"Good morning."

"Can I help you?"

Sorting through her mail, Geraldine shook her head. Winter sunlight through the windows made the rows of postal boxes gleam.

"I haven't seen Guy lately," Eppie said.

Geraldine made no response. The bell above the door rang again and Jim Scoville entered. Tipping his hat toward the two women, he went to his box and worked the combination lock. Finding nothing inside, he tipped his hat again in an old-fashioned way—the hat, too, was old-fashioned, brimmed, with a ribbon around the base of the crown—and left the two-room government building, his overcoat unbuttoned. The temperature outside was mild for February.

"Can I talk to you?" Geraldine said, following him outside. Through the plate glass window, Eppie watched.

Scoville paused. "Would you like to come to my office?"

"It won't take that long. I just wanted to tell you something I forgot to mention the other night."

The detective stepped back up onto the curb.

"In the alley, you know."

"Yes?"

"Did you notice the pillow under the—head?" she asked.

"Yes."

"I remembered later that I've seen it before. Or pillows like it."

He waited.

"At Oregon Discount."

"Can you remind me what it looks like?" he said.

"Navy blue satin, with tassels at the ends. White silk tassels. They had a large stock of them at Oregon Discount. They were on sale."

"Can you come to my office later today?" he asked.

"I'm reporting a trial starting this afternoon."

"Then drop in when it's convenient."

Tucking the mail into her shoulder bag, Geraldine crossed the street to her house.

"Did you buy one of those pillows?" he called after her.

She turned 180 degrees. "Well, yes, I did. And so did lots of other people. That's my point. In fact, I bought two."

He nodded. She reached her porch and closed the front door behind her. Scoville stood for a minute on the curb, then turned and reentered the post office.

"Back for more?" Eppie said.

"I was wondering if we could talk during your break."

She absently patted the upswept side of her hair-do. Sunny shafts of light bounced off the jeweled ornament. "How about 10:45?" she said.

"Good."

"At the Beach House."

"That's fine," said Scoville. "I'll see you there."

7

At 10:40 Eppie locked the cash drawer and taped a handwritten note on the door: 'Back soon.'

Scoville's old Chevrolet was already parked in front of the Beach House when she arrived. The restaurant was in one half of what had originally been a modest house whose two-acre lot backed up to a cliff-side road. A rusted trailer on blocks marked the back property line. Beyond the trailer, road, and cliff was ocean. The other half of the house was occupied by a souvenir shop, its gravel driveway displaying carved redwood bears standing on their hind legs. Through the plate glass window, seashells turned into knickknacks lay in profusion along shelves.

Scoville had taken a table at the far corner of the restaurant, facing the door. The sound of surf carried up the face of the cliff and across the property.

"Coffee?"

"And a piece of pie," Eppie said. "Cherry."

Scoville placed the order.

"I'm investigating the death behind the Knotty Pine Tavern," he said when the waitress left for the kitchen.

"So I've heard."

"What do you know about it?"

"Very little." Eppie unrolled the napkin wound around a knife, fork, and spoon.

"Where were you this past Thursday night?"

"Where I am every night. At the Knotty Pine dealing cards."

"Did you take a break at any point in the evening?"

"No." A glint of pride flashed in her green eyes. "I have a lot of stamina."

"What are your hours?"

"7:30 p.m. to 1:00 in the morning."

"We're out of cherry," the waitress called from a window behind the counter. "How about lemon meringue?"

"Fine," said Eppie without taking her eyes from Scoville's face.

"Did you leave at all?" he continued. "Take a short break?"

"Just to the bathroom. What time did she die, anyway?"

Scoville accepted coffee and handled the sugar jar almost without looking. "Don't know yet." He poured a granular stream into his teaspoon.

"How well do you know Dr. Brown?" he said, stirring the coffee. He watched the cautious shutting down of her face, and then the reconsideration.

"We have a romantic relationship," she said, turning loose of the silverware and napkin. In a decisive movement, she brought her hands to rest in front of her. "We've been seeing each other ever since he started playing cards on Thursday nights."

Laying his spoon in his saucer, Scoville seemed only slightly interested.

"His wife—you do know that Rhonda Rhinehart was his wife?—began coming to Brooks Beach on Thursday nights a couple of weeks later." Eppie took a swallow of black coffee. "She seems to have found her own reason for being in Brooks Beach."

Scoville pushed his saucer a little away. "Does Mrs. Brown play cards?"

"I don't know. She never played at my table."

"Did Dr. and Mrs. Brown drive together from Medford? Or did they come separately?"

"Separately. Dr. Brown stays overnight and leaves before 6:00 on Friday mornings."

"Stays with you?"

She smoothed the left side of her hair-do, such a sleek, sophisticated contrast to the thick hair swept up from her right temple. "Yes."

"What about Mrs. Brown? Did she stay overnight in Brooks Beach?"

"I believe sometimes she did."

"Do you know where she stayed?"

Eppie paused. "Ask Geraldine Manahan."

"You're not saying she stayed at Mrs. Manahan's house?"

"No, I'm not saying that. I'm saying she stayed with Mrs. Manahan's husband, and that was not in Mrs. Manahan's house."

"You're presuming that was her reason for coming to Brooks Beach on Thursdays?"

"It's a thought."

"Can you be sure of that?"

"Pretty damn sure."

The sun came and went in a clear sky filled with scuttling clouds. It sent shafts of bright light through the window onto Eppie's auburn hair. Scoville focused on the red undertones and sparkling ornament before picking up the check.

Rewinding her napkin around the knife, fork, and spoon, Eppie said, "You might be interested to know that Guy Falkenburg—"

"Thank you, Ms. Epperson," said Scoville. "You can tell me more when we meet again."

"I assume you're interested in pertinent information."

"Always, and in due time. For now, enjoy the lemon meringue." He left the Beach House, got in his old Chevy, and sat until Eppie left the restaurant. Beneath the brief wave she fluttered in his direction, Scoville detected uncertainty. She'd wanted to tell him something damaging about Guy Falkenburg. Geraldine Manahan had tried to explain away the dark blue pillow with silk tassels. Useful information was coming in. He inserted his key into the ignition and let the car run a moment before he too backed out of the parking lot and entered the road that led to Coast Highway and his office in the Courthouse.

8

By evening, the fog horn was blowing again. Humboldt stopped at the bottom of the Dentons' steep road and made a swift turn onto Coast Highway.

"Did you see that car coming from the north?" Maggie asked.

"Of course I saw it. That's why I took the turn fast."

The old Plymouth picked up speed. From the passenger side, Maggie watched individual spruce and fir come to life in the headlights before returning to the anonymous forest.

"What time did we leave Geraldine's house for the Knotty Pine?" Humboldt said after they'd driven a mile or two. These days their conversation was almost always about Thursday night.

"We crossed the Oregon State line about 9:30." Maggie stared straight ahead at the wet road. Mist swirled in the headlights. "I'd say it was 10:30 by the time we finished our hot chocolate."

"Eppie Epperson could have been in the car, hiding behind her purse," said Humboldt.

"She doesn't usually take breaks." She thought for a moment. "It might not have been a woman at all," she added. "A man can hold a purse up against a window."

The engine hummed. "I guess Eppie could have been driving," he said.

Maggie redirected the heat from their faces and let it settle around their feet. "It could have been anybody in Brooks Beach," she said.

"Scoville asked me if Geraldine was in the bar the whole time," Humboldt said in a monotone.

"He thinks she did it?"

"No. He was just asking if she was in the bar the whole time." Worry silenced both of them.

Maggie shivered. "Geraldine's not a killer."

"Of course not," said Humboldt. "She was with us the whole time."

"Not the whole time."

Humboldt hit the steering wheel with the heel of his fist. "Geraldine didn't do it and neither did Guy! Geraldine's got self-control and Guy doesn't park in alleys with women." He waited for Maggie to say something. "It's not their style!" he cried.

"He shouldn't have run off to Mexico," Maggie said. "It looks suspicious."

"He's not really in Mexico," Humboldt said more calmly.

"Geraldine told you he was."

"He isn't."

"Did he call you?"

Humboldt didn't answer.

"Oh, God, Hummer, you can't be holding back information. If you're not straight with Scoville, it'll come back to bite you."

He sniffed. "It's up to Geraldine to tell Scoville where Guy is."

"Did Guy call you?"

"No, he called Geraldine."

"And she didn't tell me?" Maggie said, disappointed. "We're the best of friends."

"She doesn't want you to know too much. 'Implicated,' she said."

"But she doesn't care if *you're* implicated."

"I can take care of myself," said Humboldt. "Guy and Geraldine don't want you implicated."

"If you're involved, then I'm involved," Maggie said. They were approaching Brooks Beach city limits. "Where is he if he's not in Mexico?"

Humboldt wouldn't say. He parked in the dirt lot behind the Knotty Pine. The rear of the car stuck out into the alley.

"You'd better pull closer to the building," Maggie advised. "The alley's a busy place." She climbed out of the passenger side and caught up to her husband. "Has Scoville traced the car?"

"Dunno."

"If Guy was driving—"

"Guy didn't need to park in an alley to make out with a girl friend," Humboldt said as he reached the side door of the Knotty Pine.

"Eppie's telling people he's the killer," said Maggie.

"Where'd you hear that?"

"At the beauty parlor."

Humboldt snorted and held the door for Maggie who preceded him to a table. "With a card game going on in the back room, are you sure you have time for me?"

"Humboldt. That's not fair." They sat down at a table for two.

"Beer?" Humboldt finally broke the silence. Maggie nodded. He stood wearily and went to the bar. When he returned, Maggie was chatting with a couple at the next table. He didn't know who they were and didn't care. But Maggie would know all about them by the time she'd finished half a beer. Then she'd carry her glass back to the card room and he'd be left alone out here without a curly-haired man in his prime who inspired him to tell stories, laugh, and feel young again.

9

Geraldine looked up from the court transcript she was proofreading. Through her back window she watched Maggie and Humboldt park their Plymouth behind the tavern. Moaning, she put her elbows on the desk and her head in her hands, unable to bear the stabbing pain when she remembered the times she and Guy had sat in the back seat of that car, parked in that very space; how they'd so often gone into the Knotty Pine, a foursome. Later they would come back to the cedar-shingled cottage and drink black coffee at the kitchen table before Maggie and Humboldt drove home to their house on the cliff. Waving good-bye from the porch, she and Guy would lock the cottage for the night, draw the drapes, and go to bed, the lamp in the bedroom casting soft light about the room.

She lifted her head and studied the window of the card room where Eppie stood behind the Black Jack table six nights a week. At the post office the next morning, she never looked tired, not even on Fridays.

Maggie had guessed at the affair with Dr. Brown long before the murder took place; long before anyone knew that Rhonda Rhinehart was his wife.

Geraldine, herself, had once thought of killing the woman. Then she'd thought of killing Guy. Then both of them. She'd wasted more than one sleepless night imagining the double murder she could commit, ridding herself of her passion for Guy, her fury toward the woman, at the same time curing herself of a sexual desire that was becoming so hateful she thought she might go mad. She physically ached. In the midst of the aching, hatred would take over; her heart would race with such fury that she heard and felt the flooding of arteries. Then, within minutes, she might grow faint from grief over Guy's unfaithfulness.

Murder would relieve all that.

Only after she remembered courtroom trials, confessions, pleas, agonized statements, did she admit that there was no relief to be had. No relief with murder; no relief without murder.

She comprehended motives and knew she could kill. She hoped Eppie and Dr. Brown could, too. She hoped one or both of them had done it. They both had a reason. Over and over, Geraldine worked out motives. But she was afraid it had been Guy.

Sometimes, staring into desolate space, she indulged in the

daydream that he'd killed his girl friend because he wanted to come back to his wife; that Rhonda Rhinehart stood in his way. She pretended that Guy still loved her. When reality reasserted itself, when the daydream crashed, then once again she wanted to kill.

But Guy had called *her, Geraldine*, when he was in trouble. He hadn't told her yet where he was hiding, but he would.

She was already covering for him. Now she couldn't find the second pillow with the silk tassels. Guy must have taken it with household furnishings when he moved out of the house.

But why had he left a pillow with the body?

She'd bought them at Oregon Discount. Anyone in town, any tourist, could have purchased one. She, a court reporter, had not lied to Detective Scoville. She could testify under oath that the tasseled pillows had been on sale; that there had been five or ten piled in the bin at Oregon Discount; that she, Geraldine Manahan, had bought two.

But she would have to testify that she didn't know where the second pillow was.

She'd intended to preempt the question of the pillow by speaking frankly. She wanted the Sheriff's Office to know that any number of people might own one. Now she thought she should have waited and let Detective Scoville ask the questions. She'd never been good at foreseeing consequences.

She and Guy would both be under suspicion, all because of a pillow. Guy could not help her. He would never be able to help her. He could not even help himself.

Dr. Brown crossed the packed dirt at the back of the Knotty Pine and entered the tavern. She sat straighter. In comparison to his bulk, the door he opened and closed seemed small. The window of the card room, blurring, shifting in her vision, went dark for a moment. She pictured the large man switching off the light, taking a giant step, reaching out with his enormous arms, committing mayhem. But no, the light was still on. It was she, herself, who had blacked it out. She tried leaning back in her straight chair, but her heart beat painfully not only in her chest but along her spine. She sat forward again to ease the pounding.

With white-hot intensity, she wanted Dr. Brown to be the murderer.

10

From his parked car at the far end of the highway frontage road, Scoville watched the tall, heavy man with dark hair leave his silver Cadillac and walk around to the rear door of the Knotty Pine. From what he'd observed, the doctor never passed through the front entrance. The dirt lot was closer to the card room.

Medford had no gambling. The Oregon State legislature allowed municipalities to pass their own gambling laws. Brooks Beach, with its fishermen and loggers, its need for money from taxes and licenses, voted in gambling. Scoville guessed that the doctor had a wild streak and needed a card game outside the reach of Medford.

He wondered how the doctor felt when his solitary Thursday nights—or not-so-solitary nights—in the rough fishing town came to the attention of his wife. How must he have reacted when she began following him over the Siskiyous to the coast? Did her presence torment him? When she began sleeping with a younger, handsomer man in Brooks Beach, was he jealous? Was he relieved?

Scoville waited a few minutes before leaving his car and entering the front entrance of the Knotty Pine. He saw the Dentons seated at a table against one wall.

"Evening," he said, approaching and nodding briefly.

"Evening," said Humboldt.

"Join us?" said Maggie.

Humboldt was pointedly silent.

"You drinking?" said Scoville. "Or just sitting?"

"Maggie's slumming," said Humboldt. "She's keeping me company for a few minutes before she plays Black Jack."

"We're pouting," Maggie said.

"I had a question or two for you," Scoville said, looking squarely at Humboldt.

"I'd buy you a drink," he added, "if it wasn't against the rules."

"I suppose it would look bad if I bought *you* one," Humboldt almost growled.

"It would look bad," Scoville agreed.

"I'll buy you both a beer," said Maggie. "I don't know a rule against *that*."

"What's your question?" Humboldt asked after she'd gone for the drinks.

"Two years ago you helped solve a crime," Scoville said.

"That's not a question."

"Here's the question. Why aren't you helping with this one?"

"I've answered your questions," said Humboldt. "I told you about Dr. Brown and Eppie." He didn't blink. "Am I under suspicion?"

"Not hardly," said the detective. "But I think you know something."

"I don't."

"If you do, it could be considered conspiracy."

Humboldt set his jaw and locked away any response.

"Where's Guy Falkenburg?"

"That's for you to find out," said Humboldt.

"Find out what?" Maggie asked cheerfully as she returned to the table with a tray, pitcher, and three glasses.

"I think you have access to Guy," Scoville said, keeping his attention on Humboldt.

"I don't."

Maggie started to speak, but Humboldt cut her off. "Nobody," he said, standing abruptly, "has access to Guy Falkenburg unless he wants them to."

"Geraldine Manahan has access," Scoville said without inflection.

"They're married," Maggie began.

"That's right," Humboldt said, taking his wife's hand and pulling her away from the table. "You've got all the resources of the Sheriff's Office behind you. You don't need to be siccing a wife on her husband."

"It's you I'm asking," Scoville said.

Maggie exerted pressure on her husband's hand. "This beer isn't going to waste,"

she said. "Not after I paid for it and carried it over here." She almost begged. "Sit down, Hummer."

But Humboldt shook her off and walked rapidly past the pool table and out the side door of the tavern.

11

In the car he sat breathing heavily, not noticing the chill. As he straightened one leg to reach in his pocket for car keys, he turned his head and saw Geraldine crossing the alley toward him, without coat or sweater.

"Where's Maggie?" She slid into the passenger seat. Humboldt started the car and turned on the heater.

"Inside with Scoville," he said sardonically, "or maybe playing Black Jack by now."

"Dr. Brown just got here," said Geraldine, running one hand through her short hair. Abruptly she began crying.

Tears always alarmed Humboldt. He settled for indirect sympathy. "Cold?" He turned up the heat. "It'll take a minute to warm up."

"I'm not crying because it's cold."

"I know it." He would have liked to pat her shoulder, but felt odd doing so; Maggie always sat in the passenger seat. Outside, the beer sign cast ruddy light onto the dirt lot.

"I can't stand having crime right here behind my house," said Geraldine.

"You should put up a no parking sign," Humboldt said, and immediately wished he'd said something intelligent.

Geraldine lifted her head. "Isn't that beside the point?"

"Yeah. It is." Country music from the juke box floated toward them each time the side door opened. Humboldt wiped his hand across the dashboard and studied the dust left on his palm. "Scoville's been asking me where Guy is."

"He won't be asking *me*," said Geraldine, blowing her nose. "There's a marital privilege."

Humboldt brushed his hands together. "I wish *I* had a privilege."

"I shouldn't have told you where he is."

"Yeah. You've implicated me." He fiddled with the knob on the stick shift.

"You were in the Knotty Pine the whole time we were there, weren't you?" he said.

"Do you think I did it?"

"Scoville asked me."

"I was with you the first time we crossed the alley, and I was with you when we found—the body." She turned sharply toward Humboldt. "I went back to the house once to use the bathroom. It's cleaner than the one in the bar."

Humboldt's eyes narrowed. "Have you told that to Scoville?"

"No. He hasn't asked." She faced forward. "There was no body in the alley then."

"Don't say anything about it."

After a silence Geraldine impulsively flung her hand over her heart. "I'm going to tell Guy to leave town," she said. "And I don't want to know where he goes."

"How do you plan to reach him?"

"I'll track him down. Through his friends."

Humboldt touched her on the shoulder. "Nah. Bad idea. It's dangerous."

"You think Guy will hurt me," she said sadly.

"Not Guy. Not the man we know. But remember: he's scared."

"Do you think he did it?" Geraldine whispered.

"Nah. Guy? Nah. He's not a killer."

"The tasseled pillow under the head… "

"Don't think about it."

"No, I mean the pillow was mine." She whispered. "I think Guy used it."

"Pillows are a dime a dozen," Humboldt said gruffly.

The car was warm now. Geraldine turned down the heater. "I can't help myself," she said softly. "I'll always want to know where he is."

"So will I." A fog had begun rolling in from the beach. Sitting in the car without talking comforted both of them.

"Why do you think Guy left me?" Geraldine eventually said.

"Restless."

"Well, I know that."

"He doesn't like himself." Humboldt leaned back against the head rest.

"Everyone likes him except himself."

"Why?"

"Dunno. Do you?"

"No. I don't understand him. He wants to be bad. That, I know."

"He married a court reporter," Humboldt said.

"An officer of the court," said Geraldine.

"I guess he wants to be caught."

"Oh, God!" she cried. "Why did he do it?"

"He didn't." After a long silence, Humboldt said, "Why did you marry him?"

"What?"

"I said why did you marry Guy?"

She shivered, then lifted her chin high. "He makes me feel two-hundred percent alive."

"You're past the honeymoon stage now," Humboldt said. He pushed down on the door handle and stepped out into the fog. "Are you comin' in?"

"No. I'm staying away from the Knotty Pine. I don't want to see anyone who has anything to do with the murder."

"Hard to know who to stay away from," Humboldt said.

Geraldine got out of the car.

"It could be almost anybody. Almost anybody but Guy," he added loyally, and left her standing where the Knotty Pine property ends and the alley begins.

12

Humboldt found Maggie still sitting at the table with the detective. He took the chair he'd vacated earlier, and she poured him a beer as if he'd never left.

"I was never introduced to her," she was saying. "But it got to be general knowledge that Rhonda Rhinehart was a girl friend of Guy's and that she came on Thursday nights."

"What's it doing outside?" Scoville asked Humboldt.

"Fog. The fog's rollin' in."

The detective turned back to Maggie. "Was Guy always here on Thursdays?"

Maggie smiled. "Guy was never always anywhere. But often he was, yes."

"And you didn't know this girl friend was Dr. Brown's wife?"

"No, that was a surprise." Maggie glanced at Humboldt. "I did think they were both having affairs. My husband will tell you I usually know just about everybody. And if I don't know them, I know something about them."

"That's what I was led to believe," Scoville said courteously.

"It's my opinion," Maggie said, leaning forward confidentially, "that Rhonda Brown was still in love with her husband."

"Hard to see why," Humboldt muttered.

"Why else would she come over the mountain?" Maggie said.

"To see Guy," said Scoville.

"To kill her husband," said Humboldt. "But instead, he killed her first."

"Is that something you know?" Scoville asked. "Or is it speculation?"

"It's a darn good guess."

"Murders aren't solved by darn good guesses," Scoville shot back, then leaned against his straight chair and stretched his legs. "I need facts," he said. "Tell me where Guy is."

"He moves about," said Humboldt. "Place to place."

"With all due respect, Detective Scoville," Maggie said, "Guy isn't the only person in this town."

"Have you talked to Eppie?" Humboldt broke in softly, as if the woman might hear from the back room.

"Yes, and I'll talk to her some more."

"How about Dr. Brown?" said Maggie.

"In due time."

"Why so patient?" said Humboldt.

"I want Brown to be worried."

"Why not due time for Guy?"

"Guy Falkenburg is already worried," said Scoville.

"The doctor isn't worried?" said Maggie.

"Don't think so," said Scoville. "What people do when they're scared can be interesting."

"You'll never know whether he's scared or not," Maggie said. "He doesn't say anything and he doesn't give any signals. I've never seen him look scared. Or confused. I've never seen him smile."

"I've seen him frown," said Humboldt

"Yes," Maggie agreed, "but that's about the limit of what he gives away."

"Do you know what Eppie sees in him?" asked Scoville.

Humboldt snorted. "Money. He's a doctor."

Maggie looked thoughtful. "In a way, I think she likes him. And it's nice to have a man in your life."

Humboldt and Scoville looked at each other blankly.

"You don't like to have a woman in your life?" she said, looking from one to the other.

Keeping his eye on the detective, Humboldt tipped his head toward his wife as if to say, *What are you gonna do?*

"So far I've escaped the blandishments of the fairer sex," Scoville said.

"What's *blandishments*?" said Humboldt.

"Good looks," said Maggie. Scoville was too polite to correct her.

"The doc had a good-lookin' wife and he's got a good-lookin' girl friend," Humboldt said. "For such an ugly fellow, he does pretty well for himself."

"Where does he stay when he's in Medford?" asked Scoville.

"Dunno," said Humboldt. "I don't follow him back over the mountain."

"You're wondering if he still lives at his home," said Maggie.

"It's a question that occurs to me."

"We don't know."

"I wish he'd done the deed in his own town," muttered Humboldt. "He's introduced a lot of problems here."

"Has Eppie been married in the past?" Scoville asked. "Had boyfriends?"

"Yes to both," said Humboldt. "She attracts men."

"She's never found the right one, though," said Maggie.

Humboldt looked surprised. "Since when do you know so much about Eppie's love life?"

"We've talked a little," said Maggie. She laid her hand on her husband's arm. "She thinks I'm lucky. I found the right man."

Scoville looked away, as if he shouldn't be listening. Humboldt frowned, pleased.

"Eppie's steady as a heartbeat," said Maggie. "The Post Office couldn't run without her."

"Depends on whose heart is beating," said Humboldt. "I could tell you stories about what Eppie did to her ex-husband."

Scoville seemed uninterested.

"He doesn't have anything good to say about her," Humboldt insisted.

The detective turned to Maggie. "Did you see Geraldine leave the bar anytime that night?"

Maggie laughed. "Surely you don't think Geraldine did it."

"I don't think anything," murmured Scoville. Humboldt settled back in his chair and began to relax under the influence of Maggie who kept the glasses filled. In no hurry to leave the warm tavern and their comfortable table for the chilly fog outside, the threesome spent another leisurely hour before standing, pushing their chairs under the table, and heading for separate cars: Scoville's out by the highway, and the Dentons' in the alley behind the Knotty Pine, across from Geraldine's garage.

13

Dr. Brown held the side door open for Eppie and followed her out of the Knotty

Pine Tavern to the parking strip alongside Coast Highway. Under the sodium lights his silver automobile took on a yellowish tinge. Most of the cars on the frontage road had left for home; a few would be there until the last call at 2:00 a.m.; three or four cars would remain overnight.

At the far end of the strip, Scoville sat with his engine running, watching Eppie and Dr. Brown get into the Cadillac.

Eppie spotted him and waved. The doctor looked without interest in his direction.

"That's the detective in charge of the case," Eppie said when Dr. Brown had started the car and begun driving south, moving ponderously through the fog. Strung out like a long necklace along Coast Highway, the town was nearly abandoned at 1:30 in the morning. A car traveling north faced them as they waited in the left-turn lane. Eppie's house sat on an incline above the highway, behind the big-box discount store.

"Tired?" she asked.

"Not too tired for you." Dr. Brown remained squarely behind the wheel as Eppie moved closer. She looked forward to bringing him alive. Under her handling, he became almost kittenish. The attention, the permissions he gave her as she slowly turned his large, stolid body into a playground, was a once-a-week pleasure she looked forward to.

The left-turn arrow flashed green. "It was a good table tonight," she said, snuggling against his shoulder. "The nights when you're here are good."

"Thursdays are good," he said.

"This isn't Thursday," she said.

He didn't respond.

"What did Rhonda and you do on Thursdays before you started coming to Brooks Beach?" she asked cautiously.

"I don't remember."

"What was Rhonda like?"

"She was a mystery." He patted Eppie's knee twice with his large hand before laying it back on the steering wheel.

"The Sheriff's Office has talked to me," Eppie said after a while.

"Yeah?"

"Yeah." She waited for him to say something. "Don't you want to know what
they asked me?"

"You'll tell me if you want me to know."

"He asked me what my hours are."

"Who's he?"

"Detective Scoville."

"What else?"

"I didn't give him a chance to wonder about us. I told him."

Dr. Brown swung into Eppie's driveway and clicked the door opener attached to his sun screen. The Cadillac rolled into the empty garage; Eppie's Ford was still parked in front of the Knotty Pine, to remain there all night.

When she slid toward the passenger door, Dr. Brown reached out to stop her. The garage door closed behind them with an electronic hum and a small thud.

"Told him what?" His hand remained on her knee.

"That you stay here on Thursday nights. That Rhonda Rhinehart is your wife. Was your wife."

"Why did you do that?"

"It's the truth. It's better to tell the truth from the beginning."

Lifting her face toward him, she invited his kiss which came swiftly, heavily.

"I told him to ask questions about Guy Falkenburg," she said, half buried in the necktie and collar he'd loosened, "not me."

He grunted and kissed her again. He rested his hand in her thighs. She didn't try to hurry him into the house. She knew that, excited, unsatisfied, he would follow her inside when she told him he must.

Later, with her clothes hung neatly in the closet and Dr. Brown's lying across the wing-back chair in one corner, his shoes and socks tucked under the bed's footboard, tidy habits she'd insisted on from the beginning, they turned off the light and entered the king-sized bed he'd purchased to accommodate his size.

It was their habit to arouse each other in the car and save intense pleasure for later. Once bedded, Eppie kissed him until he smiled; stroked him until he laughed; all but crawled about on him until he cried out. Again and again they procrastinated. But always at some point she lost control of him. Teasing, fighting, she was ultimately helpless under his weight.

Then, satisfied, they slept until morning when Dr. Brown performed once again, quickly, before leaving at six in order to drive over the mountain and arrive in Medford for early morning rounds at his private hospital

"What if Scoville asks me about your rental car?" Eppie said, sleepily watching him dress the next morning. Between the strips of Venetian blinds, no light showed. Dr Brown buttoned his shirt by the night light plugged in at the baseboard. By sunrise, his Cadillac would already be climbing the Siskiyous.

"What about the rental car?"

"Well, it's bound to make him wonder."

"Wonder about what?"

"About your wife's murder," Eppie said impatiently. "Someone saw the car."

"They didn't see *us*."

"Sure they did. It was Geraldine and the Dentons."

"They didn't know it was us."

"Maybe. Holding the purse against the window might not have fooled them." She paused. "I told Scoville I didn't leave the Knotty Pine all night."

He fastened his belt. "Just because we were in the alley doesn't prove we killed anyone."

Eppie shifted on her pillows and drew the blankets higher. "*We?*" When he didn't respond, she said, "Scoville doesn't know about your wife's visit."

He turned sharply, one hand still on his buckle. "Are you gonna tell him about that, too?"

She shook her head. She had no intention of telling Scoville that three weeks earlier, Rhonda Brown had followed them to Eppie's house. That they'd seen her headlights come slowly down the street behind them and continue on as the automatic garage door slowly lowered behind them. Minutes later, through the window of the dark bedroom, Dr. Brown had watched his wife emerge from her car at the end of the cul-de-sac and walk silently toward the house.

"She's walking on the balls of her feet," Eppie had whispered, joining him at the window. "She doesn't want anyone to hear her high heels."

He'd dropped the curtain and gone to open the front door before the bell sounded. He'd pulled her inside. "What d'ya want, Rhonda?"

"My husband back." She'd been drinking. She smiled too broadly and touched a table to prevent herself from swaying. Opening her coat to show a red sweater and glittering silver beads, she looked up at him and said, surprisingly in control of speech, "Come home, Roland. Stop gambling and sleeping around. Stop driving over to the coast."

"Look who's talking about sleeping around," Eppie said from the bedroom doorway.

But Rhonda showed an unwillingness to engage with her husband's girlfriend.

"Come home," she repeated. She lifted her head and controlled the swaying. "Come home, Roland. Let's both stop the bullshit."

Dr. Brown focused on her face and didn't seem to be aware of Eppie behind him.

"Get out of my house," Eppie said.

But the doctor ignored her. Taking a step toward his wife, he said, "Won't you miss your boyfriend at the Knotty Pine?"

Rhonda reverted to the sway and slur. "Not as much as I miss you." She leaned toward him, her breasts rich and full. Eppie knew that her own breasts were small, hard; that it was her pelvis and thighs that interested Dr. Brown. But Rhonda also had pelvis and thighs, and they were as shapely as her breasts. Eppie wished she, herself, were as ample and desirable as

Rhonda Brown. She longed for the stranger in her house to leave so she could incite her powerful, inarticulate boyfriend into a sexual fever. But, instead, she saw him lean forward; witnessed the intimacy of his and his wife's bodies across the empty space between them; watched them fasten on each others' faces.

For a moment she'd been afraid they were still in love.

After his wife left, Dr. Brown had insisted on immediate sex with Eppie, fast, and with little participation from her.

Now, weeks later, relieved that their nights in bed were once more successful, Eppie watched him put his wallet in his back pocket, pick up his keys, and sweep up his dark overcoat from the wing-back chair.

"See you tomorrow night," he said. "We don't have to wait till Thursdays anymore. Protect yourself. Don't talk too much." And without a backward glance, he left the house.

14

The Dentons sat in their car behind the Knotty Pine, engine on, waiting for the heater's roaring blower to circulate warmth, when a voice from the back seat made them jump.

"Well, hi there."

Maggie threw one hand over her heart. Bracing himself against the floorboard, Humboldt looked ready to lunge over the driver's seat.

"What the hell!"

Sitting in the corner of the back seat, as far from the neon beer sign's light as he could get, Guy sat grinning.

"What the hell!" Humboldt repeated.

"You shouldn't be here!" Maggie warned. "Scoville's just leaving! His car is out front!"

"I know where Scoville is." Guy folded his arms around his waist. He wore a leather zip-up jacket.

"We can't stay here," Humboldt said. "What do you want?"

"You don't have a bottle in the car, do you?" Guy said. "I haven't had a drink in days." He laughed. "You wouldn't have a hot meal on hand, would you?"

"You're putting Maggie at risk," Humboldt said angrily.

Guy sat in abashed silence.

"Let's take him home and cook him some dinner," said Maggie.

Humboldt abruptly faced forward. "Dinner? It's almost time for breakfast." He turned back toward Guy. "I'll take Maggie home and meet you somewhere later."

"Good enough," said Guy.

"Not good enough," said Humboldt. "Not nearly good enough. We've got a major problem."

"I'll be here in Geraldine's garage," Guy said, "if you decide to come back for me."

"Wait," said Maggie. She grasped Humboldt's arm. "What's the harm in cooking him a hot meal? We can bring him back to town afterwards."

"He's got no business being in town," said Humboldt. "He's got no business being in our house. If anyone sees him—"

"No one's going to see me," Guy said confidently. "But I'll do it your way, Hummer. I'll disappear again."

Whether it was Maggie's kindness or hearing his friend call him by his nick-name, Humboldt wavered.

"Hold on," Guy said impulsively, and was out of the car before anyone could ask what he was doing. "Give me five minutes." He shut the back door softly and was gone.

15

Giving up on her transcript, not even pretending to proofread, Geraldine imagined she could hear the fog nibble moistly around the edges of her little house. She avoided looking out at the Knotty Pine. Maggie and Humboldt would have left for home by now. Their five-mile drive would take longer than usual in the thick whiteness shrouding the coast. Geraldine was filled with a melancholy as opaque as the night.

She turned off the lamp and wheeled her desk chair around toward the bedroom door and hall. Aware of a ticking sound at the window, she stopped in half-swivel. The ticking, like fingernails on glass, stopped, followed by a single knock. A fist, knuckles just outside the window, appeared, disappeared, knocked again, while Geraldine's heart started its own knocking. With both hands at her throat, she watched Guy spring into view. He pointed toward the back door. She ran through the darkness and slipped the bolt. In a single movement he was standing in her kitchen. She uttered a cry that didn't stop even when he covered her mouth. She moaned into his hand and shook loose of it.

He was laughing. "Didn't expect me, did you?"

She pulled him away from the door and windows. "My God! What are you doing?"

He hugged her.

"You can't come here!" Her whisper held back the force of a scream. "You can't!"

Ignoring her, he pulled her close. "I'm outside in the car," he said. "With the Dentons. Get your coat."

She pushed him back and stepped to the glass panel in the kitchen door. Still parked behind the Knotty Pine, the Plymouth sat half in, half out of the neon light. "I thought they left," she said.

"Let's just say they were detained," Guy said, smiling. "They're waiting. Let's go."

True to their history together, Guy freed her of all constraint. Bubbling back to life, Geraldine grabbed a coat, eager to be in that car; to be part of the foursome she so badly missed. He closed her kitchen door quietly and locked it with his key.

Quickly they crossed to the alley. As soon as the back door of the Plymouth had been opened and closed in a muffled slam, Humboldt shifted into reverse and backed around toward the garage. Once or twice, bits of gravel pinged the underside of the car as they slowly moved forward down the alley. No one said a word until they'd passed the last traffic light in town and were on Coast Highway driving north.

"Just like old times," said Guy.

"Not quite," said Humboldt.

"I can cook steak," said Maggie. "Or we have left-over stew."

"Steak sounds good," said Guy.

"Warm up the stew," said Humboldt.

Guy laughed. No one joined him.

"We've missed you," Maggie said when the City Limit sign floated by, nearly invisible in the soupy air. Humboldt switched his lights to low beam and turned on the windshield wipers. The silence in the car stunned all of them; they'd always been a talkative group.

Guy turned to Geraldine beside him. "How've you been?" She didn't answer. She and the Dentons wanted their boisterous, incorrigible Guy Falkenburg back, not this diminished fellow straining for conversation.

Humboldt answered for her. "She hasn't been good. Neither have we. We're all worried about you."

Guy ran his hand across his forehead, then tried to straighten his legs by angling them cross-wise toward Geraldine. He put his hands in the pockets of his jacket, leaned back, and stubbornly closed his eyes.

"Where have you been, Guy?" Geraldine asked.

For a minute he didn't answer. "It's better if you don't know," he finally said. "Anyway, I'll be leaving soon."

More miles of silence.

"Will you please talk to the Sheriff's Department?" Geraldine asked when she couldn't stand the tension any longer.

Guy flared. "Hell, no. They'll nail me." He lowered his voice. "I didn't do it."

"We know that," said Humboldt from the front seat.

Guy turned to Geraldine. "You know I didn't do it."

"I don't think you did," she said, "but I don't know."

He pulled his legs in sharply and pounded one knee with his fist. "If you don't believe me, who will?" His eyes, always bright, often bloodshot, were wet.

"Take it easy," Humboldt said. Shortly they came to a lookout point that, in daylight, offered a wide-angle view of wooded hills rising to the distant, purple-shadowed Siskiyous. Tonight, however, it offered nothing but blowing tatters of fog. Humboldt stopped the car.

Guy twisted in his seat and supported his bowed head in his hands. "I screwed up!" he cried.

Geraldine wept. "You killed her, Guy?"

"No!" he shouted. "I didn't kill anyone!" The cry hung in the car. He tried to combat the silence. "I sure as hell didn't kill anyone!"

"I know that," said Humboldt.

But Guy wanted agreement from the women. "Maggie? Geraldine?" His tone changed to helplessness. Hopelessness.

"I know you didn't do it," said Maggie.

"I believe you," Geraldine said.

Humboldt lifted his foot from the brake and the car crept back onto the highway. "You can't keep running, buddy," he said after he'd driven a mile.

Guy gave a hoarse sob. "Take me back down to the courthouse."

Geraldine put her arms around him. She kissed him on his cheeks, his hair, his hands. His lips were not available. "You can call the Sheriff from my house," she said. "Our house."

Humboldt's voice was thick. "You can wake up Scoville," he said. "Make him earn his salary."

"What about the hot meal?" said Maggie.

Guy leaned forward and patted her on the shoulder. "Thank you, Mags. I've lost my appetite."

Humboldt turned back and drove into Brooks Beach. In the alley he dropped Guy and Geraldine off.

"Thanks," Guy murmured as he shut the back door of the car. "So long, Hummer." Humboldt blew his nose. Crying, Maggie slid over beside her husband. Together they pulled out onto the highway, straining to see through the layers of fog enveloping the town.

16

Once in the kitchen, Guy reached for Geraldine and held her close. "Come with me," he whispered, almost lifting her.

"You said you'd call Scoville!" she cried into his chest.

He smiled at her panic and for a moment it dissipated. "This is the last place anyone would look for me," he said. The truth of the statement stung her.

"Let me rest a minute," he said, and went ahead of her into the bedroom. She followed, closing blinds and drapes. He sat down gingerly on the edge of the bed. The infectious smile, cascading laugh, had long since disappeared. Now the physical man, whose every cell propelled him toward action and pleasure, collapsed. Falling back onto the mattress, he was careful to keep his work boots on the floor. They had seen heavy use. When he threw his arms out to each side, his left hand hit the footboard of the bed. Geraldine flinched and picked it up, almost as if it were separate from his body, and massaged it. She scooted onto the bed beside him.

"Guy—" she began, still in a seated position, but he pulled her over on top of him then rolled her under him and held her face between his hands. He didn't smell unclean: just dusty. There was dried mud on his windbreaker and pants cuffs. The work boots were beyond dirty. She could have melted into him and died.

"Let me sleep here tonight," he whispered back. "Let me sleep with you." His smile was a beggar's smile.

She pushed him off of her and he sat up.

"The body was lying on the pillow I bought," she said out of nowhere.

He shot her a puzzled look. "What pillow's that?"

"The blue one with silk tassels." She saw that he didn't remember it. "The one I bought at Oregon Discount."

He rubbed his eyes, interested in only one thing. "Sleep with me." Again he reached toward her in a gesture that made her think of a child. She could barely resist throwing herself into his arms. She sat straighter.

"We have to think," she said.

He waited for her to think.

"Either Rhonda's husband or Eppie Epperson did it," he said when she hadn't come up with anything.

"Did you love your girlfriend, Guy?"

He looked at her with amazement. "Are you kidding? No." Talking of love, he kept his hands to himself and forgot about sex.

"Do you want to stay married?"

He thought before answering. "Yes. But I've got to go away."

"You said you'd talk to the Sheriff's Department. We were going to call Scoville." She got off the bed and started toward the telephone.

"Wait."

"Why?"

He bit at a hangnail. "I'll call later."

"When?"

He sat moodily thinking. "I have to go away for a while," he repeated.

"Where?"

"Can't say."

"Mexico?"

He didn't say no.

"Just go, then!" she cried. "You're in danger of being arrested! I'm in danger, too!" He jumped up at her outburst and backed toward the door. She connected his frightened expression with another she'd seen an hour earlier: Humboldt's face when she'd started to cry. Disillusionment swept across her. Men might be taller, heavier, more sinewed, more muscled, but they were not stronger. She'd believed a myth. Guy might lift and haul; charm and seduce; sexually excite; nimbly dodge the inevitable for a while. But he could not keep himself or his wife happy and safe. She was stronger than he was.

17

They'd both wiped away their tears. In the headlight beams, fog rested in heavy layers, unruffled by coastal wind. "Slow down," said Maggie. "I can't see a thing."

"You don't need to see," said Humboldt. "I'm the one that's driving." It felt bracing to debate a small point.

"I don't like to nag—"

"Then don't," Humboldt said.

"I don't think Scoville will arrest the wrong person," Maggie said as the highway took its last curve before reaching the Dentons' steep turn-off. "I trust him."

"I trust him as much as I trust any law enforcement," said Humboldt, "He's got pressure from the Sheriff—hell, from the whole county—to find somebody who did it."

"Has he asked any more questions about Geraldine?" Maggie asked. A muscle in her neck twitched.

"Not to me," said Humboldt.

"She didn't do it," said Maggie.

"Don't worry about Geraldine," said Humboldt. "Scoville's

out to get Guy, not Geraldine."

"Guy is more likely to murder someone than Geraldine," said Maggie.

"Guy is not likely to murder anyone," Humboldt snapped, and immediately retreated into hurt silence. Climbing their steep drive, he felt as alone as their redwood house precariously facing the ocean and dark nothingness. His defense of Guy fell on deaf ears. If Maggie didn't sympathize with the man, who would? Even getting Geraldine to believe her husband was like pulling teeth.

"What have you got in the way of a drink?" he asked as they entered the house.

Maggie tried to lighten his mood. "Some of my sherry?"

"Tea," he said. He needed comforting. He would, she knew, have a sip or two, set the cup on the night stand, turn on the television, and promptly lose interest in everything except herself. They would hold each other fast while their tea cooled and the television droned on.

"Damndest thing how I get into these situations for my friends," he muttered, pulling down the bedclothes. He plumped the pillows and accepted the tea Maggie handed him, sugared the way he liked it. He sat on the edge of the bed, took a sip, and lay back. When Maggie had put her clothes away, slipped on her nightgown, brushed her hair, he patted the space beside him. She lay down and Humboldt turned out the light. He'd forgotten about television.

"What's going to happen to Guy?" Maggie whispered.

"God knows," Humboldt said quietly, sincerely. His reliance on something like faith eased his mind. For Maggie, her husband's surrender restored something like faith for her, too. The sound of the ocean moving against the rocks a hundred feet below soothed them both and they fell asleep in each other's arms.

18

"It's terrible not knowing whether Guy's in jail," Maggie said.

"Terrible," agreed Humboldt. He stopped at the traffic light, abstracted. Driving past the courthouse, he and Maggie avoided looking at the beautiful stone building with the columns and clock tower facing the street, the jail relegated to the back. Humboldt turned the corner to get away from it and stopped in front of Meg's Diner. "I'll pick you up in about an hour."

"Are you going to see Scoville?" Maggie asked. "Find out if Guy went to the Sheriff's Department last night like he said he would?"

"Dunno," said Humboldt. "I've got business at the hardware store. And the post office. I dunno if I want to ask about Guy or not."

A few minutes later, entering Meg's, she saw Eppie and Dr. Brown finishing breakfast at a table by the plate glass window in front. She waved and took a step toward the counter.

"Come sit with us," Eppie called to her. Dr. Brown looked less enthusiastic about having company.

"I'm just here for a quick cup of coffee," said Maggie. "Don't let me interrupt your breakfast."

"No interruption," said Eppie. Dr. Brown moved his water glass closer to him, more for privacy, Maggie thought, than to make room for a third person. Chilly, she seated herself and gathered the skirt of her coat around her. But Eppie seemed active and warm-blooded up here where cool air seeped in around the plate glass and an actual breeze blew each time the door opened for customers. The woman took small, quick bites of French toast and her eyes darted to and from Dr. Brown's face like a bird's on the lookout for any small movement in the vicinity. Dr. Brown had enough girth to stay warm without a coat; in fact, he was perspiring. He wiped his forehead now and then with a large, white handkerchief.

"Missed you at the table last night," Eppie said. "Busy?"

"Not particularly," Maggie said. "We lead a quiet life. I can hardly tell one day from another."

"Some days stand out, though," said Eppie, dipping her forkful of French toast in a shallow pool of syrup. She looked at Dr. Brown while she chewed. "Don't they, Roland?"

"Yeah," he said.

Anything Maggie thought of to say was fraught with danger. She smiled mechanically at the waitress who delivered her cup of coffee to the table. If she asked about the doctor's drive over the Siskiyous, or the weather in Medford, or funeral arrangements for his wife, if she chatted about his car or home, she would be touching on his wife's murder. Even his medical practice and private hospital might lead to something awkward. Finally she said, "Do you eat here often?"

But that too was an indirect comment about his overnight stays with Eppie which related to the fact that he was married or rather had been married to a woman recently murdered. Maggie put the cup of coffee to her lips and swallowed. Flinching, she set it down hard; she'd burned herself.

"Roland and I haven't had much experience eating in Brooks Beach restaurants," said Eppie. "Except, of course, at the Knotty Pine." Again she looked over at Dr. Brown.

Maggie, who had never seen Eppie Epperson rely on others for conversation, studied her while searching for small talk.

"Have we, Roland?"

"No," said Dr. Brown.

"But now Roland will have a chance to know Brooks Beach."

Roland seemed uninterested in having the chance to know Brooks Beach.

"How long have you lived in Medford?" Maggie asked sociably.

"Most of your life, isn't that right, Roland?" said Eppie.

"Yeah." He reached for the butter and tried to spread a thick layer on a biscuit that immediately crumbled in his hand.

Fragments rained onto the table and into his large lap.

"Good thing you're not a surgeon," Eppie said, and laughed. Dr. Brown glared at her. Maggie stared at this new woman. What had happened to bring about such a change in her personality? And was it really a change? Maggie had known Eppie for years, but not well.

Since her own puzzled good manners were wearing thin, Maggie said in a frank tone, "You two will be glad to get back to cards tonight. That's something we're all comfortable with."

"I'm taking a little vacation from Black Jack tonight," Eppie said.

"Well, that's a first," said Maggie.

"The table lost money," said Dr. Brown, "and she's sore."

"That's not it, and you know it," Eppie snapped.

Pushing back her chair and standing, Maggie addressed the topic of arguments in general rather than this particular one. "When my husband and I have—a difference of opinion, we usually need some time alone," she said. "You'll feel better when you sort things out." She looked at her watch ostentatiously. "Humboldt will be here any minute."

"Don't go," Eppie said, holding out her hand. By her tone of voice, she meant it.

"Roland and I will stop squabbling."

"You're the one who's squabbling," said Dr. Brown, picking up the fraction of biscuit that hadn't been destroyed and putting it in his mouth. The three sat at the table, swallowing and awkwardly glancing about.

"I've been dealing cards for twenty years," Eppie said, "and I've never had any trouble with customers." She looked haggard. Makeup could not disguise the dark circles under her eyes. Speaking directly to Maggie as if Dr. Brown weren't present, she said, "Roland says I cheated last night." She put a paper napkin to her face, pressed it against her eyes, and suddenly withdrew it. *There is no cheating at my table. Ever.*

ALWAYS ON THURSDAYS

Across the street, Maggie saw Scoville emerge from a single door beside the entrance to a florist shop and lock it behind him.

"Is that where Jim Scoville lives?" she asked, glad for the distraction. As soon as she said it, she was sorry. Nothing was more calculated to remind all three of them of murder than the detective in the Sheriff's Office.

"Yeah, I think so," Eppie said, preoccupied with folding her napkin into four equal squares. Maggie scanned the brick façade of the building across the street. With its white painted trim and wooden braces decoratively supporting the roof, it looked quaint and historic.

"So he lives above the florist shop?"

"How would she know?" said Dr. Brown.

Maggie flashed a glance at the doctor. "It was a rhetorical question." It wasn't. She hadn't known where Scoville lived. She imagined a flight of stairs to an upstairs apartment, cheerful by day with noises from the street and florist below; quiet and isolated at night. The upstairs windows, bowed out to form a bay, would be bright when he was home; a dark commercial space when he wasn't. A bachelor, would he spend his evenings alone reading and watching television? Or perhaps he went out every night rather than stay alone in rooms that never heard voices, kitchen sounds, family meals, children's pitter-patter, a woman's soft laughter.

He struck her as a man who might like being alone. She mused on his habits. She would suggest to Humboldt that they have him to dinner after this wretched business with Guy blew over. Scoville was crossing the street now. Perhaps this is where he takes his meals, she thought. Suddenly Dr. Brown pushed back his chair with an alarming screech. Other diners looked up.

In the back of the restaurant, two other chairs were suddenly pushed back. The doctor made a quick move for the door, but before he could reach it, a police officer and a diner in plainclothes came forward and took him swiftly by either arm. Dr. Brown made a gigantic movement, throwing himself forward, scuffling with the two who restrained him. But just as suddenly, he collapsed, gave up, even held out his wrists like an ashamed boy. The officer and plainclothesman positioned themselves at the right distance from the door for it to open without hitting them; for Detective Scoville to enter; for the words "You're under arrest" to be spoken in a calm, even voice; for a pair of handcuffs to be placed around Dr. Brown's thick wrists.

Eppie was standing, a fork in hand, her eyes starting from their sockets. Maggie had her hand over her mouth. Outside, a Sheriff's car glided up to the curb and Dr. Brown, without resistance, was ushered into the back seat. Within one minute the car had left the curb; the diners were left gasping and frozen in position. After the stunned silence, talk began haltingly, picking up in intensity and speed until there was a din above which Maggie and Eppie stood staring at each other.

When Humboldt drove up to the curb he beeped once for Maggie who failed to react to the sound. It was as if she'd forgotten where she was. At the second beep, still staring at Eppie, she backed toward the door without saying a word. Outside, she gave a hasty wave through the plate glass window. Humboldt reached across the passenger seat and opened the door for her, unaware that breakfast at Meg's had just been interrupted by an arrest.

19

"Honesty is the best policy," Guy said without sincerity and leaned forward, laughing, his casual view of life and irreverent mind fueling the merriment at Geraldine's kitchen table. The four of them were hysterical with relief. Humboldt cuffed Guy on the shoulder and Maggie wiped away tears.

"You pushed it to the limit," the older man exclaimed. They were celebrating Guy's release from questioning, really not surprised that he'd gotten lucky; that he'd gone to the Sheriff's Office some time in the wee hours of the morning; that he'd been released just in time to observe Dr. Brown being processed in as he, himself, was being processed out

"How did he kill her?" Humboldt asked, suddenly serious. The mood in the kitchen changed from hilarity to squeamish curiosity.

"How should I know? The Sheriff's Office doesn't confide in me," said Guy. "You're the one who talks to Scoville."

"We'll have to wait till the trial," said Geraldine.

"There's a way to find out before that," said Humboldt.

Maggie leaned forward. "What do you have in mind?"

Humboldt moved his head a notch to the right, toward the Knotty Pine. "Scoville likes his beer."

"We could invite him back here for a drink or coffee," said Geraldine.

"No you don't," said Guy. "Keep your distance."

"Right," agreed Humboldt. "We seek him out on his own ground. He doesn't come here."

After more coffee, high-pitched joking, congratulations to Guy for doing the right thing—"a rare moment of good judgment," Humboldt said, sending them all into gales of laughter that couldn't quite hide the trauma they'd been through. But Guy wouldn't admit to doing the right thing.

"Surrounded by all you respectable people, what else could I do?" he said. "Did I hear something about the Knotty Pine?" He turned to Humboldt. "How about a game of pool?"

"I wouldn't say no to a game of pool."

Geraldine and Maggie gathered up their purses and coats and the men followed them out the back door and across the strip of yard toward the tavern. All chatter ceased as they stepped into the alley. Humboldt put his arm around Guy's shoulder. "Good to have you back," he said solemnly. Geraldine slipped her arm into her husband's. He tightened his elbow around her hand but kept his own in his pocket. Maggie was behind the others until Humboldt reached around and pulled her forward, beside him. In silence the four crossed to the dirt parking lot and entered the back door of the bar.

Geraldine's color was high and her eyes shone. There was no thought of a single woman sitting at a table, eyeing the curly-headed man with the laugh and the physique and the charm of a male in his best years.

The pool table was busy. The men went for beers and came back to Maggie and Geraldine who had taken a table by the wall near the front entrance. Maggie showed no inclination to go back to the card room. Geraldine pulled her chair closer to Guy. With their coats hanging on pegs nearby, their legs in easy positions, their eyes roving the room, coming back always to their table and each other, the four settled in. Geraldine felt like a wife and fell deeply in love with her husband all over again. He cast a private, coded look of achievement in her direction before he was off again, laughing and refusing to be drawn into her web.

Scoville entered the bar. Guy grew still.

"Join us?" Humboldt said.

Scoville nodded in the affirmative. They made room for a fifth chair while he went to the bar and ordered his beer.

"Well, I guess you wrapped 'er up," Humboldt said jovially when Scoville returned to his place at the table. Geraldine suddenly thought of Rhonda Rhinehart wrapped in a blanket, head resting on the tasseled pillow, and felt, not jealousy, but compassion for Guy. He sat quietly, inward rather than guarded.

Humboldt congratulated Scoville again. "Nice work." It never occurred to him that Scoville might be thinking something like "no thanks to you," but in fact the man looked as if he had no thought whatsoever as he sat drinking his beer and looking blandly around the room.

"Can you tell us about the arrest?" said Maggie, incautious, confident that she could talk to him. "Can you tell us anything about the murder? How he did it? Did he confess?"

"It's no secret," said Scoville. "The lab report came back. The victim was dosed with an anesthetic. The doctor brought her body to Brooks Beach in the trunk of a rental car. He confessed."

His listeners didn't stir as they absorbed the information.

"What about the car in the alley?" asked Maggie. "The car that backed out when we were on our way to the bar?"

"The rental car," said Scoville. "Dr. Brown and his girl friend."

"Eppie?" Maggie said. "For Heaven's sake."

"It seems he likes to be in the front seat of a car with a woman," said Scoville.

Guy roused himself from his private thoughts and reverted to his irreverent style. "Foreplay," he said, but his tone was grim and no one laughed.

"What about the pillow?" said Geraldine.

"Sometime during the evening he drove back to the alley, took his wife's body out of the trunk, and laid it near the garage." Scoville didn't seem aware of either the drama in the alley or the drama here around the table. "People surprise you," he said, no man less likely to be surprised. "The doctor looked in the garage for something to cover her with. Found the blanket and pillow."

Guy sent a blameworthy glance toward Geraldine, but, self-contained, she accepted no blame. He stared at her, unused to her new sense of self-preservation.

"He told you all this?" said Humboldt.

"Yesterday."

"You left him until the end," said Maggie.

"Left him until the report on his private hospital came in." They all sat waiting. "He was being shut down."

"Drugs?" said Humboldt.

"Too many patients died," said Scoville, "under questionable circumstances. Rhonda Brown worked as a nurse. She made copies of forged death certificates."

"She was blackmailing her husband?" Maggie asked in a stunned tone. Scoville said nothing.

"Wisht they'd kept their dirty business in Medford," said Humboldt. "Not bring it over the mountain."

Until now, Geraldine had remained silent. In a thoughtful voice she said, "Maybe he planned Thursday nights at the Knotty Pine just so he could get his wife out of Medford and"—she stared at Guy—"get rid of her in Brooks Beach." She turned sharply toward Scoville. "Did he want his wife to have an affair in Brooks Beach?" She looked back at Guy. "Did he put her in the alley so he could tie it to"—she looked at the ceiling, the wall, the table—"funny business at the Knotty Pine?"

But Scoville had lost interest in the conversation. Before long the four set about discussing whether to go back to Geraldine's house for more coffee, stay in the Knotty Pine for cards and pool, go to their separate homes, or simply stay put and order more beer.

After another half hour, home won out. Maggie and Humboldt got their coats from the pegs on the wall and said good-night. Some last-minute kidding, congratulations, and another heartfelt clap to Guy's shoulder preceded their trip to the Plymouth parked in the dirt lot. Scoville unwound his thin, sinewy frame from the chair and put on his overcoat. Winding a wool scarf around his leathery neck he said, looking vaguely toward Guy and Geraldine, "Till later."

"Not if I can help it," Guy murmured to Geraldine on their way out the back door.

Geraldine moved nearer. Though separated from him by the thickness of their jackets, the thought of his body warmed her. He reached out and pulled her close. They stopped to say goodbye to the Dentons who sat running the engine.

"Come up for dinner tomorrow night," Maggie said, leaning down so she could see them through the driver's window. "Six-thirty." Humboldt backed into the alley, followed it to the street, and turned toward Coast Highway, his taillights growing smaller and smaller until they disappeared. Geraldine and Guy crossed the alley and retraced their steps to the cedar-shingled cottage and bed.

Scoville stepped into his car and turned the key in the ignition. He sat for a moment, glancing around at the few parked cars remaining in front of the Knotty Pine. Traffic had quieted by now. The fog horn down at the harbor blew its long, sad notes and the wash of the ocean against the shore carried up to him as he entered Coast Highway and drove toward the dark apartment across the street from Meg's Diner, in the heart of town, directly above the florist shop.

RECESSES OF THE MIND

1

The patient stirs behind the railing of the hospital bed. Outside, gray light could be either dawn or dusk. At this best of all moments, when the pain-killer begins to take effect but before mental fog obscures thought, a voice whispers, "It's not safe. Tell them..." And yet words remain just beyond reach, like a blanket that cannot quite be grasped when the room grows too cold for comfort.

2

Humboldt Denton stood at the plate glass window of his redwood home and stared out over the Pacific. From their perch high on a Southern Oregon cliff, he and Maggie often heard the surf more clearly than they could see it. In squalls, thick air and sleet obliterated the view. But on a day like today, blue and gold, all glittering water and smiling sky, the surf far below sloshed merrily and the little armada of fishing boats floating on the water rested as if held in a cupped hand.

"What time is he coming?" Humboldt asked, wandering into the kitchen where Maggie stood crimping the edges of a cherry pie.

"Six o'clock." She took a sideways step to the stove. "Scoville is never late."

Absently watching the pie-making operation, he stood rubbing his light growth of beard. By the time she'd adjusted the metal racks, tucked the pie in the oven, and stepped into the dining room, his electric razor was already buzzing faintly from the back of the house.

Flushed from the warm kitchen, Maggie fluttered a cloth over the dining room table where tonight they would not need the extension leaf for their party of three. In the bathroom, Humboldt leaned into the mirror and went over his upper lip again.

He and Maggie were thinking the same thing: what had Jim Scoville, detective in the Crescent County Sheriff's Office, learned about the recent crime that, for the first time in twenty-five years of criminal investigations, touched him personally? Should they mention it? Would he want to talk about the murder and kidnapping in the house where he'd grown up? His mother had been injured and a renter in her house killed; the woman renter's little son had been kidnapped. It was hard to believe, and hard to connect the private, imperturbable Scoville with such events in his own life.

Separately, in the bathroom, in the dining room, they came to the same conclusion: follow their guest's lead. Only Scoville knew whether he wanted to talk about the tragedy or not.

3

It turned out he did want to talk about the tragedy, although through dinner nothing was said about the desecration of his boyhood home in Portland three hundred fifty miles to the north. Rather, conversation focused on the local Brooks Beach economy—fishing, logging, illicit marijuana crops—until dessert when Scoville leaned back in his chair and drew in a deep breath of air still laced with cooked cherry.

"Homemade pie is a favorite of mine," he said.

Maggie, who stood at his elbow with a fresh pot of coffee, sensed an opening for discussion of mothers and, indirectly, the crime in Portland. "As children, I think we all grew up eating our mothers' homemade pies."

"Bought pies can't hold a candle to homemade pies," said Humboldt, in case Scoville would rather talk about pie than mothers.

"My mother baked a good cherry pie," Scoville murmured, satisfying everyone. "By the way, they have a suspect."

"Oh?" Maggie whispered.

"Who is it?" said her husband.

"Our Brooks Beach killer."

"But he's in state prison," Maggie objected.

Scoville unfolded, then refolded his linen napkin. "He escaped three nights ago."

Maggie swayed, dropped into the vacant fourth chair, and studied the detective's weathered face: dark eyes set within the chiseled lines one develops from squinting, from looking hard and thinking hard. "How did he get from the prison to Portland?"

"Not known yet."

"Hitch-hiked, probably," said Humboldt, who'd left home at fifteen, hitching rides back and forth across the country, greasing cars from coast to coast to support himself.

Maggie smoothed a wrinkle in the tablecloth. "Where is your mother now?"

"Here," Scoville said. "In Brooks Beach." He lifted his coffee cup but immediately set it back in its saucer. "I had an ambulance bring her from Portland to the nursing home."

"The killer wants to get even with you," said Humboldt.

Scoville nodded, impassive and remote.

Maggie began to worry. Perhaps he was sorry to be here. Sorry to be talking about the violence in Portland. She stood, forgetting the coffee but unable to forget the crime. "How did he find out where your mother lives?"

"I told him."

"You're kidding," said Humboldt.

"He picked up a detail when I was on the witness stand," said Scoville, and fell back into silent detachment.

"I guess they didn't need to worry about his mental status after all," said Humboldt. The criminal trial had lasted three weeks because the jury couldn't agree on the defendant's mental competence.

"He was smarter than we thought," Scoville said.

"How badly is your mother hurt?" Maggie asked.

The detective took a swallow from his cup and methodically corrected the ratio of sugar to coffee. "Three cracked ribs." In response to Maggie's sympathetic expression he added, "Her bedroom is off the living room. When she heard the door forced open, she tried to get out of bed. He came into the room, threw her to the floor... " He trailed off.

"And the renter?" Maggie gently asked when he'd returned the spoon to the sugar bowl. "The woman who looked after your mother?"

"He shot her," Scoville said. "And then he kidnapped her little boy." Lifting the cup to his mouth, he tried to hide the lower third of his face as it collapsed.

4

A year earlier, in Room 8 of a dank, failed Brooks Beach motel, a murder had been committed. The stucco units overlooking the Pacific were flaking and stained. In the forty-year-old bathrooms, mildewed grout between tiles harbored fungus.

The victim, a poor, single man, as failed as the motel, was cremated in the local mortuary and his ashes scattered just below the unstable seam that had so far prevented the little town from sliding down the continental shelf into the Pacific Ocean. Detective Jim Scoville had been the chief investigator.

"I didn't hear you say anything about your mother when you testified," Humboldt said as Maggie carried the diminished cherry pie back into the kitchen.

Scoville shook his head. He all but wagged his finger at Humboldt. "It's in the transcript."

"What's in the transcript?" said Maggie, returning for the empty dessert plates.

"Where I told the killer that my mother lives in Portland."

"I never heard it," Humboldt repeated.

Maggie paused, holding the plates in midair. "We can ask Geraldine," she said. "It's her transcript."

Scoville sat in silence.

"Whatever you said will be in her notes," Maggie restated. "We can ask her what you said."

"I'd rather not," said Scoville.

"Just to clear things up."

He glanced at the ceiling, then back to the table. "I'm going to try to forget the whole experience."

"I can ask her when I'm in town tomorrow. You know, if you don't want to," said Maggie. "She and I are good friends."

"I'd rather you didn't."

"After all, you're the investigative detective of the Sheriff's Department—"

"Not anymore."

"What do you mean, 'not anymore'?"

"The Sheriff's taking this one over."

Maggie studied him for a moment, then turned her back on the table and proceeded into the kitchen where she opened the dishwasher with a decisive motion and pulled out the bottom rack. The chatter of ceramic and chime of silverware emphasized the silence in the dining room.

Finally Humboldt said, "We'll all feel better when this guy is caught."

"Re-caught," Scoville said. He pushed himself away from the table. "I don't like to eat and run, but I'm not very good company tonight. I'll just thank your wife for the fine meal and say good-bye." The two men stood and moved toward the front hallway. From the kitchen Maggie heard them stirring and came out with cheerful demeanor and extended hand.

"We loved seeing you," she said. "Next time the circumstances will be better."

Scoville took her hand in both of his, an old-fashioned gesture that gave him a courtly air. As he passed through the door Humboldt held open, Maggie's eyes narrowed.

"Whether or not he wants me to," she said when the door closed, "I'm going to pay a visit to Geraldine."

Humboldt turned the lock.

"Don't you want to know why?"

"Why?" he said indulgently.

"To see her verbatim notes."

"You can't read them, can you?"

"Well, no. But she can."

"Why don't you just go to the courthouse and read the transcript?"

"I'd rather not have the staff know what I'm doing."

"Strategy," said Humboldt.

"Exactly," she said. "There's a bookcase in Geraldine's spare bedroom devoted to raw notes. That's what she calls them. Raw notes." Turning back toward the kitchen, she added, as if providing crucial testimony, "You know, Humboldt, the law requires court reporters to keep their notes for five years."

Bowing to her superior knowledge, he turned off the hall light and returned to the plate glass window. North toward Portland, the land mass stretched dark and unknown. To the south, Brooks Beach street lights and house lights twinkled, amused winks at the edge of solitude. Maggie finished washing the last of the pots and pans and joined him at the window.

"Scoville's alone with all that sadness," she murmured.

"He's used to being alone," said Humboldt.

"Is he on leave from the case?" asked Maggie. "Or on leave from the County?"

"Both. I'll stop by his apartment tomorrow," said Humboldt. "Time's going to weigh heavy for him."

They moved closer. Hands touching, they watched the surf far below as it thrashed at the foot of the cliff, regular in its restlessness; phosphorescent and beautiful in the moonlight.

5

"Are you home?" Maggie sang out from Geraldine's front steps. It was another spring day in Southern Oregon. No rain, fog, wind, salt spray. Just lightness and gardens heating up. A sky-, ocean-, land-perfect day for commercial fishing boats and marijuana crops that stretch east to the Siskiyous. Ignoring the door, Maggie stepped to the living room window and knocked on the glass. She could hear the tapping of typewriter keys in the back of the house where Geraldine transcribed shorthand code from the continuous narrow paper disgorged by her stenotype machine during legal proceedings. By the time the typing stopped, Maggie was already inside the house, knowing she was welcome; so welcome that within seconds she was standing in the doorway of the back bedroom where Geraldine, still wearing her pajamas, sat at the old desk Humboldt had located on one of his excursions to the basement flea market held every Saturday in City Hall.

"Hell of a deal," he'd told her two years earlier, out of breath from excitement over his find and from rushing to the pay phone in the rotunda so she could authorize him to buy it before anyone else wanted to. "A roll-top desk in good condition! Just like my dad's back in Vermont! It'll last a lifetime!"

"Hi, Mags." Geraldine looked up from the typewriter.

"Do you have time to find something in your notes?" Maggie asked.

"Sure." Geraldine stood and went to the bookcase. "What's the date?"

Maggie absently stared out the window and followed the progress of a Golden Retriever wandering along the alley. Before this Brooks Beach murder, it had been several years since a capital crime had occurred in Crescent County.

"I don't know exactly," she said. "The trial where Detective Scoville testified about the Portland murder. Was it early

November?"

"Maybe November 10th," Geraldine said. "Did you want something from the first day?"

"No, something from Scoville's testimony."

"That would be the third day," Geraldine said, scanning the shelves for November notes. "It took them two days to voir dire the jury." After pulling out, then rejecting several packets of notes, she said, "You could go to the Courthouse and read the transcript."

"I'd rather just keep this between you and me."

Geraldine hesitated. "It might be better if you went to the public record. I've never read notes to a private person. I mean, I've read notes to attorneys and even the judge before the transcript was prepared, but… "

Maggie turned aside, disappointed.

Geraldine sighed. "Can you tell me what you're looking for?"

"Scoville thinks he said something during the trial about his mother. He thinks he told the killer where his mother lives."

Geraldine frowned. "I don't remember him saying anything about his mother."

"Neither does Humboldt. Neither do I."

"Was he on the witness stand when he said it?"

"He says he was. For some reason he feels responsible for what happened in Portland."

"You can feel guilty about almost anything if you think about it long enough," said Geraldine.

Maggie occupied herself with a fingernail and cuticle. "That's why I want to know what he actually said."

Geraldine slowly pulled out the packet of notes marked November 13th, 1986 and for a moment stood transferring it back and forth between her hands like a hot potato. Finally she unwound the rubber band and set the packet on the desk. Laying back the continuous sheets, unfolding each, reading quickly, she passed through the first few minutes of court. "He wasn't sworn in until after morning recess," she said, skipping long chunks of colloquy and proceeding faster. "I'll get to it in a minute."

While she waited, Maggie moved to the back window. The alley behind Geraldine's one-car garage separated the strip of back yard from the dirt lot of the Knotty Pine Tavern. Letting her attention float from the low cement building to the garage, drifting en route across the spot behind the tavern where she and Humboldt parked on the nights she played Black Jack, Maggie absently watched the retriever leave the alley to nose around the front tire of the only car in the parking lot. She pictured the driver inside on this beautiful spring day, drinking alone in the dark, piney room, smoking and contributing to the stale air, watching a rerun of a police show on the TV above the bar... She turned away from the window, assailed by thoughts of Scoville's mother lying in the nursing home a few blocks away. And somewhere was a little boy from Portland who had seen his mother shot; a child who, if he were even alive, was now in the custody of a killer. Chirping voices of children passing by on the sidewalk in front of Geraldine's house sounded bittersweet. Maggie thought of the baby she and Humboldt had lost so many years ago. The birth of three thriving daughters had not erased the sadness. She sank onto the edge of the guest bed.

Geraldine looked over her shoulder. "Do you feel all right, Maggie?"

Maggie nodded. Trying to retain the agreeable outlines of her life, she concentrated on Humboldt. At this very moment he would be having coffee in Scoville's apartment above the florist shop. Later he would stop for her at Geraldine's and drive her up the Chetco for farm produce and freshly laid eggs. On the dinner menu tonight she planned roast chicken and a green salad. The setting sun would be casting a rosy glow over the cliff and redwood house while tendrils of last light slipped into the kitchen, touching fresh asparagus, savory herbed potatoes on the stove...

Until a few days ago, Scoville's world had been comfortable, too. Often after a game of Black Jack, Maggie would come out of the card room at the back of the Knotty Pine and join Humboldt and the detective—neither of whom gambled—at their table where the three would chat or sit in a satisfying silence, now and then welcoming a friend to sit down and share their pitcher of beer.

"Here it is," said Geraldine. "Scoville's testimony. It's short."

Maggie got up from the edge of the bed and went to stand beside Geraldine, peering down at the ink marks she couldn't read.

"The prosecution is questioning," Geraldine explained.

"Tell us, Detective Scoville, how long you've been with the Crescent County Sheriff's Office."

"More than twenty years."

"Where were you employed before you joined the Sheriff's Office?"

"I was a parole officer in Portland, Oregon."

"Did you grow up in Portland?"

"Yes."

Geraldine looked up from her notes. "That's it. The next question is about his duties here in Crescent County."

Maggie searched Geraldine's face. "That's all?"

"That's all."

"He didn't say anything about his mother?"

"No," said Geraldine. "He's an experienced witness. He didn't say more than he needed to."

"Oh, God!" Maggie exclaimed, and burst into tears. "Then I'm the one who told him! The murderer learned it from me!"

6

Humboldt hurried up the porch steps of Geraldine's house and was soon standing in the middle of the living room, one arm extended toward his wife who came stumbling out of the back bedroom. He led her to the sofa, tucked her into the corner next to the armrest, and dropped onto the cushion beside her.

"When she couldn't stop crying, I called you," Geraldine said, coming in from the kitchen where she was making tea. She'd changed from pajamas to corduroy slacks and a jersey top. Humboldt leaned forward, pulled a white handkerchief out of his back pocket, and unfolded it.

"She doesn't cry very often," he said, dabbing at his wife's tears. Maggie took the handkerchief from him and brought it up to her eyes.

"She blames herself," Geraldine said, seating herself in the wing-back chair, repeating what she'd told him on the phone. Her hair, held by a few pins in an unstable swirl at the crown of her head, trembled.

"It wouldn't have happened if I hadn't talked about ... about ... oh, that poor little boy and his d-dead mother."

"Maggie," Humboldt said, patting her knee over and over, his face drained of color. "Maggie, you mustn't blame yourself."

Geraldine leaned forward. "Tell Humboldt what you were telling me."

Humboldt's handkerchief was a damp, wadded-up ball in Maggie's hand before she was able to lean back against the sofa and tame her ragged breathing. "It was when I helped Tammy in her café at the motel," she began. Humboldt and Geraldine looked at each other without comprehension.

Maggie shifted in the sofa corner and looked directly into her husband's eyes. "It was the day you and Jim Scoville drove to Portland. Remember? He drove up to settle his mother at home after surgery. You were with him."

"I remember," Humboldt said.

"I told Tammy where the two of you went." The effort to follow his wife's story was bringing color back to Humboldt's face. "You know, the day Tammy needed help in the café and I offered to wait tables."

Geraldine leaned forward and laid her hand on the coffee table. "Maggie, tell us what the café has to do with the killer and Scoville's mother."

"He was there!" Maggie exclaimed, as if they should know. "The killer was having lunch! He heard me talking to Tammy!"

"What were you saying to Tammy?" asked Humboldt.

"We were talking behind the counter. Tammy said she appreciated my help and I should call you to come have lunch at the café, without paying, you know, to show her appreciation, but I told her you couldn't come for lunch because you were with Scoville in Portland."

"What else?" Geraldine asked.

Maggie threw herself against Humboldt. "I said you were visiting Jim Scoville's mother who was an invalid! I said it was nice that Jim could still go back to his childhood home for a visit!"

Humboldt alternated between patting and gripping Maggie's knee. She couldn't be stopped now. "Tammy wanted to know who Jim Scoville was, and I told her, and she sounded interested. She wanted to know if he was married, and I said no—"

Humboldt's jaw muscles began to work. "For God's sake, Maggie, stick to the point… "

"Where was the man sitting?" asked Geraldine.

"In the booth by the window."

"How long was this before the murder?"

"I don't know. He'd been staying there in the motel. Tammy said he took his meals in the café." Abruptly she stopped talking and bowed her head as if bearing physical pain.

Humboldt stood and dug in his pocket for car keys. "I have

to take her home," he said to Geraldine.

"Do you want me to ride with you?"

"I'd appreciate it. I'll bring you back to town later."

From the back door the three walked unevenly to the Denton car parked in the alley. Once the car was in motion, Maggie calmed. Driving north along Highway 1, spruces glided alongside the shoulder of the road while to their left, the sunny sky swept high above the ocean. Directly in front of them, a chip truck on its way to the paper plant smelled gluey, its scent of wood chips mingling with the odd smell of simmering Brussels sprouts from the factory at the end of the county turn-off; such familiar odors that no one in Brooks Beach smelled them anymore.

Geraldine leaned against the window, legs stretched out across the back seat, arms folded at her waist. As Humboldt turned into the steep drive leading to the house, Maggie, calmer now, said, "I'd like to tell Jim Scoville what I've told you, without the tears. Heaven knows he has enough emotion to deal with. It may help in the investigation. And I want to apologize."

Humboldt concentrated on the graveled incline. Geraldine leaned forward and patted Maggie's shoulder before returning to her restful position, aware of being comfortable, wishing this peaceful moment wouldn't end. A sense of something important about to happen, of cloth being torn apart, a ragged seam splitting, lurked beneath the quietude in the car, along with a sense that she was going to have to sew something up. Repair damage. Thirty-four, divorced, she was living on the surface of her life. Work; a few friends; daily tasks; Monday-through-Friday, then Monday all over again.

"Call Scoville," Maggie said to Humboldt as the car rolled into the garage. "Ask him if he'll drive up and have a drink with us."

"He told me he was going to the Knotty Pine," Humboldt said.

"Tell him to come here instead." The words, though spoken

quietly, were phrased as a requirement. As soon as she entered the house, Maggie went to a corner of the living room and stretched out in the reclining chair, exhausted. Geraldine sat down near her while Humboldt disappeared in back.

Here on the cliff, there was almost always wind. The plate glass windows creaked. Several seagulls landed on the deck rail, then lifted into the air again, mewing. Geraldine heard Humboldt speak to Scoville from the telephone in the bedroom. Maggie, eyes closed, had apparently achieved temporary peace. Geraldine listened to the wind that seemed to move in a circle around the house and imagined she could hear the ocean washing against the base of the cliff far below. And something else. A quiet tearing sound. A seam coming apart.

7

Scoville mounted the stairs to the deck and front door. He climbed slowly and knocked twice. When Humboldt answered, he stepped inside, not out of breath, but looking haggard.

"Glad you could come," Humboldt said, shaking his hand. There was something formal about Scoville since he'd gotten the bad news from Portland.

"My pleasure," Scoville murmured. As he approached the center of the living room, Maggie reared up out of her recliner. Standing in front of him, she inhaled sharply, one dry sob, before restraining herself and extending her hand.

"What is it, Maggie?"

"I have to tell you something," she said.

Her husband took her by the arm and guided her back to the recliner while indicating for Scoville to sit in the maroon leather swivel chair.

"What can I get you to drink?" he asked.

"Beer," said Scoville.

"Geraldine?"

"If Maggie's having her afternoon sherry, I'll have some, too."

"It's not afternoon yet," said Humboldt, leaving for the kitchen. "You can have morning sherry."

Scoville looked from one woman to the other. "Windy afternoon," he finally said. The plate glass still creaked and the seagulls, gathering and dispersing, still cried into the wind. The clinking of bottles and glasses coming from the kitchen sounded more nervous than hospitable. Scoville waited for Humboldt to join them again.

"What do you want to tell me?" he finally said, swiveling toward Maggie.

Upright in the recliner, ankles crossed tidily, sherry glass on the small table beside her, Maggie spoke carefully. "I'm sorry to say that I'm the person who gave the information out about your mother living in Portland." She cast a wild glance at the birds out the window before facing the detective again. "It wasn't you," she whispered.

He took a sip of the beer Humboldt had poured into a tall glass as if a bottle would be too casual for the purpose of this visit.

"You didn't say anything about your mother when you were in court," Maggie repeated, as if he might not have understood the first time.

Scoville set his glass of beer with its live foam on the table beside Maggie's sherry. "What are you saying, Mrs. Denton?" He never called her "Mrs. Denton."

"The killer," she said, "overheard me in the café when I was talking."

"What café is this?"

"The café in the motel where he stayed."

"What was he doing in the café?"

"Eating lunch."

Scoville watched one seagull chase another straight up into

the sunlight. "Why were you talking about my mother?"

"I was helping the owner. I was waiting tables. She said to call Humboldt and invite him for lunch, and I told her that you and Humboldt had driven to Portland to see your mother."

Scoville rubbed his eyes with the thumb and fingertip of one hand. "I'm sure I said something about her when I testified," he murmured.

"You didn't," Maggie said. "Geraldine read her notes to me. You didn't say anything at all about your mother."

Glancing toward Geraldine on the sofa, he reached for his glass, then turned back to Maggie. "I asked you not to talk to anyone about it," he said.

"I'm sorry," Maggie whispered.

Humboldt fidgeted. Geraldine began to perspire. Perhaps she'd been wrong to read the notes to Maggie. She'd wondered at the time if she should. Was Scoville angry? Or just depressed? The man was harder to read than someone else's stenotype notes.

"We're sorry," Humboldt said. "She was only trying to help."

When Scoville did finally speak he said, "Tell the Sheriff, not me. He's the one who's investigating." He held no one and no thing in his dark gaze. He seemed empty. The others didn't know what to do or say. There was a ghost in the room: Scoville. And with him were four more ghosts: an old woman, a young woman, a child, and a killer.

"Let's talk about something else," he said and lifted his beer as if toasting a new subject. Maggie picked up her glass of sherry and, without pleasure, took a sip.

"The weather," Humboldt said glumly, looking toward the window and the sunlight, so different from the room now shadow-filled. "We can talk about the weather."

Geraldine checked her watch.

"Do you need to get home?" Humboldt said.

She didn't need to get home but she saw no reason to stay. "I'll finish my transcript," she said vaguely. The word "transcript" threw them all into another silence.

Scoville stood. "I'll drive you back to town," he said.

Geraldine wondered how he knew she needed a ride.

"I'm a detective," he explained, as if he'd heard her thoughts. "I saw your car in town." His smile was the forgiveness Maggie craved. They began to feel better, so when Humboldt said, "Stay at least long enough to finish your beer," Scoville sat back down and they all remained where they were, quietly sipping from their glasses, resuscitating themselves and each other.

8

"I've never seen Maggie so upset," Geraldine said as the old Chevrolet paused at the foot of the Dentons' steep gravel road.

Scoville shifted into first and turned onto Coast Highway. After moving through gears, his hand returned to the steering wheel and his left foot came to rest on the floorboard again.

"There's a lot to be upset about," he said.

"I regret reading my notes to her."

Scoville looked in the rear view mirror at a lumber truck bearing down on them and pressed the accelerator. "There's nothing in your notes that she wouldn't have learned from the court transcript," he said as the truck receded into the distance behind them.

"Still, I don't think I'll do that again." It was difficult to talk about the Portland crime and impossible to think of anything else. Scoville's silence was louder than the hum of the car. Geraldine looked out her window and watched the ocean's blueness begin thinning toward gray until she felt she was being rude and turned back toward the windshield, where she ended up watching the white line in the middle of the highway rush into the past. She wished the day were over, but spruce trees along the opposite shoulder of the road trying to form a line of defense against daylight failed; their rough tops and jagged limbs couldn't create night when it was only late afternoon.

"I can't think straight," Scoville said.

"It's no wonder," said Geraldine.

In front of her house she opened the car door and thanked him for the ride. Hesitating, she added, "If you'd like company, you're welcome to come in."

He surprised her by nodding his thanks, turning off the ignition, and following her up the porch steps. Inside she turned on a lamp, though it wasn't needed yet, and went into the kitchen to start coffee. He must be lonely to accept her invitation, she thought. We pass in the courthouse halls, but we don't know each other at all.

As if he'd been thinking the same thing, he said, "I could have taken you to the Red Door Cafe but I didn't think of it in time."

"No, this is fine," said Geraldine. "We'll be comfortable here." She smiled. "My coffee isn't too bad." She picked up Maggie's teacup from earlier in the day—"I haven't cleaned up from the earlier shift," she said—and carried it to the kitchen.

Even in the best of times, Scoville didn't banter. Returning, she sat down in the wing-back chair and looked into his face. Since the man hadn't spoken six sentences from the time they'd entered Coast Highway to the time he'd parked in front of her house, Geraldine decided he was incapacitated and it was up to her to talk.

"I haven't seen you in the courthouse the last few days," she said. "What have you been doing since all this happened?"

He was sitting on the sofa, the same corner of the sofa where Maggie had sat earlier in the day.

Geraldine rephrased: "How have you been occupying your time?"

"I visit my mother every day in the nursing home. And this morning Humboldt came and had coffee with me. I just got back from beer with the Dentons"—his face softened into something not quite resembling amusement—"and now I'm here having coffee again. It's been a busy day."

"How is your mother?"

"Surprisingly well. She knows me and she can talk."

"Is she able to—identify who broke into the house?"

"She's picked out the suspect's photograph."

"Do you think they'll find him?" Her question sounded silly to her, but Scoville took it seriously.

"It's difficult because he has the child. We don't want the child hurt." And then, abruptly, he did cry. In a gesture that matched Humboldt's earlier one, except that he was wearing a sports jacket and had to brush it aside, he leaned forward and pulled a folded white handkerchief out of his back pocket. He was unashamed and so Geraldine didn't regret asking the question. It was perhaps what he needed.

His tears didn't last long. "My mother is fond of the boy. We haven't told her about the kidnapping."

"Did you know the child?"

Scoville's voice changed from the refined bass of his normal tone, from the moist and thickened sounding board of a moment earlier, to tenderness. "How is that coffee coming?" he said.

Geraldine had forgotten about the coffee. A sense of alertness, of pending events, made her steps to the kitchen light and quick. She came back with a tray and set it on the low table in front of the sofa. In his methodical way Scoville added sugar to his cup and stirred thoughtfully, as if trying to decide what to tell her.

"The little boy is my son," he finally said.

Geraldine stared. "So—oh, God, his mother is—gone."

He nodded.

"Maggie doesn't know?" Geraldine said.

"No, and neither does Humboldt. No one knows except my—the mother and I." He corrected himself. "Only I know now. And you."

"How old is your son?"

Scoville looked grateful. "I like hearing him referred to as my son," he said, and cleared his throat. "Three-and-a-half years old."

"You've told the Sheriff?"

"It's immaterial," he said.

Geraldine knew it was not immaterial.

"If you feel you have to tell anyone," he said, "I'll be sorry I confided in you." He drew himself up, preparing to stand.

"If asked, I can't lie," she said. He seemed to accept that. But he stood nevertheless.

"Am I the only person besides you who knows?"

"Yes."

"Does your mother know?"

He sat back down. "No."

"And your son?"

Scoville looked thoughtfully into space. "He calls me Jim, but I believe he's beginning to"—he paused and cleared his throat—"has begun to regard me as his father."

Geraldine stared at the craggy face, the deep lines in the cheeks and around the full lips. "We're going to have to find that child," she said.

He stood again, put his hands in the pockets of his tweed jacket, and began to pace up and down the living room. It was a small room and he had to turn often: at the kitchen door, at the door to the hallway, around the sofa, to the front door, and back again. "She never wanted it known. Neither did I." He stopped in front of the window. "My mother wouldn't have understood. The boy's mother didn't want to lose her job. She loved my mother and my mother loved her."

"Did you help support the child?"

"Of course. And now I'll raise him."

If he lives, Geraldine thought silently, aware of a low-grade nausea beginning to seethe. Her mind raced into the future. If he were found unharmed, the grandmother would have to be told she had a grandson.

"Your mother may have guessed," she said.

But Scoville's attention was on the boy. "If I disappear for a while, it will be because I have some idea of where they are." He made a gentle fist with one hand and closed the other around it.

"*Do* you know where they are?" Geraldine asked sharply.

"Not yet." He almost pled with her. "It's important that you not divulge what I've told you."

Obviously, Geraldine thought to herself, he was not thinking straight. If he disappeared, Humboldt and Maggie would be forced to tell the Sheriff they'd seen him in the afternoon and that he'd driven Geraldine home. If asked what she'd talked about with him, she would not lie. The Sheriff would learn that Scoville was the father of the kidnapped child.

"Were you still having a relationship with the mother?" she asked.

"Off and on," Scoville said. "I would have liked to marry her and give my son a family, but she wasn't interested." He stopped pacing and stood at the window next to the front door. "She was only twenty-eight." His silhouette expressed sadness beyond words, but when he turned, his face reflected his mind. Emotions weighed in; he managed them all. If shock was still operating—and it was—the capacity to think clearly and to endure hovered, ready to slip back into action when the trauma wore off.

Geraldine admired him for wanting to take action; for having an idea where his son and the killer were. It didn't seem to have occurred to him that the boy might not be alive. She admired him for that, too. Her nausea quieted. Her numb hands rested in her lap.

"So if you disappear for a while, where will you be?" she asked.

But he only shook his head as he prepared to leave. "I've been investigating crime for twenty-five years," he said, and offered no further explanation.

9

The telephone wakened the Dentons at 12:30 a.m. They were both old enough to fear a call in the middle of the night. In the early years of the twentieth century, when their ideas about the world were being formed, people did not call at 12:30 a.m. unless there was a death or an accident.

"Who is it?" Maggie asked, alarmed and fumbling with the bedside lamp.

Humboldt motioned for her to stop talking and leaned closer into the receiver. "Who?" he said, supporting his weight on one elbow and shielding his eyes from the lamplight. By now Maggie was sitting up against the pillows. He shifted and turned. "It's Scoville," he mouthed. Maggie inhaled sharply. The delicate skin around her eyes was still puckered from sleep, but the eyes themselves were wide.

"Yeah," he said into the phone. "Yeah." And yet again, "Yeah." Scoville did not characteristically speak rapidly, but Humboldt had to say, "Slow down, Jim. Slow down." Then, "Uh-huh. Uh-huh. Okay."

When he finally hung up, he scooted against the pillows Maggie had arranged against the headboard. There was no thought of turning off the light.

"He's awful upset," he said, reaching for Maggie's hand on the bedspread.

She leaned close and kissed him gently on the lips. "You're not going out, are you?"

"Scoville is beside himself," Humboldt said. "No, I'm not going out. I told him to come to the house."

"I didn't hear you invite him."

"I didn't exactly invite him. I said 'uh-huh' when he asked if he could come."

"Poor man," Maggie said, shaking her head slowly. "I wonder if he'll want something to eat."

"Doubt it. You don't need to get up."

"Do you really think I can fall back asleep?" She pivoted and swung her legs out from under the covers. "Are you sure I can't fix something for the two of you?"

"No. I'll make him a stiff drink. Stay in bed."

"Don't let him drink on an empty stomach," she said for lack of any other advice. "He has to drive home."

"He can stay in the guest room if he needs to," said Humboldt. "Go back to sleep, Mags." She swung her legs back under the covers and watched her husband bustle from bureau to closet.

"Call me if the two of you get hungry."

"I can rustle up something," Humboldt said. "Scrambled eggs and toast."

Having exhausted the subject of food, Maggie grew quiet. "I wonder," she said in a drowsy tone, "if he had any sort of relationship with the dead woman. With his mother's caretaker."

"Scoville? Nah," said Humboldt. "He's a confirmed bachelor."

Her eyes flew open. "You don't have to be married to have a relationship." "Yeah, well, maybe," he said on his way out the door.

In the living room he switched on all the lights before going into the kitchen and turning on more. In spite of what he'd told Maggie, he opened the refrigerator door and moved a few Tupperware containers about. Finding what he wanted, he peeled a boiled egg at the sink and shook salt over one end. While he chewed, he looked out the window and gazed across the Pacific, its sudsy fringe glowing white in the moonlight. In this moment of solitude, before any knock on the door, before any encounter with Scoville's agony, his defenses broke down. He coughed hard-boiled egg into the sink. Decades ago his baby daughter had died. Her birthday was June 24th. Forty-five years old this year. If she'd lived. But that was just it. For him, for Maggie, she would always live, just as the three who'd survived still lived.

There was a knock on the door. When he opened it to Scoville, he decided against taking the time to mix a strong drink. The man looked as if he needed something right away. Humboldt ushered him straight to the swivel chair and opened the third bottle of beer for the day. This time he wouldn't bother pouring it into a glass.

"Turn on the TV," the detective said. But the only thing Humboldt could find was a test pattern.

"Concentrate on that," Humboldt said wryly, and Scoville's dry smile made Humboldt think the man might be more mentally organized than he appeared with his eyes wild and his hair, usually well parted and brushed, as rough as a bird's nest.

After a few minutes in the chair, rocking a little, turning now and then, Scoville said he didn't need the test pattern any longer; he thought he could focus his mind without outside support. "In fact," he said, swiveling toward Humboldt who now sat in the recliner keeping a hand on his bottled beer and a watchful eye on Scoville, "I'm feeling a hell of a lot better. I lost it alone in my apartment."

"Yeah, well, we can all use a good friend now and then."

"Glad you're here on the cliff." The quiet statement reassured Humboldt, though the next one undermined the effect: "I'm leaving on a short trip."

"Oh?" Humboldt took a swallow of beer. "Where to?"

"I'll let you know when I get there," said Scoville.

"Portland?"

"Not known," said Scoville.

"When will you be back?"

"I don't have a plan right now. This is an exploratory trip."

"You want company?"

"Nope."

"Maggie wanted to cook something for you," Humboldt said.

"Maggie's a good woman," said Scoville. They sat in silence for a while.

"Where did you say you were going?" Humboldt asked, and they both smiled.

With his feet on the floor, Scoville stabilized himself while leaning as far back as the mechanism of the chair allowed. "Water seeks its own level," he murmured.

Humboldt cocked his head to one side. "A riddle," he said. "Meaning what?" Scoville didn't explain.

"You have ties to the state prison," said Humboldt. "I guess you have some information."

Scoville didn't confirm or deny.

"Somebody there knows where the guy is," Humboldt said.

He'd gone too far. Scoville stood up from the leather chair and left it rocking on its own. "Good of you to let me drop in."

"Let me give you a thermos of coffee to take with you," Humboldt said.

"Appreciate it," said Scoville.

Later, Scoville shook hands in the doorway and stepped out onto the deck. As the detective climbed down the outside staircase leading to the driveway, Humboldt experienced a sudden, young man's desire for adventure. But he couldn't leave Maggie alone while he traipsed north on some doubtful quest. And he wasn't a young man. Anyway, his desire was irrelevant: Scoville would not permit him to ride along.

At the foot of the steps the detective turned and waved up to Humboldt. The only thing he'd said yes to all evening was the thermos he now carried to the Chevrolet and set in the empty passenger seat.

10

An hour after Humboldt had climbed back into bed, the Dentons were roused by another phone call. A sudden April storm had whipped in from the ocean, rattling the windows and flinging rain against the glass.

"What in the world?" Maggie murmured on the third ring. Lying half-awake after the strange night, entwined together, they brought their slow love-making to an end. In the darkness Humboldt rolled over, felt for the phone, and lifted the receiver. Maggie remained still, eyes closed, listening.

There was a silence while Humboldt strained to hear. "Can you speak up? We've got a storm coming off the pond." Then, "Say again? Where did he call from?

"What time?"

Silence. "Yeah, he was here. 'Till about 2:00."

More silence. "I would recommend you go to work today, like usual, Geraldine. Scoville wouldn't want your help." Then, "He doesn't want anyone's help."

Silence. "Yeah, I agree with you on that."

He said good-bye and hung up.

"What do you agree with Geraldine about?" Maggie asked without opening her eyes.

"Arithmetic."

Her eyelids fluttered.

"I agree with her that if he left our house at 2:00 a.m. and just now called her, that he could be an hour north of here."

"He didn't say he was going north," Maggie pointed out. "You were the one who mentioned Portland."

"You're pretty well informed, Mrs. Denton. You weren't eavesdropping, were you?"

"Well, I have to be alert. You're apt to jump in the car and try to follow him."

Humboldt lay back against his wife. Eventually he felt

her fall asleep and wished he could, too, but his mind was on Scoville out there, probably on Highway 1, crawling along the rim of the Pacific, the only car for miles in a storm at three in the morning.

He stared into the darkness and tried to enter the recesses of Scoville's mind. Alone, without the accustomed support of the Sheriff's Office, he must be feeling severely tested. The car's headlights would be inadequate in the lashing rain. Windshield wipers falling further and further behind. His childhood home a warm, sad memory he couldn't afford to indulge in. A kidnapped child being hauled around by a violent man or, worse, not being hauled around but tied up somewhere in a damp basement, crying for his mother...

Humboldt shivered and wondered how well Scoville knew the kidnapped child and mother. Maggie liked to speculate: she'd been speculating when she said something about a relationship between Scoville and the woman in Portland. He sat on the edge of the bed and looked over to see if his wife was still asleep. She was pretty good at speculation, but he, himself, had never heard Scoville say anything about a woman, much less a woman who rented rooms in his childhood home and looked after his aged mother.

Without waking Maggie, he moved his feet about on the carpet, feeling for slippers. Carrying his robe to the living room, he stood at the window for a while, perversely enjoying the whistle and thump of the storm on the other side of the glass until he thought about Scoville out there in the weather and turned away. Pushing his arms through the sleeves of his robe and tying the belt, he walked to the recliner in the corner. What motivates a man to be a criminal investigator? he wondered. To live alone in an apartment in a little town at the edge of the continent? To set out alone, without backup, on a two-lane highway at the edge of the ocean? To engage in the briefest of human contacts before driving north in the middle of the night?

Humboldt sat down, worried. Worried but proud to have

been Scoville's brief human contact. And puzzled. The man was in a fragile state. Unlike Humboldt himself, Scoville was used to being on the good side of the law. Humboldt adjusted the lever on the recliner and lay back as far as the chair would go. As a young man, a boy, really, he'd been forced to hold together when crime touched him personally. Hell, didn't just touch him. Originated with him. He'd stolen some money from a filling station on his way to California. Far from his home in Vermont, unable to find work as a mechanic, broke, he'd gotten off the Greyhound bus in Battle Mountain, Nevada and stolen $40 from the till in a Phillips 66 station where the owner had just turned him down before leaving his desk to fill up a black Oldsmobile at the pump. Humboldt could still see that black Oldsmobile. The driver had money. The station owner had money. Everybody had money except him. He'd been caught before he could get out of town and ended up in the county jail because he was one year too old to be considered a juvenile.

He hadn't called home for help. The judge let him off with a slap on the wrist and community service. He got back on the Greyhound, found a job greasing cars in Reno, and screwed up one more time—bad friends, a drunken party, a stolen car, then hiding from the law at his uncle's sheep ranch in Wyoming for a few months—before he found himself in Los Angeles, this time selling cars. He'd bought a suit and stayed on the right side of the law. More important, he'd met Maggie who wouldn't put up with his shenanigans.

11

In the bedroom Maggie listened for her husband in the kitchen making coffee or opening the refrigerator; even creeping down the back stairs to the garage and the car. He'd done it before, gone off to help a friend in the middle of the night in spite of her pleading. She scooted over to his side of the bed that had grown cold and picked up the receiver. There was just enough gray light for her to see the dial. Squinting, she put in a call. With her hand shielding her mouth she said quietly, "Geraldine?"

"I can't hear you," Geraldine said. "Is that you, Jim?"

"It's Maggie."

"Oh. Maggie." Geraldine fell silent, probably wishing she hadn't said "Jim."

"Do you know where he is?" Maggie asked. "The phone's been ringing off the hook."

"No. Has he called you?" Geraldine asked.

"Just once, before he came up and talked to Humboldt. Then he left, and then you called." She plumped the pillow behind her. "Do you have any information about him?"

"No information," Geraldine said. "He called but wouldn't tell me where he was."

"We don't know where he is, either," said Maggie. "I just hope Humboldt doesn't go out looking for him."

Geraldine remained silent.

"You're not going out to look for him, are you?" said Maggie.

Geraldine hesitated. "It would be silly," she said.

"Yes. In this storm and not knowing where he is."

"He must have called from a pay phone," said Geraldine. "There aren't that many pay phones on Coast Highway between here and the Oddfellow River."

"Or farther," said Maggie.

"If I drove a little way north and looked for a pay phone and his car—"

"You make it sound like a nice ride," Maggie interrupted. "Look out the window. We have a storm going on."

"It's almost light," Geraldine said weakly.

"I would recommend against leaving home now." Maggie waited for the younger woman to say something. "Just what did he tell you?" she finally asked.

The conversation changed, like a power source that kicks in:

two women plugged into confidential talk about a man. "He sounded disturbed," said Geraldine. "He had to be disturbed to call at all. He said he wanted someone to know he had useful information and that he hadn't told the Sheriff's Office because it was a delicate situation; it was work for just one person. Then he said he was sorry he called and to forget what he'd said."

"As if you could forget a call like that," said Maggie.

"That's what I told him. When I started to ask questions and offered to help, he hung up."

"Just hung up?"

"Well, he's a polite man," Geraldine said. "He thanked me and then hung up. And he said he didn't know why he was so indiscreet—he's already told me that once before—and then he hung up."

"It sounds like he hung up more than once," Maggie said.

"Just once," said Geraldine.

"He's trying to handle this thing alone."

"I'm afraid so."

"You're not going to try to help him, are you?"

"Look, Mags. I'll talk to you later. Don't worry. I'll be in touch."

"Don't worry!" said Maggie, then muffled her voice again. "I'm worried about Scoville and I'm worried about my husband. He's just apt to set off north and get himself involved in something dangerous." She paused, listening for agreement that the situation was dangerous. "It's dangerous, Geraldine. Right? You agree that it's dangerous?"

"Yes, it's dangerous," said Geraldine, and wouldn't say anything more. Maggie hung up the phone, got out of bed, and went to the living room where Humboldt lay snoring in the corner. Freshly distraught over her role in the crime—she was the cause of it—she returned to the bedroom and made the bed. In the bathroom she stood in a hot shower for several minutes, debating what to say to her husband when, inevitably, he decided to go looking for Scoville. She knew him, and she knew he wouldn't be able to stay at home or be satisfied with the daily trip to the post office, the morning stop at the coffee shop, a drive up the Chetco for farm produce. She turned off the water, reached for a towel, and groaned with guilt. Of course she would go with him.

12

In pleasant weather Geraldine had seen surf lifted by the breeze and carried from the water's edge up to the highway. On such days, bubbling froth, like clean dishwater from the ocean, blew and bounced across the asphalt high above the beach. But now there were no bubbles. Just the driving rain that overpowers windshield wipers, and a wet darkness working against everyone and everything; nothing like the amiable light off the Pacific on a fine day.

She slowed at the first of three outposts that punctuated the lonely stretch of highway between Brooks Beach and the Oddfellow River. Beyond the Oddfellow was the Salmon, and beyond that, the Outlaw. Every thirty miles was another river coming down from the Siskiyous and emptying into the ocean. Humboldt had told her about the bridges built as World War II approached, replacing the old ferries with a rapid means of transportation for any wartime materiel that might be needed against a Japanese attack.

No worn Chevrolet was parked near the solitary gas pump and pay phone in front of the first café. Its "Open" sign in the window that someone had forgotten to turn off blinked a bright welcome; the café was anything but open. Pressing the accelerator, Geraldine re-entered the highway. The narrow band of oncoming daylight she'd relied on a few miles back had disappeared. If anything, the storm was worse than when she'd left home. Passing the Dentons' road, she'd looked up longingly, as if she could see their friendly lights. She'd almost smelled Maggie's coffee and breakfast. How she loved the Dentons and their home, especially now that she couldn't go there because she'd set off on this dark drive that was no one's idea but her own.

Mile after mile unraveled behind her with no sign of Scoville. At the next stopping place, another café, this one with lights burning and a pickup truck sitting at the gas pump, she turned and parked in front of the plate glass window with the flickering neon beer sign. She hurried out of the car and ducked into the cement-block building, thoroughly wetted by the downpour. After accepting coffee at the counter from a slow-moving waitress who'd been exchanging a few tired words with the cook in the kitchen, Geraldine rotated her bar stool toward the door and stared out at the rain bouncing off her car. "Eggs over easy and rye toast," she said, rotating back to face the waitress.

"We got any rye?" the woman called over her shoulder. She and her uniform looked as if they'd been up all night.

"No rye," said the aging male cook whose straggling gray hair was without any kind of restraint. Here on the isolated Southern Oregon coast it wouldn't be surprising to find rules not followed, state laws about hygiene in restaurants unobserved, federal laws about almost anything ignored.

"Whatever bread you have," said Geraldine. While the eggs sizzled in the kitchen and the toaster on the pass-through shelf popped, she twisted her stool back toward the plate glass and stared at the pickup by the gas pump, fantasizing that the murderer and little boy were inside; that, before daylight, they'd crept out onto the highway from a hole in an Oregon cliff to get a little gas, a little food, and would soon be nosing up some side road bordered by dirt banks where exposed tree roots clutch the earth like gnarled toes and mini-watercourses break through, washing mud onto the road... She should have followed

Humboldt and Maggie's advice: don't leave home in this storm. What had she hoped to accomplish? It was her own anxiety, her own loneliness, her own empty life that had propelled her to drive north in a blinding storm.

Finishing her breakfast, soaking up egg yolk with a half piece of toast in an impolite but satisfying practice that she indulged in when eating alone, she felt someone come up behind her and hesitate at the counter two stools away. She glanced to the right.

"I saw your car out front," said Scoville. Laying his felt hat on an empty stool to his right, a brown, wide-brimmed hat for keeping off rain, he slid onto the stool next to her. "What are you doing out in this weather?"

Stalling, she wiped egg from the corners of her mouth and drained the last of her coffee. "I ignored all advice. And may I ask what you're doing here?"

Disregarding her false hauteur, he glanced at the waitress and cook, who weren't listening. "Looking for a dangerous man," he said quietly, "with a little boy who doesn't belong to him."

Geraldine dropped the pose. "Do you know where they are?"

"I think so," said Scoville. On his way to the restroom he spoke to the waitress busy filling sugar jars at the end of the counter. "I'll have coffee, scrambled eggs, and toast." His face relaxed. "Second breakfast."

"Was he here earlier?" Geraldine asked out of his hearing.

The waitress nodded. "We open at 5:00."

When he came back, Geraldine asked if he was on his way home. For the first time he betrayed fatigue. "I don't know." Rubbing his eyes with thumb and finger of one hand, he added, "I think I'd better keep going toward Brooks Beach."

She frowned. "Why do you say that?"

"Well, you're here."

"What does that mean?" she flared.

"Because anything I might try to do has to be done alone."

"I can leave you alone," she said, sounding sullen. He and

the Dentons were right. She should have stayed home.

"I'm not sure why I called you," he said.

"Stress," she said.

He rubbed his eyes again. "Maybe."

She leaned toward him. "Are you going to tell the Sheriff you know where they are?"

He pulled his hand away from his face and looked at her with cold detachment. "Who said I know where they are?"

"I thought you just did."

He leaned back as the waitress slid his breakfast plate in front of him. "I don't know for sure where they are. I drove north past the Outlaw River, but I think the road I want is closer to home." He picked up his fork, then laid it down again. "I appreciate your help, but too many people will scare the guy. It's a risk to the boy."

The plate glass window at the front of the restaurant rattled in a sudden gust. Scoville pushed his plate away. "Can't eat."

"I'm going back to Brooks Beach," Geraldine said impulsively and laid money on the counter. Outside, rain battered her burning face. She felt useless and exposed. Over-eagerness to help had showed Scoville and the Dentons how lonely she was; how empty. And, too, how selfish, thinking of herself. She slipped at the edge of a puddle and almost fell. Scoville reached out and steadied her. In the rain, she hadn't heard him behind her. His hand at her elbow increased her confusion. He held the door until she was behind the wheel. Without looking up, she nodded curt thanks. As soon as he'd closed the door, she turned the key in the ignition and drove off.

13

She'd driven several miles when she saw in the rear view mirror that Scoville, who had been behind her since she left the café, was turning onto a side road. Since he must know she was driving ahead of him, she wondered why he let her see him turn. She pulled off at a lookout point about a half mile south of where his Chevrolet had left the road and considered the options. Perhaps he wanted her to turn around and come back to where he was. More likely he would want her to continue south. Certainly the Dentons would want her to continue south. She, herself, believed she should continue south. Checking her mirrors, she made a U-turn north and cautiously retraced Coast Highway to where she'd seen him turn.

She nosed along the gravel road and found, too late to resurrect any dignity, that he was waiting for her on a muddy shoulder. While she hesitated beside him, windshield wipers flailing, he got out of his car, opened her passenger door, and ducked in out of the rain. His jacket and hat filled her car with the scent of wool working to repel water and of wet pine needles, wet sticks, wet forest. He reached over the front seat and laid his hat in back.

"You again," he said.

She pulled ahead and parked in front of his car. "Were you waiting for me?" she asked.

"No."

"Why are you here?" she said.

"I was deciding what to do."

"Have you decided?"

"I'm deciding." For a moment the rain stopped. In the silence, cedar and redwood seemed to take a deep breath before the sky opened again and released another reservoir. Geraldine wondered how much rain it would take to wash away a car and a gravel road.

"What am I going to do with you?" Scoville said.

I don't know, she thought.

"I can't let you go back to Brooks Beach knowing what you know."

"What do I know?"

"Where I am."

"Didn't you see me ahead of you?"

What she wanted to ask was *why are you here? What now? What's next?* She waited for him to say something. He might not be thinking straight, but as far as she could tell, he was alert. Steely.

"You're in danger," he said. "I'm looking for a murderer."

"But I want to help," she said.

He studied her face. "Stay here, then. If I don't come back in half an hour, go to the Sheriff's Office. If someone else comes down the road, leave." In a single gesture he turned off the ignition and reached for her hand. Drawing close, he put his arm around her and rested his cheek on the crown of her head. She turned her face into the damp wool of his jacket, slipped one arm behind his back, one around his waist. After a few minutes they pulled apart.

"Drive on down this road," he said. "There's an empty shed."

She didn't ask how he knew.

When they reached the shed he directed her to park behind it. The gray, distressed walls of the old building leaned eastward from years of enduring wind off the ocean.

Scoville reached around for his hat and opened the passenger door. "The trailer is about a quarter of a mile in," he said. "I'll be back with my son," and he left the car before she could ask questions. He walked toward a bend in the road ahead. When his lean silhouette with the brown, brimmed hat disappeared, Geraldine sat back, stunned by the fact of where she was; where he was. Fear of criminality released itself in a rush and she breathed too fast for comfort.

Slanting rain against her face, against her hands on the steering wheel, helped. She kept the window lowered, trying to breathe slowly, listening for any sound that might come from wherever Scoville was. She wanted to be useful but didn't know what might help; what might hinder.

14

Set against a muddy bank at the road's dead end, the aged trailer looked abandoned. Circling behind it, Scoville climbed and reached a grove of mature alders. He was grateful for bad weather and a dark sky; grateful that, in the storm, seeing and hearing would be as hard for anyone else as it was for him. From under a dripping tree, he studied the trailer's two back windows. One was covered by an uneven curtain, striped, the other by a torn paper shade. His inclination was to wait as long as necessary until he was sure this was the right road and trailer. He trusted the information he'd received, but criminal activity, by its very nature, is unreliable. Good information one minute can turn bad the next.

The trailer rocked once. Someone inside had moved; more than just a turn in bed from stomach to back. More like getting out of bed. Getting out of bed and then just standing there, because the trailer was once more still. Scoville watched and waited. Beyond the tree's drip line, rainwater thudded into the absorbent forest floor and sprang noisily off the metal roof and sides of the trailer.

Something inside animated the trailer once again. And had he imagined the torn shade moving? More stillness. No shiver of the trailer; no stirring of a window covering. Five minutes passed. By giving Geraldine thirty minutes, he'd given himself fifteen. Assuming she followed directions—and she didn't seem too good at following directions—he would have to leave the trailer site with his son very soon in order to get back to the shed before she left.

It didn't occur to him that his son might not be in the trailer. Might not be alive.

So intently did he wait for another tremor that the entire woods seemed to be watching and waiting with him.

Then the door at the front of the trailer slammed closed.

Immediately he was scrambling down the bank, sliding, grabbing at tree roots. Running around the corner of the trailer with his revolver out, he shouted at the man who was just becoming aware that a figure in brown hat and jacket was almost upon him; that before he could draw a weapon of his own, or a breath, he was being rushed by someone who weighed less but was more violent than he was.

When Scoville had shoved the stunned man into the trailer, face against aluminum, he frisked back pants pockets; front pants pockets; jacket pockets, front and sides. Belt line. Thighs. Ankles.

"What d'you—"

"Shut up!" said Scoville. The lean, sinewy strength in his arms and legs was hidden by clothing, but the speed and certainty weren't. From his back pocket he retrieved handcuffs, locked the man's wrists behind him, and ordered him inside the trailer where he pushed him face-down onto the dirty carpet. Scoville was distracted by a child's cry, and his hesitant step into the back of the trailer gave the man time to slither on his belly and kick the hall door shut. Scoville whirled. A glimpse into a bedroom where his son sat tied to a chair registered swiftly.

From inside the hallway Scoville turned the doorknob and kicked against the door and body braced on the living room side. The cheap wood splintered and he leaped forward, face grazed by a jagged piece of plywood.

Breathing noisily, the man was getting to his knees when Scoville landed on him. A fist to the side of the face; fist to the eye, temple, ear; fists that Scoville couldn't control. He finally rocked back on his heels when he felt the man go slack. Bracing his hands against his knees, he stood and walked back through the splintered doorway to his son sitting beside a window, crying like a small animal, the sound weak and thin. On the floor beside the chair, a plate of food scraps held rat droppings. The little boy's pants were saturated.

"Robbie, it's me." Scoville's voice cracked as he cut the ropes with a pocket knife. "Robbie, remember me? You're all right now. We're all right now." He continued to murmur phrases he wasn't aware of—"We're leaving now, stand on the chair, let me hold you"—and he stepped carefully through the jagged plywood, pushing his son's head into his own shoulder to avoid sharp fragments of ruined door.

"Daddy," the little boy said, and the father was stunned. The child had never called him anything but Jim. Outside, he bent to pick up his hat that had fallen on the ground. The rain pounded on him and on the child as they moved fast around the trailer and toward Geraldine's car a quarter of a mile down the gravel road.

The sound of running steps came up behind him and Scoville turned to face the man he'd put in state prison. Somehow he'd gotten free of the handcuffs. At a disadvantage, Scoville set the boy on his feet and pushed him to the side of the road where the child silently landed on his back, too weak, or too cagey, to cry.

The man shot Scoville in the chest. When he was sure he'd killed him, he ran back to the trailer and started up an engine. Jumping into first gear, spitting gravel, his truck careened around the corner and entered the road. He was intent on running over Scoville, but the detective wasn't where he'd fallen. Swearing, the driver swerved toward the ditch where he saw the body and the little boy sitting beside it. Scoville's bullet pinged off a wheel well. The Brooks Beach killer stepped on the accelerator and raced up the road as he fled through the rain toward Coast Highway.

15

Geraldine saw the truck hurtle by, headlights off, hard rain mauling the dented pickup. Even in the rain she saw and smelled the tailpipe's black smoke. Hunched over the wheel, the driver looked neither right nor left. She waited a minute to see if he would come back, then decided she couldn't wait any longer. As she pulled around the shed, her tires spun in the mud. Praying she wouldn't get stuck, she rocked the car back and forth, quick forward, quick back; played with the steering wheel; tried not to dig the same trench. Finally the car shot forward. When the tires touched gravel, she turned left in the direction Scoville had walked. Her heartbeat was faster than the windshield wipers but she noticed the strength and steadiness of her hands on the wheel. Reaching the bend in the road, she methodically searched the edge of the woods, right and left.

Ahead, the road ended. Momentarily focused on a trailer set against a muddy bank, she almost missed the movement at the side of the road. First she saw the child, then Scoville, and braked hard. She pushed down on the door handle, leaned against the door, and leaped onto the road.

"Jim!"

The little boy began crying, a sound as rough and gravelly as the road, before he abruptly stopped and drained away into a whimper. Geraldine tried to reassure the child by cupping his head for a moment, then knelt in the rain beside Scoville. "Jim," she whispered. "Let go of the gun, Jim." She was afraid to take it from him; she could not control it. His hand loosened, and he laid it aside.

A fine mist of blood came out in a wheezing sound as he tried to speak. Geraldine bent low over him, but he couldn't make himself understood. She picked up the child and set him in the passenger seat.

"Stay here. Stay here."

In the driver's seat again, she moved the car a few inches forward until the back door was even with where Scoville lay. She turned off the engine, put on the hand brake, then jumped out. Kneeling again beside him, she said, "I'll pull you onto the back seat, Jim."

The blood beginning to stain the front of his jacket in a slow seep frightened her. Medically, she was incompetent and did not even unbutton the coat to look at the wound. She repositioned him on the gravel. Crawling into the opposite side of the car, stretching out on her stomach the length of the back seat, she reached down and heaved him toward her by his armpits. She was appalled to see his head fall back and hit the bottom edge of the door. He was so pale. His eyelids fluttered once. She pulled again, and tugged. Tugged horribly. She could not imagine the damage she was doing. Backing out the door, rushing around the car to where he half-hung from the back seat, she pushed and lifted, bent his legs at the knees until he looked like a burial figure in some ancient culture. She longed for him to draw a deep, free breath.

Closing the back door, she returned to the driver's seat. Trying to smile at his little boy beside her, she drove to the trailer, made a wide U-turn, and came back down the road. Before she stopped at the highway, she tried to pull the little boy close, but he remained rigidly upright.

She turned north. They were closer to the town of Oddfellow, where there was a hospital, than they were to Brooks Beach. Though she hardly believed she was this far north on Highway 1, she couldn't quite disbelieve it, either. She suspended all but the most mechanical of thoughts. Soon they would be at the hospital. Soon Scoville would be cared for and comfortable. Soon he would regain life. Soon his little child would be clean, warm, fed, and sleeping in her arms.

16

The Dentons were preparing to drive north in search of Scoville when the telephone rang. Humboldt answered. "Where are you?"

He turned in the swivel chair, the coiled cord swaying between the hand set and telephone resting on the end table. He exchanged a look with Maggie.

"All right. Uh-huh. Okay. We're on our way."

Maggie asked no questions. It was almost as if she'd heard what her husband heard. "We're driving north, aren't we?" she said.

He nodded. "To Oddfellow."

Two hours later when they'd crossed the frothing Oddfellow River downstream from the town, it had stopped raining. As the still-gleaming, still-slick highway ran inland, trees on both sides of the highway dripped onto the pavement. At intervals Humboldt turned on the wipers to clear the windshield.

Oddfellow Community Hospital, a geographically isolated weapon against illness and death, was housed in a one-story red-brick building just north of the river. Its banks full from the Siskiyous' spring thaw, the river thundered toward coastal rocks before throwing itself with its baggage of swirling sticks and logs into the Pacific.

Seated in an orange plastic chair in the waiting room shared by the emergency room and main wing of the little hospital, Geraldine kept an eye out for Humboldt and Maggie. Fed and bathed, Scoville's son slept in her arms. After an interview by child protective services from the County office, an aide in the pediatric ward had found short pants, shirt, and soft jacket that more or less fit the boy.

"Hello," Geraldine said in a tired, flat voice when she saw the Dentons come through the double doors. Putting out her hand to each of them in turn, she held on, not wanting to let them go. Maggie sat down beside her. Humboldt remained standing.

"Is this the child who was kidnapped?" Maggie asked, focusing the attention of an experienced mother and grandmother on the little boy.

Geraldine looked at the Dentons with an intimate, stunned expression. "Scoville's son."

They were speechless. "He has a son?" Humboldt finally said. Geraldine nodded.

"Was Jim married to the boy's mother?" Maggie whispered, too surprised to look at her husband or to even think of saying *I told you so*.

"They weren't married," said Geraldine.

Humboldt said abruptly, "What's the medical report on Scoville?"

"He's critical," said Geraldine. "He's in surgery." They spoke in low voices, not wanting to wake the child. Mostly they were shielding the little boy and themselves from knowing how close he was to being an orphan.

"What is his name?" said Maggie, reaching out, not quite touching the sleeping child's hair.

"I don't know. He's three-and-a-half," Geraldine said.

Humboldt dropped into the empty chair on the other side of Geraldine. The three watched a nurse take the blood pressure of an old woman who had walked in alone. The smell of a hospital's daily struggle against filth and infection wafted into the waiting room in spite of closed doors to the emergency room and sick wards. Once the three were used to being together in these new surroundings, they began talking in low voices, stumbling over each other, speaking almost at the same time.

"How did you find Scoville?"

"He found me. In the café not too far from here—"

"But the trailer—"

"South of here, closer to Oddfellow than—"

"Otherwise you would have taken him to Brooks Beach. Where did—"

Maggie asked a clear question that took precedence: "What happened to him?"

"He was shot," said Geraldine. "He was bleeding in the chest. I—"

"God," breathed Maggie.

"How did you get him in the car?" said Humboldt.

Geraldine explained, and, being careful not to jar the sleeping child, put one hand over her face when she talked about how Scoville's head had hit the door frame. She described the pickup she'd seen, and the man hunched over the wheel.

"Did he see you?" Maggie asked.

"No, but I was afraid he would come back."

"He'll have to stop for gas," said Humboldt.

"I forgot to call the Sheriff," Geraldine said absently.

"Humboldt called him," said Maggie. Involuntarily she reached toward the child again but at the last minute prevented herself from waking him. "Are you going to stay here at the hospital?"

Geraldine looked surprised. What she would do next hadn't occurred to her. "I don't know." All three looked down at the sleeping child. "What should I do?"

"Keep the boy with you," said Humboldt. "You and Maggie can take him back to Brooks Beach. I'll stay with Scoville."

"I have the keys to his car," said Geraldine. "Somebody needs to get his car."

"You can drop me off at the car and I'll follow you home," said Maggie.

"No, you won't," said Humboldt. "No one but the Sheriff is entering that road. He's probably there now."

"But I have the car keys," Geraldine repeated.

"Keep them," said Humboldt. "Take my word for it. They'll get the car back to Brooks Beach."

The three remained seated, enervated, with no incentive to move. A doctor came out from the glass doors. "Mr. Scoville's visitors?"

"That's us," said Humboldt. "How is he?"

"I understand he doesn't have family in the area," said the doctor.

"That's right. We're his closest friends," said Humboldt.

"He's in the recovery room," said the doctor. "The outlook is cautious. We removed the bullet and repaired the lung. He's on a ventilator now." He scanned their faces. "People recover from these kinds of injuries. It was a small-caliber gun. The main danger now is collateral damage. Clots in the leg. Pulmonary embolus. Pneumonia. We'll try to minimize those things."

"Is he conscious?" said Geraldine. "Can we see him?"

"He's conscious, but we've got him on some pretty strong painkillers. He can have visitors later today." He looked at the little boy in Geraldine's lap.

"This is his son," Geraldine said. "I'll be watching him until his father is out of the hospital. There are no other relatives besides an invalid grandmother."

"We're helping," put in Maggie.

"Back-up," said Humboldt.

After the doctor returned through the glass doors, the three sat in silence, separately processing the information.

"You might as well start back," Humboldt said after a while.

"Wait until the boy wakes up," said Geraldine. "I'm so grateful that you're here and …"

She couldn't finish the sentence.

17

While Geraldine and Maggie drove south toward Brooks Beach with Scoville's son in the front seat between them, Humboldt prowled the hospital waiting room, wondering how he was going to kill the hours between now and the time he might be allowed to visit Scoville. The Sheriff's Office would be investigating the road and trailer where Scoville had been shot; Humboldt had forwarded the information he'd gained from Geraldine's phone call early this morning. They would also be contacting law enforcement both north and south of where the killer's truck had entered Coast Highway.

But sheriffs' departments, like city police, were strung thin up and down the Southern Oregon coast, burdened with crimes of the poor, and with the misdemeanors of hitch-hikers trudging along the shoulder of Highway 1, their dirty packs higher than their heads, lower than their knees. Illegal marijuana crops and sales attracted crime. The spotty economy was a source of unemployment and layoffs for everyone, including sheriffs' departments.

Even Scoville, investigator for the County District Attorney, had little respect for law enforcement here on the coast. Though he built the cases for Superior Court prosecutions, too often, he'd privately told Humboldt, felonies were pled down to misdemeanors. It was cheaper to let a defendant slip away than to try him.

Humboldt stepped outside, hands in his pockets, head bent against a strong wind blowing in from the ocean.

Unlike the landscaped entrance, here against the hospital's back walls, patches of weeds and packed dirt won out over flowers and shrubs. Farther back, lined up against the metal fence whose base was choked with swaying weeds, its gate padlocked, were garbage dumpsters labeled Bio-Hazard and Medical Waste. Circling the hospital, his hair and pants cuffs blowing, he tried not to look interested in what was behind the windows. Sick rooms, nurses' stations, a small cafeteria passed in a haze. He changed direction and circled the other way. On this second circuit, he shot frank glances into the sickrooms, hoping to find Scoville.

How, he wondered, had the detective located the killer in a remote trailer between Brooks Beach and Oddfellow? How did he know to turn down that particular road? At the house last night—was it just last night?—Scoville hadn't known where he was driving. He must have had a tip from someone in prison.

Someone who heard the killer talk about a road, a trailer on the way to Oddfellow. Someone who slipped information to Scoville. He tried to imagine an anonymous phone call to Scoville's apartment. A note under the door, maybe. A late-night knock. He shook his head sharply. He was writing a damn movie. Maggie was definitely better at speculation than he was. She'd guessed that Scoville had a relationship with the little boy's mother. It wouldn't have occurred to Humboldt that the detective had a love life in Portland, much less a son young enough to be his grandchild.

Humboldt took people at face value. In the last few hours, he'd begun to harbor a few doubts about Jim Scoville. Maggie and Geraldine were all sympathy. He, too, had a certain amount of sympathy, but why would the man lead such a secretive life? Why couldn't he just have a wife and kids like most men? Humboldt had always trusted Scoville, but now, to his sorrow, he was beginning to wonder.

You live in a bachelor apartment in town. You drink beer by yourself or with a few friends almost every evening at the same tavern. You occasionally visit an aged mother in Portland. And you do something more: you sleep with her caretaker, father a child, and come back to a little town at the edge of the continent. Five days a week you unlock your gray, single-room office on the first floor of the Courthouse and go through criminal files while your little boy in Portland wonders why he doesn't have a father like the other kids.

An ambulance pulled up the circular drive in front of Oddfellow Hospital and stopped at the Emergency Room entrance. Humboldt watched a gurney being removed. Two attendants clicked the legs and wheels into place and rolled the patient and intravenous pole through the automatic doors. Humboldt idly re-entered the waiting room. Giving a little tug to the knees of his slacks, he sat down in a molded plastic chair, bright orange. Too much orange, Humboldt thought. Trying too hard to cheer people up.

The Oddfellow Hospital wasn't soundproofed. He could hear almost everything the attendants were saying to the admissions clerk on the other side of the glass partition. Highway accident. Truck traveling north found in a wooded gully eighty miles south of Portland. No driver's license or ID of any kind. Bored and nosey, Humboldt stood up and strolled around the perimeter of the waiting room. At the glass partition he looked in at the patient on the gurney. The man was pale. His few days' growth of beard was very dark against the pallor. A flash of light went off in Humboldt's head, an electric shock of recognition so unexpected that he almost stumbled. Yes, the same lank hair growing from a widow's peak. Cheek bones as craggy as rock. Thick eyebrows growing in a straight line, hairs straggling across what should be hairless space above the nose. Gray skin. The man looked dead.

"Truck was totaled," one of the attendants said. He looked at Humboldt through the glass; a cool, expressionless stare that meant, "What are *you* looking at?"

Humboldt walked on, weak from surprise. It was the Brooks Beach killer that Scoville had put in state prison. He went straight to the pay phone and called the Crescent County Sheriff's Office. Injured or not, in or out of the hospital, the guy was an escaped prisoner.

He finally reached dispatch and, following a long wait, a deputy who didn't seem motivated to do much more than write down information. After his report, Humboldt followed a back hallway to a modest breakfast line in the cafeteria. Only God knew how long it would take the Department to get this far north.

Returning to the waiting room with coffee and two doughnuts, he took a different orange chair. But now the scene was deserted. Nothing to watch or hear. The gurney and attendants had been absorbed into the hospital. The clock on the wall said 10:15. He chewed slowly, brought back a refill from the cafeteria, and drank it. By that time it was 10:30. Slumping in the plastic chair, he rested his chin on his chest and dozed.

When he woke, the clock said fifteen minutes to eleven. He pulled in his legs and sat up straight. Another party had entered the waiting room while he was sleeping, a family of Indians, probably from upriver: parents, a grandmother, and three kids. Every now and then they talked in low voices. Behind them, against the back wall, a man of about forty sat, doing nothing. Before another half hour passed, three more people had come through the double entrance doors and sat shifting uncomfortably in their plastic chairs.

Humboldt went outside and took another stroll around the hospital. He still couldn't find Scoville. He did, however, see the newly admitted patient in a southwest corner room being examined by a doctor with a nurse standing attentively to one side. When she saw him outside looking in, she came to the window and dropped the blinds. He ought to return to the waiting room, he thought to himself, before he gained a reputation as a peeping Tom. In the hall he paused to let the Indian family file out of the cafeteria, snacks in their hands.

Following them back to the waiting room, he returned to his chair. The single man had left. Unchanging boredom. Maggie and Geraldine and the boy had probably reached Brooks Beach by now. He wondered if Geraldine would drop Maggie off at the house or stay for a while. What would they do with the child? There was always television. The Dentons still had a toy box and child's bed left over from their youngest grandchild. Maybe Geraldine would leave the boy with Maggie.

Who, he wondered, would baby-sit when Geraldine had to work? He and Maggie? He hoped not. How long could the women improvise a life for the boy? Children need a regular schedule, friends, a family. The child's mother was dead, his father's outcome still uncertain, his grandmother in a convalescent home. Geraldine had never been a mother. He and Maggie had the time and experience to care for the boy, but

Humboldt had no incentive to act as a grandfather to someone else's child. Even more, he had no incentive for his wife to mother a young child again.

Scoville would have to get well; that was all there was to it. He went to the admissions desk behind the glass partition and asked if there was any change in Jim Scoville's condition. When the clerk said she had no information, he asked if he could visit the patient. She directed him to the nurses' station at the end of a hallway that had a blind turn. "Follow the painted red line on the floor," she said. Smells—high, professional odor of medicine mixed with the lower smell of cleansers—led him to a busy counter. Nurses and doctors bent over medical records or sat at two computer terminals, something he'd begun to notice in town at the bank and in some offices. Computers were the coming thing.

18

"They told me I could see you," Humboldt said at Scoville's bedside. Entering the room, he'd immediately looked out the window and memorized what he saw: the padlocked gate, blowing weeds, and dumpsters marked Bio-Hazard and Bio-Waste. It gave him momentary confidence: the future was manageable. Since he knew he would be taking walks around the hospital to kill time, and since he now had markers opposite the window, he'd be able to check on Scoville whenever he wanted to. The pleasure of predictability swam through his system. Scoville would pull through this emergency; his little boy would be fine; his own and Maggie's pleasant life would resume. Once the Portland mystery was solved, he would understand Scoville's actions and be able to regard him once more as a trusted friend.

Filled with the optimism inherent in his temperament,

Humboldt bent over Scoville. "They told me I could see you for a minute," he said, enunciating carefully. "I'll be coming back for short visits through the day."

Scoville opened his eyes. Humboldt saw the lack of comprehension. "It's me, Humboldt. You're in the hospital after an injury to your chest."

Slowly Scoville's eyes focused on the face before him. He made a sound. Humboldt reached for a Kleenex and wiped spittle from the corners of the cracked lips. Scoville's focus drifted before he regained it. Lifting one hand, he tried to speak. The hand fell back on the bedding.

"Your son is fine," Humboldt said. "He's with Maggie and Geraldine."

Scoville closed his eyes. When he opened them again, ten minutes had passed. Humboldt saw him look at the bright ceiling light. He doesn't know if it's day or night, Humboldt thought.

"It's almost noon, Jim," he said. Absently patting Scoville's shoulder, smoothing a wrinkle in the hospital gown—been living with Maggie too long, he thought to himself—he added, "I'll be back soon." Scoville's eyes had rolled shut again.

At the pay phone in the waiting room, Humboldt fed quarters into the coin slot. "Did you and Geraldine get home all right?" he asked Maggie.

He listened to her say all three of them were fine, they'd reached Brooks Beach around 11:00, and Geraldine and Robbie—for that was the boy's name—were staying at the house tonight. Humboldt, in turn, gave her a report on his endless day and told her he'd already gotten himself a motel room for the night. Overloaded with emergencies, he didn't mention the killer's highway accident and the ambulance that had brought the guy here to the Oddfellow Hospital.

"Geraldine can drive up tomorrow and keep you company," Maggie was saying. "She doesn't have a trial or deposition."

"You're coming, too, aren't you?"

"Somebody has to take care of Robbie," Maggie said. "Oh, Humboldt, he's such a nice little boy. He's staying in the kids' room and playing with their old toys."

Humboldt grunted into the telephone, something about not getting used to it; that Scoville was doing pretty well and would be able to take on the duties of fatherhood before long.

When he hung up the phone he'd failed to convince her to drive to Oddfellow with Geraldine the next day. Wait till Scoville is out of the woods, she'd said. Then when he sees his son, it will really mean something to him.

It'll help him more if you bring him now, he'd insisted, but Maggie disagreed. She promised to bring Robbie day after tomorrow.

Humboldt checked the coin slot for quarters and turned back to the waiting room. The man who'd been hanging about the hospital almost as long as Humboldt was back again, sitting in the far corner. Well built, with strong shoulders and upper arms, he had a face without definition. The expression was vague, as if his mind were somewhere else, probably on a sick relative. Going through magazines on a nearby table, Humboldt nodded and said, "Afternoon" without getting a response. "Long day."

Back at his seat, reading *Forest and Stream,* he grew absorbed in an article about cut-throat trout. But he could read only so long. He looked around. A nurse was pushing a youthful woman in a wheel chair out onto the circular drive where an equally young man in a station wagon waited for her. A pang, short-lived but agonizing, struck him when he saw her drawn face, jaundiced skin, bony chest. She was being released from the hospital but he knew she was deathly ill. He pitied the young couple to the point of inhaling too sharply; swallowing too quickly. He coughed and returned to his magazine where tears blurred the print.

After riffling aimlessly through pages, front to back, back to front, he stood again and walked down the hall leading to the cafeteria. He ducked in for pie and watched a game show on a TV mounted high on the wall above stacked trays. Instead of returning to the waiting room, he followed the hall toward the back of the hospital. At the door he put his hand on the bar to exit but stopped himself. The man with the strong body and vague face was at the fence. He seemed to be examining the gate. Bored, Humboldt thought. Killing time, like me. The guy stepped over to the dumpsters and examined them, too. There was something unsettling about it, almost as if he was contemplating getting in. *Don't do it*, Humboldt imagined himself saying, running across the weeds and dirt to keep the man from jumping into the bio-waste. *There are better ways to hurt yourself.* The man was strange, unfriendly, and Humboldt's mind had cooked up a strange, unfriendly scene here at the back of the hospital.

Before he went to his motel room for the night, he asked for and was granted permission to visit Scoville again.

"The doctors say you're going to be fine, Jim. You're in basic good health and you're stubborn. It's a good combination."

Scoville looked as if he wanted to smile but couldn't remember how. He lifted the same hand he'd lifted in the morning, though this time he was able to keep it aloft. "Boy?" he murmured.

"Your boy is fine," Humboldt said. "Geraldine and Maggie are taking care of him. Robbie, isn't it? That's your son's name? Robbie?"

Humboldt watched him close his eyes and struggle mentally. Then, yes, he seemed to say. Robbie. Making an effort, he reached for Humboldt and grasped his jacket sleeve at the cuff. Riveting attention on Humboldt's face, he tugged him down nearer his own level. "Not safe," he whispered.

"Don't worry, Jim," Humboldt said, without mentioning that the killer was here in the Oddfellow Hospital, tucked away in a hospital bed. "The killer, the kidnapper, was in a car accident. He totaled his truck. He's out of commission."

"Not safe," Scoville repeated.

Humboldt frowned and covered Scoville's hand with his own. "What's not safe, Jim?"

But Scoville had expended all his energy and his eyes rolled closed.

19

Outside, gray light might be either dawn or dusk. At this best of all moments, when the painkiller begins to take effect but before mental fog obscures thought, a voice whispers, "It's not safe. Tell them..." And yet, he cannot convey his thoughts. Words remain just beyond reach, like a blanket that cannot quite be grasped when the room grows too warm or too cold for comfort.

20

Maggie took pity on Humboldt and surprised him.

"I couldn't let you wander around the hospital another day all by yourself," she said when her husband, rested, shaved, and showered from a restorative night in the motel, met her at the front entrance to the hospital. Since breakfast he'd kept an eye on the double doors. When Geraldine's car had pulled up in the circular drive with Maggie and Robbie in the front seat beside her, the Oregon day didn't need to be sunny, which it was, for him to feel that all was going to be right with the world. Maggie and Geraldine entered with Robbie between them holding their hands.

"How is Scoville?" Maggie asked, leaning into her husband's hug.

"I haven't seen him yet this morning, but last night he was a little better."

Robbie looked up into the faces of the two new women in his life. Bending down, they gave him their full measure of motherly and grandmotherly attention.

"I think Robbie would like something to eat," Geraldine said. On the way to the cafeteria they passed through the waiting room where a new flux of family groups occupied the orange chairs. Once they'd served themselves in the breakfast line, they moved to a table in the center of the dining room.

"I visited Scoville's mother at the nursing home," Maggie said quietly while Robbie played with his silverware and Geraldine tucked a napkin under his chin. "I have something to tell you."

"I have some news, too," Humboldt murmured. When Robbie was out of earshot, he would tell his wife and Geraldine about the killer here in an Oddfellow Hospital bed and about Scoville's incoherent warning.

Before they'd arrived this morning, he'd taken another stroll around the hospital, past the killer's window. The guy was still alive. The Sheriff had sent a deputy from Brooks Beach with paperwork for the prisoner. And handcuffs, one for a wrist, one for the bed railing. Until now, Humboldt had never wished anyone dead, but he'd been sorry to see the body still there in its hospital bed.

While Robbie followed Geraldine to the pick-up window for their food, Maggie said, "Mrs. Scoville knows more than anyone thinks she does."

Leave it to Maggie, Humboldt thought, to get useful information in a nursing home. Uneasiness lodged in his mind as he ate his second breakfast and wondered what Jim's mother had said and whether Scoville's warning had been nothing more than drug-induced rambling.

Robbie whispered something to Geraldine who immediately turned to Humboldt.

"Can you take Robbie to the men's room?"

In the bathroom, Humboldt noted with satisfaction that the boy had been taught to use the toilet and wash his hands. He was a good kid. Without a mom now, without a dad present, he seemed well in control of himself for a three-and-a-half-year-old. As Humboldt helped Robbie zip up his khaki shorts—probably something Maggie had retrieved from a stash of clothes left over from one of the grandkids—the door to the stall behind them opened and the single guy with the vague face came out, buckling his belt. In the mirror he met Humboldt's eyes, then dropped contact to the level of the sink.

"Hi, Daniel," Robbie said, and reached up for the door handle like a confident little man.

21

Humboldt wheeled. "How do you know the boy?"

"He's got me mixed up with someone else," the man said, bending to splash water on his face. Robbie grew still as he watched the man reach for a paper towel before leaving the bathroom.

Humboldt led Robbie to the waiting room where he took an orange chair and patted a second one beside him. "Who is Daniel?" he asked as Robbie climbed up into the plastic seat. The man was nowhere in sight. Robbie didn't answer.

"You can tell me," Humboldt said. "It's important."

"He's Daniel," Robbie said.

"Who is Daniel?"

Robbie considered. "He brings Mommy... " He trailed off.

"What does Daniel bring Mommy?"

Robbie got up on his knees and looked over the back of the chair, turned around, and sat back down again. "Toys."

"What kind of toys?"

Robbie thought for a moment. A gleam of pride passed across his face. "Toys for me!" He dug in the pocket of his shorts. As he hauled out a bright red miniature racing car, he eyed the hand extended toward him and reluctantly placed his treasure on the flat surface of Humboldt's palm.

"When did Daniel give you this?"

Robbie took back the miniature car and didn't answer.

"Did he give it to you here in the hospital?"

Robbie vigorously shook his head.

"At home?"

"At home." Robbie slid off the chair and set off with a sense of purpose toward the cafeteria. Humboldt followed.

"Robbie knows a man here at the hospital," Humboldt said to Geraldine and Maggie in a pseudo-hearty voice when they'd reached the table.

"You mean your daddy?" Geraldine said.

"It's someone else," Humboldt said less heartily. "His name is Daniel." He touched Robbie's shoulder and the boy looked up at him. "When we're finished with breakfast let's go to a playroom I saw here in the hospital. There's a fish tank and a table full of Legos."

"Nice idea," said Geraldine. "Finish your breakfast and then we'll go play."

When Robbie had cleaned his plate, the four passed back through the waiting room and into the adjacent play area.

"There's a lot we don't know," Humboldt said in a low voice when Robbie had come to a stop at the Legos. The little boy pulled out the miniature car from his pocket and set it beside the plastic component parts on the shelf.

"Don't get your car mixed up with the other toys," Maggie said from across the room. Robbie shrugged as if it could never happen.

"That toy car he carries with him," Humboldt said in a low voice, "was given to him by this Daniel who's been lurking around the hospital. He knows the boy, though he says he doesn't." He described the incident in the men's room.

Geraldine leaned forward sharply. "Who is he and what's he doing here?"

"He may be here because of the automobile accident," said Humboldt. Maggie took rapid, shallow breaths as Humboldt told them about the ambulance bringing in the Brooks Beach killer from the highway. "I'm betting this Daniel is here because the killer's here."

"The killer killed Robbie's mother," said Geraldine. "She could be this Daniel's girl friend, couldn't she?" Her eyes explored a far corner of the play area. "And how did he know the killer was at the hospital?"

Humboldt, too, stared into space as he tried to imagine different scenarios.

"Maybe he saw the accident when he was driving," suggested Maggie.

"That's too much of a coincidence," said Geraldine.

Maggie hesitated. "Maybe he's here because Scoville is here."

"Why?"

"Well," Maggie said, her expression anything but certain, "maybe he was in the trailer with the killer."

Geraldine sat straighter. "God. You mean he might have seen me pulling Scoville into the back seat?" Her eyes darted about the room. "If he's a friend of the killer, he wouldn't have let me take Scoville to a hospital."

"Maybe he's not a friend," said Humboldt. "Maybe he's just pretending to be a friend."

"Why?" said Maggie.

"Money," said Humboldt. "Blackmail."

"Who would he blackmail?" said Geraldine.

"Scoville's mother?" said Maggie. "She would be sick with worry about the child. She'd pay to get him back."

"Scoville," said Geraldine. "He'd pay to find his child."

"The killer," said Humboldt. "This Daniel had information about the killer."

The three sat in urgent thought. "Scoville's mother told me about her handy-man in Portland," Maggie added after a moment. She tried to slow her breathing by holding a hand to her breast bone. "He rented a room in the house and did yard work and repairs." But the hand at the breast bone wasn't working. She was panting now. "Mrs. Scoville said the handy-man and Robbie's mother had an on-again off-again relationship."

"Daniel," Humboldt said, as if he was sure.

"Robbie's mother was playing a dangerous game," Geraldine murmured. The Dentons looked at her, surprised.

"You know about Robbie's mother?" said Humboldt.

"Slightly," Geraldine admitted.

"You need to tell what you know, Geraldine," Humboldt said. "I think the boy is in danger."

Geraldine stared at her hands. The fingernails had turned blue. Across the room, the child connected Lego after Lego with a click, then pulled them apart again. His skillful little fingers found the seams and joints he looked for. Humboldt took a step into the waiting room. Daniel—Humboldt was already calling him Daniel in his mind—was nowhere to be seen. The guy would not be seen again, Humboldt felt sure.

22

"We need to tell the Sheriff," Maggie said, coming to the doorway beside her husband and taking his hand in hers. "This is more complicated than anyone thought."

"Give me one or two more times with Scoville. He might be able to tell me something."

"Can he think clearly?" Maggie asked.

"He's getting close," said Humboldt. "He doesn't want to have law enforcement get involved yet. They'll have to work with the Portland police and—"

"And what?" said Maggie. "Scoville can't do any useful work now. We can't protect Robbie if someone wants to harm him."

They went back into the playroom and sat down beside Geraldine. But soon Humboldt was up again, taking rapid steps to the fish tank. Four carp flitted among the swaying vegetation, hiding, emerging, digging into the phony ocean floor, seeking something in the decorative gravel, never finding it. He looked at his watch.

"I'm going to see if they'll let me talk to Jim," he said. "It's 11:00."

"Let me go with you," said Geraldine.

"Why?"

Geraldine looked nonplussed. "Well, do I have to have a reason?"

"She saved his life," Maggie gently reminded her husband. "I'll watch Robbie. You two go ahead."

Humboldt and Geraldine passed through the door of the glass partition and followed the painted red line on the floor to the nurses' station. When permission had been granted, they continued toward Scoville, trying not to look into the sick rooms they passed, fighting down the low-grade panic generated by sounds and smells of the ill who remind us that, ultimately, we all lose control of our flesh and fluids.

They both stood on the same side of Scoville's bed, Geraldine slightly behind Humboldt.

"How are you, Jim?" Humboldt placed his hand on the patient's shoulder, then the upper arm.

Scoville stared.

"We're all here. Maggie, Geraldine, and I are here in the hospital. And Robbie. Your boy, Robbie. We're all here."

Scoville moved his dry lips. "Okay," he whispered, but the effort cost him because he had to cough and the cough produced pain in his chest. The cause and effect played out in his drawn face.

"Don't try to talk," said Humboldt. Geraldine stood, silent and out of Scoville's range of vision. "Just listen."

Scoville closed his eyes, then opened them again.

"Your son is fine."

"Not safe," Scoville whispered. His left hand played nervously with the edge of the sheet that was folded to the level of his upper chest. No bandage was visible.

Humboldt looked at Geraldine, then back to Scoville. "Who's Daniel?" he said.

Scoville didn't respond. He seemed not to have understood the question. Slowly he grasped Humboldt's sleeve as he had the day before, at the cuff where it was buttoned, and tugged. Humboldt bent low, obscuring Geraldine's sight line.

"Daniel," the patient whispered. "Here."

"Who is he?" Humboldt asked.

Scoville made a short, repeated motion to the side of the bed. "Here."

"He stood here?"

"Here," said Scoville.

Humboldt swallowed.

"Wants more money. Wants Robbie."

"More money?" said Humboldt. "Did you give him money?"

But Scoville didn't answer. When Humboldt stepped back, the patient saw Geraldine. He focused all his attention on her. *"Boy not safe."* Turning back to Humboldt, he said with a groan that cost him nearly everything, *"Not safe."* He seemed to fall asleep again.

While Humboldt and Geraldine quietly debated what to do next, Scoville whispered, eyes still closed, "Geraldine."

"She's right here, Jim."

"Talk. Alone."

Humboldt frowned. "You want to talk to Geraldine? Alone?"

Scoville nodded.

Humboldt hesitated, then walked out. In the doorway he glanced back at the bed and saw Scoville reach for her hand.

"Well, shit," he thought to himself. *"As if we don't have enough problems."* He returned along the painted red line. *"Scoville*

should have asked me to drive north with him yesterday morning. Should have asked me to help with the dangerous work. Whatever happened to men doing the dangerous work?"

23

"Find Daniel," Scoville whispered to Geraldine, who had moved to Humboldt's empty spot near the head of the bed.

"Who is he?" Geraldine whispered back.

"Wants Robbie. In hospital." Scoville held her hand for minutes before uttering again, "Not safe."

Geraldine withdrew her hand and laid it for a moment on Scoville's arm. "I'll try, Jim."

"Bring here."

"But if he's dangerous—"

"Bring here."

She had questions, but Scoville had fallen asleep and there was no one to answer them. She left the room and went in search of a man she'd never seen, a man in the hospital or on the grounds. She passed through the waiting room, on beyond the cafeteria before opening the door to the scruffy back side of the hospital. Except for two garbage bins and blowing dirt and weeds, the unlandscaped expanse was empty. She circled the building, looking in windows to find Scoville's room. She looked for the killer, too. After all, she remembered his face from the trial. But she didn't see either of them.

As she hesitated at the brick wall, Humboldt came rushing around the corner. "Where's Robbie?" he said.

"Robbie? Isn't he with you and Maggie?"

Humboldt glanced desperately here and there, his focus disorganized. Geraldine gripped his arm.

"We don't know where he is!" Humboldt said through clamped teeth. The two wheeled toward the entrance.

"Have you asked the front desk?" said Geraldine.

"Maggie did. They announced it. But this Daniel is on the road by now."

"You think he took Robbie with him?"

"Oh, yeah. He's long gone."

Just before re-entering the hospital, Geraldine put her hands to her head and lifted her face. "Call the Sheriff!" she cried out, as if by sobbing into the air overhead, the message would be transmitted faster.

"I called all the Departments between Portland and Brooks Beach," he said, "and between here and the Siskiyous. They say the road blocks will be up."

"What's he driving?" asked Geraldine.

"I'm guessing a pickup," said Humboldt. "I checked the parking lot, but—"

In the waiting room, Geraldine's name was being called over the loudspeaker.

"What now?" said Humboldt as they walked to the front desk.

"You're wanted in the men's ward," said the receptionist.

Humboldt started to accompany Geraldine but the woman added quickly, "Just Ms. Manahan."

"*Shit*," Humboldt said to himself. "*Scoville's out of his mind.*" Contempt for the detective was replacing sympathy. The guy had screwed up his son's life, his son's mother's life, his own mother's life, and possibly his friends' lives. Now he was relying on a woman whose only experience with bad guys was listening to them from behind a shorthand machine in a courtroom. Humboldt almost stomped holes in the waiting room floor as he went looking for Maggie. He longed to go home. Scoville didn't want his help. In fact, there was not much he could do now beyond calling the Sheriff, which he'd already done. Even Scoville didn't have confidence in law enforcement up here, and he *worked* with them.

Behind him Geraldine passed through the door in the glass

divider and followed the red line on the floor to the nurses' station.

"He asked for you," the head nurse said stiffly from behind the counter. "We've given him medication, but"—from a chain around her neck, reading glasses dangled against her starched white chest—"he wants to see you."

"I'll try to calm him," said Geraldine.

"The meds will do that," the nurse said pointedly.

At Scoville's bedside, Geraldine took his hand. "I'm here, Jim."

He frowned, tried to speak, and pressed her hand. His breathing was labored.

"Money. Robbie."

"What money? What about Robbie?"

He tried to say more. He seemed frantic. It took fifteen minutes before he stopped trying to manage his thoughts and, instead, crossed the line into drugged sleep.

24

Standing in the middle of the waiting room, Humboldt shook his head. "Hell, no, you're not going to keep looking for Daniel."

"Jim needs me to," Geraldine said urgently. She'd just returned from his bedside.

"What are you going to do with this guy when you find him?"

Geraldine's eyes burned with a mission. "I don't know. Report him." Her shoulders sagged. "Jim asked me to."

"Just now he asked you?"

"Not in so many words. He's under heavy medication. But I know he wants me to."

Humboldt shook off Geraldine's imploring hand and reared back. "Jim wants!" he snorted. "Have you noticed he doesn't mind putting you in danger?"

Geraldine stared.

"He wants you to find Daniel. Yesterday he had you drive down a dead-end road where a killer was holed up in a trailer. I'd never ask Maggie to do that."

"It's because he needs help," Geraldine said.

"He could have asked me!" Humboldt almost hissed.

"You weren't there at 6:00 yesterday morning," Geraldine said.

"No, I was there at 2:00 yesterday morning! I offered to drive north with him!" *Was it only yesterday?* "No chance of finding the guy, anyway," he said, lowering the volume. "He's long gone with the boy."

Geraldine sat down in the nearest chair. "Shall we tell Scoville everything?" she said in a shaking voice.

"He can't handle it," said Humboldt.

"Not now. But soon. I think we should tell him. Gently."

"Geraldine, how do you tell someone gently that his son has been kidnapped for the second time?" But he took her arm. "Let's go look for Daniel. We won't find him, but we'll look."

25

Maggie stood in the women's bathroom staring at herself in the mirror. If she was going to find Robbie, she had to do it before Humboldt came back. She squinted. My goodness, she had wrinkles. She'd been alive for a long time; Robbie was just beginning his life.

She thought she knew where the boy was. He'd been talking about his grandma; he would see her soon. Pulling out a second red racing car from his pocket, identical to the first, he'd indulged in sing-song play, running the two cars along the edge of the shelf, flinging Legos out of the way, meaningless barriers, chanting under his breath, "We're going to see Grandma. We're going to see Grandma."

When Maggie had turned away just long enough to watch the carp slither among grasses swaying delicately in the fish tank, the child was gone.

She bent toward the sink and cried. This was all her fault. When she lifted her head and saw her face in the mirror, she knew what to do. Because she knew where Robbie and Daniel were. Mrs. Scoville had talked about both of them. They would go to her room in the nursing home. And so she would go there, too. Hurrying out of the bathroom, she sat down on the nearest chair and wrote a note to her husband on a deposit slip from their checkbook.

"Hummer. I've gone to Brooks Beach. You're needed here. Call me tonight. I think R. is with Scoville's mother."

She folded the note and took it to the receptionist at the front desk. "Do you have an envelope?" she asked politely. After addressing it to *Humboldt Denton*, inserting the note and licking the gluey strip, she returned it to the woman behind the desk. "This is very important," she said. "Can you please page Humboldt Denton and give him this envelope?" She turned on her heel, walked briskly to the parking lot, got in her car, and drove south out of Oddfellow.

Mentally she apologized to Humboldt for running out on him, but Scoville and Geraldine needed him here. He would be furious with her. Hurt. But in this case she could not avoid helping Robbie. It was she who had put this whole nightmare into motion. And now she'd lost the child. Another child.

She drove carefully, knowing she was upset, knowing that the road was misleadingly safe now that fine Oregon weather— than which none is finer—had broken over the coast, drying ocean trash thrown high against rocks by the storm. Today the Pacific sparkled. Fishing boats were out making money for their crews. A beautiful, hopeful swath of sunlight cut through weeks of on-and-off slashing rain when fishing and logging had come to a halt and the only thing that thrived was the marijuana crop.

"You need to stay in Oddfellow, Hummer," she apologized. *"You're needed in Oddfellow."* After fifty years of marriage she talked to her husband and to herself in the same breath. She knew he was growing tired of so much disaster. That he would stand beside Scoville as long as necessary she had no doubt. But she knew he was wearying of one emergency after another.

She stopped once for coffee and took it in a cup to go. Her progress down the coast was slow and steady. True to what Humboldt had said about law enforcement on the Coast, she encountered no road blocks, no police officers looking for a man with a little boy who didn't belong to him. She passed her house at two o'clock in the afternoon. The glimpse of redwood walls and slanted roof through a brief opening in the trees made her homesick. How nice it would be to stop at home and forget all the trouble surrounding Scoville. What a nice life she and Humboldt had enjoyed; how delicate was the thread that stitches joy into life's fabric; how she loved the world and living.

She focused back on the highway. It was very important that Robbie have a chance to love life, too. He was taking the place of her little daughter who had died. The thread was delicate but stronger than it seemed.

26

Geraldine said she was going to freshen up, but hell, she was probably prowling the halls again looking for a guy she'd never seen. A guy that was long gone. Humboldt threw himself onto an orange plastic chair. His stare, hard as nails, was directed at nothing until the receptionist came toward him with an envelope.

"Your wife asked me to give you this," she said.

Humboldt took the envelope. Willing his old heart to beat steadily, he opened it. Even after he'd read it, he remained seated. Scoville had put everyone at risk: Maggie; Geraldine; the boy. And since there was no guarantee that Scoville would ever get out of the hospital alive, he'd risked himself most of all. None of it would have happened if he'd stuck to business. Not fallen in love with a woman he never married. Not had a child with her.

He himself had married Maggie and had his daughters the usual way. Why couldn't Scoville have done the same?

Thinking of Maggie driving south on winding Coast Highway made him weak. His vision fogged over. He couldn't handle all this worry: Maggie following a criminal down Coast Highway; little Robbie in a car with a kidnapper; Geraldine in love with Scoville, losing all common sense. There wasn't anyone he could trust.

27

At the nurses' station where the three-o'clock shift was taking over behind the high desk, lazy afternoon sunlight filtered through the west windows, softening starched white uniforms. Recognized but ignored, Geraldine quietly continued on down the hall and entered Scoville's room.

"Jim?" she said when she reached his bedside. As she debated whether to wake him, he stirred on the pillow and saw her. "I need to talk to you," she said softly. "The man who shot you outside the trailer is in the hospital."

"Why?"

"He was in a highway accident," Geraldine said.

"Robbie?" said Scoville.

"The accident is unrelated to Robbie," Geraldine said, dismissing it with a hand gesture. "Here's the important thing.

I looked for Daniel but he isn't in the hospital anymore. He's taken Robbie and gone."

By his stony expression, Geraldine couldn't tell if he was stunned or calculating.

"Thinks he's father," Scoville eventually whispered.

"The police have been notified," Geraldine said. She watched him try to control the chaos in the recesses of his mind where, like portraits in an out-of-focus gallery, Robbie, Daniel, Robbie's mother, his own mother, the killer, hung in crooked disarray. His eyes seemed to sink more deeply into his forehead. He gave her a stricken look before retreating into unconsciousness.

Humboldt had been right. She'd told him too much.

28

Maggie pulled into the nearly-empty parking lot of the Brooks Beach nursing home. No unwashed pick-up truck or once-luxurious but now-battered four-door car, the kind of vehicle Maggie imagined criminals drive, was parked in the lot. She followed the brick sidewalk past tall plantings of azalea and rhododendron to the front entrance of a fine old house built by a sea captain who had wanted always to be able to gaze out to sea. Now converted into a nursing home, its nineteenth-century oak beams had been logged and sawn in the Siskiyous from where they'd been floated downriver to the coast.

No one questioned her presence. She turned down a hallway, shafts of sunlight striking the honey-colored hardwood floor from rippled old clerestory windows. At Room 25 she knocked on the door jamb and positioned herself so that Mrs. Scoville could locate her from across the room. The nearer bed was occupied by a sleeping woman younger but less alert than Scoville's mother.

"Hello, Mrs. Scoville," Maggie called out. "I'm Maggie

Denton. May I come in?"

"Yes. Yes. Come in and let me see you." The old lady sat in a nearly upright position against the bed's elevated head rest. She smoothed her hair and straightened the neckline of her hospital gown. "My eyesight isn't good."

"I'm Maggie Denton. I visited you—"

"Of course. Maggie Denton," said the old woman. "I remember you very well. Sit down. Sit down," and she gestured toward an upholstered chair in front of the window.

"You look wonderful, Mrs. Scoville," Maggie said, taking a seat. "I gather you're feeling better and better?"

"I am," said Mrs. Scoville. Folding her hands on the turned-down sheet and light blanket, she said, "Have you seen my son, Jim?"

"My husband has seen him," Maggie said. "How much do you know of his whereabouts?"

Mrs. Scoville looked out the window. In spite of not seeing what was outside the room, not even seeing clearly what was inside the room, she answered crisply. "I haven't seen him lately. That is unusual for Jim." Less crisply she added, "Do you know anything about him?"

"Yes," said Maggie. "I think I can tell you where he is. And I need some information from you."

The old woman strained toward the younger woman, her eyes bright.

"Your son is in the hospital recovering nicely."

"Hospital?"

"Yes, he has had a… run-in with a man he put in prison. But as I said, he's recovering nicely."

"I knew something was wrong," said Mrs. Scoville. "What hospital? The one here in Brooks Beach?"

"He's in the Oddfellow Hospital, Mrs. Scoville. Oddfellow. Between here and Portland."

For the first time, Mrs. Scoville seemed confused.

"He was taken there after an injury," Maggie said.

"What kind of injury?"

"A chest injury. He's recovering nicely."

"Was he shot?" she whispered.

"Can I get you a swallow of water, Mrs. Scoville?"

The old woman accepted the glass, rejecting the bent straw. "Was he shot?" she repeated and held the glass herself.

"Yes," said Maggie, watching the aged throat muscles go into a brief spasm as she drank. "But he's strong and stubborn. It happened when he was rescuing your grandson."

"Rescuing him from what?"

"The man who broke into your house."

"Where is Robbie?"

"I think he's here in Brooks Beach."

"Brooks Beach," Mrs. Scoville said, frowning. Bewildered, she settled on a smaller point. "What makes you think Robbie is my grandson?"

"Isn't he?" Maggie sat biting her bottom lip. Perhaps she'd revealed information she shouldn't have. Again. Talking too much.

"Perhaps." After a minute had passed Mrs. Scoville said, "I'm surprised Daniel would shoot anyone."

"What makes you think Daniel shot someone?" said Maggie.

"If he didn't, who shot my son?"

"The same man who shot Robbie's mother," said Maggie.

"The man who broke into my house?"

"Yes. That one."

Mrs. Scoville looked up into Maggie's face. "Daniel may not have shot him, but he wants to do Jim harm." She rubbed her face with one arthritic hand. "Daniel loves Robbie, but he is very jealous of Jim." She returned both hands to the bedclothes. "I warned Jim he was playing with fire." It was hard to tell if Mrs. Scoville was crying or if it was just rheumy old eyes leaking. "Robbie's mother was very good to me. But with men she was a slut. I told Jim he was playing with fire."

Both women sat absorbing new information until Maggie asked a practical question. "Have you seen Daniel and Robbie recently?"

"Is that why you're here?" said the old woman. Maggie nodded.

"They were here just this morning," said Mrs. Scoville. "They only stayed five minutes. Daniel wants money. He's going to leave Robbie with me."

"Robbie is your grandson, then?" Maggie said.

"I'm not sure. I consider him my grandson."

"Geraldine Manahan and I have been caring for him, but"— Maggie's voice dropped—"I just turned my back for a minute this morning and I lost Robbie." Her face began to crumble. With an effort she told Mrs. Scoville about Oddfellow Hospital and the second abduction.

The old woman reached out her arm. "All will be well," she said, feeling for Maggie's hand, missing what she sought, stroking the wrist and forearm instead. "They're coming back. Daniel won't hurt Robbie. I'm going to write him a check and he's going to leave Robbie with me. Can you help me take care of him?"

29

Maggie rummaged through her purse, not looking for anything except time to think. She took out a cough drop she didn't need and offered one to Mrs. Scoville who didn't need it, either.

"When do you expect them back?" Maggie asked.

"Tonight."

"You're sure he'll bring the child?"

Mrs. Scoville's weak eyes narrowed. "I can't imagine why he wouldn't. He needs money and I need my grandson. Daniel and I understand each other."

"You could call it blackmail."

"You could call it blackmail," Mrs. Scoville repeated. She didn't seem bothered. "I'm afraid they'll catch him, though. He's not intelligent."

"He's committed a crime," Maggie insisted.

"Yes, it's a crime..."

Maggie doubted Daniel would leave the boy with Mrs. Scoville. She could almost hear Humboldt say, *"Intelligent or not, Maggie, he knows the boy is his meal ticket."*

The fellow was running a risk lingering here in Oregon when, in thirty minutes, he could be out of the state, in California. Of course, she mused, the police in California were more efficient. Perhaps he was better off in Oregon.

"Daniel loves Robbie. And he loves me," said Mrs. Scoville. "But he makes up his own facts. He likes to pretend we're related. Mother and son. And he thinks he's Robbie's father." Mrs. Scoville shook her head and said, almost to herself, "I should have asked him to move out of the house before we all got so—settled in." She crossed her arms over her skinny chest. "For a long time it was a nice little world." She looked directly into what she took to be Maggie's eyes and said with a sardonic murmur, "Daniel was not the only one who made up facts."

"*Is* he Robbie's father?" Maggie asked.

The old woman looked up. "I'm not sure," she whispered.

"We have to tell the police," Maggie said impulsively. "Robbie needs to be protected. We don't know what Daniel is planning. We don't know who he's seeing or what he's thinking."

"If he's planning, he's not planning very well," the old woman said, sounding strangely sad.

"I want to take Robbie home with me and keep him safe until Jim is out of the hospital, Mrs. Scoville."

"I won't be able to call you when they come back. The phone is in the hall. I can't trust the staff with something this important. I don't see how I can contact you."

A brightness swept across Maggie's face. "I'm going to take

my car home and have a friend drop me back here. I'll wait for them near the front door."

"Won't he recognize you?" said Mrs. Scoville, her eyes closed now.

"I'll wear a wig," said Maggie, getting into the swing of things. "And maybe a little padding. I can make myself look different. Daniel has barely seen me."

Mrs. Scoville's eyelids flew open. "This isn't a movie, Mrs. Denton." Maggie lowered her head. It's exactly what Humboldt would have said. But when he called tonight from Oddfellow, she wanted to have something to report. She wanted to have called the Sheriff of Crescent County; to have seen Daniel led away from the nursing home in handcuffs; to report Robbie bathed, wearing clean pajamas, fast asleep in the Dentons' guest room where their grandchildren had stayed so many times when they were little.

30

The Greyhound bus drove south, leaning in toward the ocean, leaning out, following the curves of Highway One toward Brooks Beach; toward the California state line; toward Eureka, Redding, Sacramento, San Francisco, and beyond.

At a window seat behind and across the aisle from the driver, Humboldt watched the breakers frothing and pulsing below. A moment of intense homesickness struck: he had often watched the same scene from his living room windows, the Pacific tossing its ribbon of white against the base of the cliff. His cliff. His and Maggie's cliff.

He leaned back against the seat. God. Let Maggie be all right.

The Brooks Beach bus station was in the center of town, not far from the convalescent hospital where he was afraid...

hopeful... afraid he would find his wife. He got off the bus and walked up the hill toward the imposing building with its landscaped lawns and polished windows that, in another hour or two, would reflect the orange sun sinking into the ocean.

He stopped at the entrance, slightly out of breath from the hilly approach and the short flight of brick steps leading up from the street. When he was breathing evenly he opened the carved wooden door. A bell rang musically and he stepped inside. Though the old building was an architectural gem, it still smelled like a nursing home. Cleaning materials with an underlay of bodily function. A neatly lettered sign on the front desk said, "We'll be right with you."

"*Oh, no, you won't,*" Humboldt muttered, and rushed past the desk, heading deeper into the building. Paying no attention to the parchment faces on pillows, he looked for Maggie. When he reached the last room, he encountered a nurse in a crisp white uniform.

"Are you looking for someone?" she asked coldly.

"Mrs. Scoville," Humboldt said. "There was no one at the front desk."

"And there was no sign asking you to wait?"

"I was in a hurry."

"Follow me," she said, and led him back to the front entrance. "Someone will be right with you."

While she watched, he gingerly took the antique chair nearest the door. One other person sat quietly in the corner reading a magazine. Humboldt, feeling as if he'd done nothing but read magazines in waiting rooms for the past two days, picked up a copy of something called *Healthy Living*. While he rustled pages, he let his eyes wander to the woman who sat reading in the dark. Above her, on the mantel of the marble-faced fireplace, a lamp sat unused. He debated whether to turn it on for her. It wasn't his business whether she could see what she was reading. Maybe, he thought idly, she was too short to reach the lamp. He wondered how tall she was and checked her shoes. They were dark, with medium heels and a strap across the instep. Like Maggie's. Even the legs were like Maggie's. He followed the legs up to the hem of the skirt.

What the hell? They *were* Maggie's. He inhaled sharply and dropped the copy of *Healthy Living*. Immediately he bent to pick it up and rushed through pages without seeing print while his circulation thundered in his ears. By degrees Maggie was inching away from him, her face partially hidden by her shoulder—her padded shoulder. She looked like a football player who'd lost mental functioning along with proper body proportions.

Humboldt thought he was dreaming, sitting here in a dark, ornate room with a woman in a wig who knew he was her husband but didn't know he knew she was his wife.

Of course. She was hiding from Daniel. Good God. Was Daniel coming here to see Mrs. Scoville? The dangerous game Maggie was playing! How did she think she was going to apprehend the guy? One thing he knew: Daniel might not recognize the disguised woman in the corner, but he would surely recognize Humboldt.

Humboldt stepped outside to think.

He decided the best place for him was in Mrs. Scoville's room, and so he stepped back inside, ignored the sign on the desk, and entered a long hallway. Peering at the occupants of each room, trying not to act like the intruder he was, he found Mrs. Scoville in the bed at the far side of Room 25.

"Mrs. Scoville?" he said.

"Daniel?"

"It's Humboldt Denton," he said. "Maggie Denton's husband."

Alarmed, the old woman struggled up from where she was lying on her back. "What's happened to Maggie?" she asked.

"Maggie's fine," he said, passing around the nearer bed and approaching Mrs. Scoville. "How are you?"

She didn't answer but, letting her head fall back on the

pillow, drew the sheet and bedspread higher. "Why are you here?"

"I'm helping Maggie," he said. "I'm looking for a man who we think has your grandson."

"Oh. That would be Daniel." She pulled one arm out from under the covers and felt along the frame of the bed. Expertly pushing buttons, she adjusted the headrest to a higher elevation. "I'm waiting for him, too."

"May I wait with you?"

"Well," she said frankly, "I don't think so, Mr. Denton. If he sees you he may leave and take Robbie with him."

"May I wait beside your neighbor's bed?" he asked, looking around the room and settling quickly on the best hiding place. "If I pretend to be visiting her, Daniel might not recognize me."

"Is she awake?" Mrs. Scoville whispered, as if they could erase the noise they'd been making by whispering now.

"She's asleep." Before Mrs. Scoville could object, he took a straight chair from the corner and positioned it, back to the door, at the neighboring bed. Beyond that, he had no idea what he would do.

"Do you know where the nearest phone is?" he asked.

"In the hall."

Humboldt stepped back into the hallway. The telephone was on the wall two rooms down. Returning to Room 25, he took a seat at the nearer bed and waited.

31

From time to time Mrs. Scoville reached out to her bedside table and touched a checkbook. She fingered the pen resting beside it, repositioned her arm under the covers, withdrew it again, and repeated the sequence.

"Mr. Denton?" she whispered hoarsely.

"Call me Humboldt."

"Well, Humboldt, do you expect Daniel and Robbie soon?"

"I don't know, Mrs. Scoville."

The old woman was silent for several minutes. "Humboldt?"

"Yes?"

The room was growing dim. The sun must be in its last moments above the Pacific, broadening, flattening at the top just before it slides past the edge of what we know.

"Where is Maggie?"

"In the waiting room."

"Is she wearing a ridiculous disguise?"

"Yes. Yes, she is." He rested his forearms on his thighs, let his hands hang between his knees, and bowed his head. He did not want to talk. A few minutes later, when the bell at the front entrance of the facility rang faintly, he lifted his head. Mrs. Scoville's hearing, unlike her eyesight, was intact and she, too, lifted her head.

Footsteps approached. A child's voice piped questions: "Is Grandma here?" Less certainly: "Where's Mommy?" For the first time, Humboldt thought, Robbie sounded anxious. He knew that his wife in the waiting room would have heard the anxiety, too. Sure enough, here came her footsteps. He hunched down toward the sleeping woman he pretended to be visiting.

Holding Robbie's hand, Daniel entered behind Humboldt and passed around the foot of the first bed. Humboldt stood and left the room, not before saying to the strange-looking woman following the man and child, the woman wearing a large black dress oddly bulky above the waist, her hair a strange shade of brown with a wide center part the color and texture of an ironing board cover, "I'm going to call the Sheriff from the hall, Maggie. Get out of the building."

Maggie nearly lost her padding. Silent, disobedient, she took Humboldt's vacated chair. As he called the Sheriff's Department from the telephone, he heard in the background Mrs. Scoville cry out with mixed pleasure and longing. Little Robbie's "Look what Daniel gave me" was muffled, probably by bedclothes and a hug. The room hummed with sounds of a reunion.

"Everyone is worried about you and Robbie," he heard Mrs. Scoville say.

"Yeah, well, here he is." Oddly gentle, Daniel added, "I guess you know what I need."

"How do you do," Maggie interrupted. "I'm a friend of Mrs. Scoville." To

Humboldt outside Room 25, it seemed his wife had gotten up from the chair and moved closer to Mrs. Scoville's bed. "Can I help her with the payment?"

"No," Daniel said.

There was a silence in which Humboldt imagined the old woman reaching for the checkbook.

"Can you turn on the light, Maggie?" she said.

"No," said Daniel. "No light."

"But I can't see," said Mrs. Scoville.

"You write it," Daniel said, apparently to Maggie. Silence. "Let her sign it."

"How much?" said Maggie.

"Two thousand dollars," said Mrs. Scoville.

"That's about right," said Daniel. Another silence before he added in a changed tone, "Please sign it, Mrs. Scoville." After a long moment Humboldt heard the tearing of a check from its glued edge. The room was peaceful. Not what he'd expected. Daniel was making sounds of saying good-bye. He'd probably picked up Robbie; the child's "'Bye" was indistinct. God, the Sheriff is going to be too late, he thought.

"You probably don't remember me," Maggie was saying. Oh, hell, she was going to put herself—and everyone else—at risk, trying to stall for time. He shouldn't have told her he was calling the Sheriff.

"I'm Mrs. Scoville's friend. And Robbie's."

"That's right," said Mrs. Scoville.

"Hi, Robbie," Maggie said. But Robbie apparently didn't recognize her.

"I gotta go," said Daniel.

"Where will you go?" Mrs. Scoville asked.

"I'll be okay," Daniel mumbled. "I got help from you and—Jim. I'll miss you, Mrs. Scoville."

As his voice came nearer, Humboldt moved away. When he'd backed up almost to the telephone again, he saw the Sheriff approach from the waiting room. Waving, shouting a warning, pointing to Daniel who by now had stepped out of Room 25 and had begun running down the hall, he watched the Sheriff spin around as the younger man merely grazed him in his sprint for the front door. But a more substantially built, firmly rooted deputy was waiting for him. Wrestling him to the floor, he brought out a pair of handcuffs.

Humboldt re-entered Room 25 and walked toward the bed by the window. He took Maggie by the arm. "What do you think you're doing, Mrs. Denton?" he said and took a light jab at her shoulder padding.

"Help," whispered Mrs. Denton, turning to the old woman in the bed. "Do you think we can get the Sheriff back here to arrest this man?"

Mrs. Scoville looked without comprehension into the room's dimness. Robbie stood beside his grandmother, their hands linked on the bedspread. Maggie removed her wig.

"Hello, Robbie," she said.

Robbie stared and did for his grandmother what she could not do for herself: used his young eyes to take in every detail of Maggie and Humboldt.

"Do you know where my mother is?" he asked gravely.

"We know where your father is," said Maggie, disengaging herself from Humboldt. "He's in the hospital getting stronger and stronger. You're the reason he is getting well. You and your grandmother. He wants very much to see both of you."

"Where's Mommy?" Robbie said. After days of grown-up behavior, he was finally crying and could not be coaxed out of his grief.

32

Scoville kept his eyes closed against the light from the recessed fluorescent tube above his bed. Every time he tried to tell the night nurse or aide to turn it off, he lost words, lost strength, and fell asleep before he could deliver the message.

He heard a metallic clink at his bedside, a new sound he didn't recognize. He opened his eyes. The fluorescent light still bothered him.

There was the clink again. He turned his head and focused. A figure stood beside him. Not the night nurse. Not Geraldine or Humboldt. He called up all his abilities.

A new person. In a hospital gown.

The metallic ringing was the bed rail. An arm and hand were moving in time to the sound of the rail.

Bed rails don't make sounds. The arm and hand were causing the sound. Scoville knew the sound, yet he didn't know it.

"Detective Scoville," said the voice.

Against his will, his eyes closed. He slept, yet he didn't sleep.

"Remember me?"

"No," Scoville said. But he was beginning to. Not exactly this person. Many people like him. Many years.

An arm lifted. The free end of a handcuff dangled. A smirk. A cough.

Scoville felt for the buzzer and couldn't find it.

The figure held up a small key and laughed. "Hell of a security system." Swaying like the bags on the pole he held onto, he stared down at the prone body of Scoville. "You're done for," he said.

"You're free," Scoville whispered. But the man looked done for; looked anything but free.

"Hah!"

"If you want to be."

The figure showed interest. Scoville struggled to think. He'd known something. Known this might happen.

"You're done for," the figure said again.

"Have something. For you." But what? Where was it? He scrabbled hard with his left hand.

"If you like this," he said after great effort, "there's more." Transferring into his free hand what he'd been hoarding, he grabbed the man's wrist, forced the hand open, and dropped something into the trembling palm.

The two men stared at each other, pushed to extremities.

33

Geraldine hung up the telephone in her motel room and remained seated on the bed where she'd been talking to Maggie. Still twining the phone cord around her fingers, she resisted the impulse to run out into the parking lot, jump in her car, and drive to the hospital. She wanted Jim to know that Robbie was with Maggie and Humboldt and that the fellow named Daniel had been caught by the Crescent County Sheriff.

But it was too late to disturb him, wasn't it?

A sob of joy surprised her. Then she laughed. Imagine his disbelief. A successful police action.

She got up from the bed and went to run a hot bath. But no sooner had she turned on the water than she turned it off again. Grabbing her car keys and purse by the door, she ran out of the motel to the parking lot where she jumped in her car and drove to the Oddfellow Hospital.

It was a few minutes after visiting hours but no one stopped her as she followed the red line on the floor to Jim's room. Only one other person was in the hall, a patient walking slowly, pulling his intravenous pole with one hand, holding his hospital gown closed in back with the other. She turned into Scoville's room. In the fluorescent light from a tube above the bed, his face was craggy—becoming craggier and craggier as he continued to lose weight—and pale. Geraldine went to stand at the bedside. His breathing was irregular and moist with phlegm.

She tested his alertness with a touch to the shoulder. He moaned briefly, turned his head to the side, and opened his eyes.

"Hello, Jim."

In the half-dark he focused on her face and eventually nodded. She stepped to the corner sink and moistened a wash cloth. Back at the bed, she dabbed at the cracked corners of his mouth and bathed his forehead, cheeks, and throat. He was sweating. She rinsed the cloth and came back to clear the corners of his eyes.

"Drink," he whispered, and for the first time swallowed water from the bent straw in the glass.

"Jim," she said quietly, "Robbie is with Maggie and Humboldt. He's safe."

She wished he would smile.

"The Crescent County Sheriff arrested Daniel. Now all you have to do is rest and gain strength."

He reached for her hand and held it through a long silence. For the last two days she'd watched him struggle. She'd struggled with him; acted for him. Now they could both rest. Robbie was with the Dentons.

He pulled on her hand. His breathing grew labored again. "Not safe," he said, and moved his legs spasmodically.

"Jim?" Now that there was every reason to be quiet and grateful, he seemed more upset than ever. "Jim," she repeated. "There is no emergency."

Something like his old self appeared in his face. "Killer," he said. "Here," and he pointed to where she stood.

She tensed. "He's in a hospital bed, Jim. He's under guard."

Though Scoville didn't answer, he managed to show contempt.

"He's under guard," she repeated. The very phrase was reassuring.

He turned his head away. She felt his disgust.

"What is it, Jim?" she said, offended.

He made a vague gesture.

"I'll go ask about him," she said.

He held her fast until she shook loose. "If he's waltzing into your room, the hospital needs to know. The police should be called. The prison system, too."

Scoville thrashed his head back and forth on the pillow.

"Stop!" she said and held his head firmly between her hands.

He took one of her hands and moved it to the bed rail, an action, a location she didn't understand. He pressed and moved her hand lower down to the frame.

"Did he leave something here at the bed?" Geraldine asked.

"I did."

Geraldine replaced her hand on top of his as he scrabbled among button controls and screws and welds in a snagging, bruising search she didn't understand. She made him stop. "What are you looking for, Jim?"

He let out an exhausted breath and gave in to her strength. In the moment of relinquishment, the word he couldn't remember came to him. "Percocet."

She frowned. "We can ask the nurse for medication," she said, and saw by his expression that she'd missed the mark. She felt obtuse and, at the same time, irrationally angry at him for not being able to tell her what he wanted. Obviously there were no drugs in the bedframe. He was so wrong. She felt humiliated for him.

He turned his head away.

"Did you hide something, Jim?"

He turned back, hopeful. She saw his hope. "Did you hide a Percocet?"

"Hide," he said. "Gone."

"Gone?" She tried to connect his words. Had he been hoarding pain-killers? But he couldn't have hoarded pills; remembered where they were; found them; gotten them to his mouth; swallowed them.

He released her hand and fell into a condition that was neither sleep nor wakefulness. His features were as muddled as his mind. She turned her back on the diminished man behind her and went in search of help.

34

"I'm concerned about a patient," she said to the nurse behind the computer. She'd followed the red line on the floor back from Scoville's room to the nurses' station. "He came here two days ago from an accident on the highway. I believe he's under guard."

The nurse looked up at Geraldine. "Why do you ask?"

"He may have been in Mr. Scoville's room recently," Geraldine said.

The nurse stood. "I can't speak to you about another patient," she said.

"Will you just look to see that everything is as it should be?" Geraldine asked. "Mr. Scoville said something about the prisoner being in his room. I don't know if it's accurate or not."

"What did he say?"

"Just that the man was in his room."

The nurse frowned and said under her breath, "He's restrained." Ostentatiously glancing at the clock on the wall, she said, "Visiting hours are over. I'll look into it."

As Geraldine passed through the waiting room, empty at

this hour, no visitors, no emergencies, just rows of empty orange plastic chairs that gleamed under the ceiling lights, she thought about how happy she'd been to bring Scoville good news about his son, and how subdued she now felt. She got in her car and drove slowly off the hospital grounds. She was about to spend the night in a motel room where even a long soak in a hot bath could not hide the fact that she was alone on a lonely coast in a town named Oddfellow or that the man she loved was lying in a hospital bed, confused, unprotected from a killer he thought had somehow gotten free to wander around the hospital at will.

35

Aloof, detached, Scoville wasn't holding her hand today. Sitting up now, he'd finished the cup of coffee served with a lunch he'd eaten without help, but he was not being himself with her. Not himself as she'd come to know him.

Not himself as she'd come to love him.

In Brooks Beach he'd always been aloof and detached, but since that early morning weeks ago on Highway 1 when she'd rescued him—or had he rescued her?—he'd ceased to be aloof.

But today he barely looked at her. "Have you seen my mother?" he asked after a long silence that did not appear to have rested him.

"No," she said, "but Maggie has. They've become good friends."

"How is she?"

"Recovering well. She's in good spirits, especially now that you're coming home."

He gave a nod and pushed his lunch tray a few inches away. "The Portland house will have to be sold."

"Everything in good time," said Geraldine.

He pushed the lunch tray another inch. "Does she need help

writing checks? Paying bills?"

"I don't think so. Maggie says she's very alert."

Geraldine was sorry to see the tension on Scoville's face as he expelled a breath loaded with worry and effort.

The next day, seated in the passenger seat of her car as they drove toward Brooks Beach, he sighed heavily and gave little attention to where they were. Geraldine wondered if he'd been released too soon.

"Robbie's doing well," she said, keeping her attention on the road. "I found a good preschool and he's—well, he's making a life for himself."

Scoville looked out his window. "Does he ask for his mother?"

"At night. He cries at night. He often wakes up crying for her."

"What do you do when that happens?" he asked.

"I go against recommended practice and lie down beside him."

Scoville moved his head a few degrees and stared straight ahead. "And that comforts him?"

"Yes, that comforts him."

Carrying his small bag of belongings upstairs to his apartment above the florist shop, she stayed behind him so she could break the fall if he lost his balance. He'd grown so thin she thought it would be easy to catch him. But when they got upstairs, feeling trembly, it was she who almost fell. Scoville reached out and steadied her.

"I'm supposed to be helping *you*," she laughed.

But he didn't laugh as he lowered himself into an easy chair and laid his head back against the upholstery. After a short rest during which Geraldine wondered if she should leave or stay, he said, "Look in the bag. There's a pocket in the lining."

She unzipped the bag and found the pocket.

"Take out the loose pills in the bottom."

She followed his instructions, thinking, as she handed them

over, *God, I don't want him to be addicted to pain-killers.*

He looked at her curiously. "They're not for me," he said.

"Who are they for?"

He laid his head back again and closed his eyes. "For anyone who might hurt my son."

Geraldine had never thought of pills as a weapon.

He opened his eyes and gave her a penetrating gaze. "Robbie was at risk in the hospital, you know."

All those times he'd seemed incapacitated, he'd been watching out for his son.

"Can you help me to the bathroom?" he said, getting to his feet. She walked beside him as he slowly made his way down the hall. "Wait outside the door."

"I'll call Humboldt for you," she said.

"Later," he said.

"Maybe you should go to the convalescent hospital," she suggested when he came out of the bathroom.

"No," he said. "I don't need to go to the convalescent hospital. I'm already regaining my strength. Humboldt can help me. You and Humboldt."

"Yes," said Geraldine.

When he was safely in bed she kissed him on the cheek. "You can reach the telephone?" she said softly.

He demonstrated.

"Well, then, I'll call you. When you're ready, the Dentons and I will bring Robbie to see you."

He smiled a little, closed his eyes, and fell asleep.

36

Weeks later, Geraldine, Scoville, and the Dentons sat at Geraldine's kitchen table finishing coffee and dessert. With the distant sound of the ocean coming through the open windows, with the Douglas fir between the house and alley unusually still in the windless summer evening, Scoville began to express himself as he had not done since his hospitalization.

"I'm very grateful," he said, and cleared his throat. "I can't thank you adequately." He took Geraldine's hand in his, laid it against his chest, then nodded his head in the direction of her extra bedroom where Robbie was sleeping.

Humboldt shifted. Geraldine saw the older man's discomfort and, wanting to avoid conflict, tried to withdraw her hand and move toward the coffeepot for refills. But Scoville wouldn't release her.

"Are you going to keep your boy in the apartment with you?" Humboldt asked.

Maggie interrupted. "Hummer—"

"It's a serious question," he insisted.

"The child is just getting used to Geraldine's house," Maggie said. "Leave him here for a while."

"He's welcome to stay as long as necessary," said Geraldine.

"He's welcome at our house, for that matter," said Maggie.

Humboldt flinched. "He's Jim's son," he said. The three looked at Scoville, but if they expected him to thank them more than once in one evening or to disclose a plan for his son, they were mistaken.

"I wouldn't ask you for more help than you've already given," Scoville said, including each of them in a slow-moving gaze around the table.

"I just wish you'd asked me for help when you were in the hospital," said Humboldt.

"I didn't feel I could," said Scoville.

"Why the hell not?"

"Maggie doesn't need to be a widow," he said.

"But it's all right for Geraldine to die," Humboldt retorted.

"I didn't die," Geraldine reminded him.

"You could have. Maggie could have died, too, wearing that moronic disguise"—he paused, impressed by his unexpected vocabulary— "and being in the same room with ..." He refused to say the name Daniel.

"Hummer," Maggie said in a low voice, "Scoville couldn't predict what would happen."

Humboldt sat staring at his dessert plate, flushed.

"I'm sorry, Humboldt," said Scoville. "I can never apologize enough."

"Well, you shouldn't ask women to do dangerous work," Humboldt said stiffly, though after an awkward silence, curiosity won out. "How did you know where the trailer was?"

"Money," Scoville said. "Daniel hates me but not my money." He looked at the older man with caution, unsure how the information would be taken. "He contacted me and told me where Robbie was. I gave him $3000 just before I came to your house."

"The night you drove north?"

"The night I drove north."

"Humph," said Humboldt.

"He got another $2000 from Mrs. Scoville," said Maggie.

"He hated the man who killed his girlfriend, but he made money off of it," said Geraldine.

"How did Daniel make the connection between the killer and you?" said Geraldine.

"An old cellmate helped the killer escape and drove him to Portland. After all"—he refrained from looking at Maggie—"the killer knew where my mother lived."

Maggie bowed her head.

"And that's where he met Daniel," said Geraldine, "scouting

around your mother's house."

"Both men hated you," said Humboldt.

"Daniel didn't hate my money."

Maggie lifted her head. "Or your mother's."

"Daniel drove him to the trailer?" said Humboldt.

"Yes," said Scoville.

"I guess Daniel was going to blackmail the killer as well as you."

"Correct," said Scoville. "He wanted money from everyone."

Lights in the parking lot of the Knotty Pine came on, illuminating the alley and Douglas fir. Geraldine, Maggie, and Humboldt sat musing on facts they now better understood. A light breeze began to play across the window sill behind Geraldine. Scoville watched it lift her hair.

Humboldt leaned back in his chair. "Well, Mrs. Denton, how about a game of black jack before we head home?"

Maggie smiled and stacked her coffee cup, saucer, and dessert plate. "It's been lovely, Geraldine."

"Delicious meal," Humboldt said, standing.

Slowly the four walked outside. Geraldine and Scoville stopped at the alley and watched the Dentons disappear into the tavern. Scoville put his arm around Geraldine's shoulders and they turned back to the house. In the doorway to the kitchen they paused. Scoville kissed her, then they withdrew from each other and he followed her through the house into her bedroom. Lying down beside her, he took her in his arms.

"I don't want to hurt you," she whispered, pulling away from the wound that was still healing. Later, when they'd undressed, he positioned her and they made love, touching, guiding, careful always to protect his chest.

"Will you help me raise my son?" he whispered later.

"That depends," she said.

"On what?"

"On whether you marry me."

Scoville lay thinking. Gravely he repositioned her.

"Will you marry me, Jim?" she said.

"Yes, I will marry you, Geraldine."

"All right, then," she said, and after another long kiss, they fell asleep.

ABOUT THE AUTHOR

Marlene Lee has worked as a court reporter, teacher, college instructor, and writer. A graduate of Kansas Wesleyan University (BA), University of Kansas (MA), and Brooklyn College (MFA), she currently lives in Columbia, Missouri and New York City. After graduating from Kansas Wesleyan, she taught English at Salina Senior High School. Her poems, stories, and essays have appeared in numerous publications.

Other books by Marlene Lee:

The Absent Woman
Published by Holland House April 2013

Virginia Johnstone doesn't need a rest, she needs a change; not comfort, but purpose. Divorced, and a visitor in her children's lives, she decides to leave Seattle and spend three months in the harbor town of Hilliard. There, on the edge of Puget Sound, she sublets rooms in an old hotel, rooms belonging to a woman who has vanished without explanation. In search of someone who can take her piano-playing to the next level, Virginia encounters Twilah Chan, an inspiring teacher and disturbing presence. Twilah's son, Greg, an exciting but also disturbing presence, re-awakens Virginia's romantic life. When she discovers a connection between the absent woman of the old hotel, Twilah, and Greg, she must decide whether to pursue the uncertain course she has set for herself or return to the safety of Seattle.

In a novel which is both elegiac and passionate, insightful and wryly humorous, Marlene Lee explores the need for change and the emotional consequences of leaving an old life in order to embrace a new one.

Praise for The Absent Woman:

"I couldn't put down The Absent Woman. I relished every scene, every word. It's one of the most compelling novels that I've read..."
Ella Leffland, author of *Rumors of Peace; The Knight, Death, and the Devi*l, and others

"Lee writes quite beautifully, with grace and wit and precision. I thought it was a very brave book, and very honest. Virginia's feelings about leaving her boys were especially resonant. And she

writes about music wonderfully. The book will stay with me for a long time."
Alex George, author of A Good American

"In Marlene Lee's psychologically astute debut, THE ABSENT WOMAN, Virginia Johnstone finds herself straining against the limitations of her existence as a comfortable suburban wife and mother. She leaves her husband and her boys to embark on a sometimes exhilarating, sometimes excruciating, and always compelling journey of self-examination. In lucid prose, Lee tells a marvelous story with echoes of Kate Chopin's THE AWAKENING."
Keija Parsinnen, author of *The Ruins of Us*.

Rebecca's Road
Published by Holland House November 2013

> "You're beginning to understand the world."
> "Am I? Then I don't like it."
> "That's precisely why your mother and I kept it from you."

Rebecca has always been looked after, cared for, shielded from the world; to avoid the realities, Mother would take her shopping, and her parents built a wing of their house just for her. But now Mother is dead and Rebecca, fifty years old, wants to take one of those trips she and Mother had often talked about. So she bargains with her father for the trust money he is withholding and buys a motor home in which she sets off to learn about life, love, and the world beyond the family peach orchard; to see if there is a different Rebecca to be found along the way.

Illustrated by B Lloyd